Evan was *not* someone she could think of as anything more than a client...

Evan was getting married.

"I apologize for sending a text so late," Sophie said quietly. "I hope I didn't wake you."

"You didn't wake me." He sounded sad over the phone, and it made her curious. "I have too much on my mind to sleep."

Sophia fought the urge to ask him what was wrong. He was not her friend. He was her client.

"Well, good night, Mr. Anderson."

"You know you can call me Evan," he said.

"I know," she replied. Her chest tightened. She could never enjoy the luxury of casualness with him again. "I'll be in touch during business hours to set up that visit to the estate."

Evan paused. "Of course. Good night, Sophia."

She ended the call and tossed her phone on the other side of the couch. She never should have contacted him.

Why did he have to feel right...when she knew he was wrong?

Dear Reader,

I think this Stop the Wedding! series is bringing me too much joy. Should I be having this much fun stopping weddings from happening? In *A Marriage of Inconvenience*, I have two characters who won't really be heartbroken over their wedding being stopped, but there is a lot at stake if it doesn't happen. At the same time, how does someone ignore something as powerful as love at first sight?

That's part of the dilemma that Evan faces. He thought he was doing the right thing by helping out his friend and setting himself up to be able to care for his brother without worry. Then he meets Sophia Reed. She was not expected at all, but she makes his heart sing. He can't have it all, though. A choice has to be made and there are things he'll have to live with...or, maybe more important, live without.

Thank you for picking up this book. Whether it's your first time stopping weddings with me or you're coming along with me to bust up another wedding—welcome and enjoy the ride!

I love to connect with my readers. You can find me on Facebook, Facebook.com/amyvastineauthor, or Twitter, @vastine7. Please stop by my website, amyvastine.com, and sign up for my newsletter, as well!

xoxo,

Amy Vastine

HEARTWARMING

A Marriage of Inconvenience

—

Amy Vastine

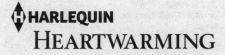

HARLEQUIN
HEARTWARMING

HARLEQUIN®
HEARTWARMING™

Recycling programs for this product may not exist in your area.

ISBN-13: 978-1-335-17985-2

A Marriage of Inconvenience

Copyright © 2021 by Amy Vastine

For questions and comments about the quality of this book, please contact us at CustomerService@Harlequin.com.

Harlequin Enterprises ULC
22 Adelaide St. West, 40th Floor
Toronto, Ontario M5H 4E3, Canada
www.Harlequin.com

Printed in U.S.A.

Amy Vastine has been plotting stories in her head for as long as she can remember. An eternal optimist, she studied social work, hoping to teach others how to find their silver lining. Now she enjoys creating happily-ever-afters for all to read. Amy lives outside Chicago with her high-school-sweetheart husband, three teenagers who keep her on her toes and their two sweet but mischievous pups. Visit her at amyvastine.com.

Books by Amy Vastine

Harlequin Heartwarming

Stop the Wedding!

A Bridesmaid to Remember
His Brother's Bride

Return of the Blackwell Brothers

The Rancher's Fake Fiancée

Grace Note Records

The Girl He Used to Love
Catch a Fallen Star
Love Songs and Lullabies
Falling for Her Bodyguard

Visit the Author Profile page
at Harlequin.com for more titles.

To my daughter who wants to be an event planner someday. I sure hope you never fall in love with a groom-to-be!

CHAPTER ONE

"I'M RUNNING TO the bank now to deposit the check from the Mahoneys and get pennies for the Westbergs' wishing well. I should be back in the office in about twenty minutes." Sophia Reed pulled open the door to the Wharton Bank and Trust. "Can you ask Cassie to check with the Chalet and make sure there will be someone to let us into that private dining room Friday *before* the actual dinner? I don't want to end up standing outside a venue for an hour like we did last weekend."

"I'm on it." Fallon Best always lived up to her name. She was the best business partner a woman could ask for. The two of them had started Engaging Events eight years ago after meeting in college. What began as only the two of them working out of their apartment was now a real company with an office and four full-time employees on staff.

Being at Wharton Bank reminded Sophia

of one more thing. "Did we ever hear back from Miss Wharton about the meeting tomorrow?"

"All confirmed," Fallon replied, and Sophia sighed with relief. The possibility of planning a wedding for the Wharton family had her absolutely giddy.

She got in line behind a man who glanced back at her and gave her a friendly smile and nod. His gray suit was expensive-looking, giving him the first impression of being someone who wasn't afraid to spend money to look good. His shoes, however, gave him away as someone a bit more practical. This guy wanted to fit in with people who had money, but perhaps didn't have as much as the crowd he ran in.

Sophia could tell everything she needed to know about a person by the way they dressed. It was her gift.

Sophia turned her attention back to her phone. "Great. See you soon," she said.

"Okay, b—" That was all Sophia heard Fallon say before a gunshot rang out, causing her to nearly jump out of her skin.

"Everyone down on the ground! Down on the ground right now!" someone shouted.

Four men had entered the lobby dressed head to toe in black and each wearing an animal mask. The one in the tiger mask had a gun pointed at the security guard.

"Hands where I can see them," the man in the monkey mask said to the teller behind the counter. "Everyone else down on the ground like my friend the giraffe said!"

Sophia's heart stopped before jumping back to life and beating at a pace that it hit only during her toughest spin classes. The shock had her frozen in place. The man in front of her took her by the hand.

"Let's do as they say and they won't hurt us," he said, guiding her down to the ground.

There was kindness in his eyes. Kindness was something she'd never take for granted again. This was a bank robbery. A real-life bank robbery. Sophia knew they happened, but she never thought she'd actually witness one.

The two of them and the woman who had been at the counter were the only customers in the lobby. The robber in the lion mask led two bankers and a customer out of the cubicles where people opened accounts and applied for mortgages.

Sophia had done that recently. She had gotten a mortgage from the banker with the blue tie so she could buy her first house. A real house with three bedrooms and two and a half baths. It was charming in its own special way. She loved it. Wouldn't it be a terrible twist of fate if she died in a bank robbery less than a month after she bought her first home?

"You aren't going to die," the kind-eyed man said. He squeezed her hand. "You'll be home before you know it."

Had he heard her thoughts or had she said them out loud? It didn't matter. The way he reassured her made her believe she'd sleep in her bed tonight.

"Okay, people, listen up. Toss your wallets and jewelry on the floor." The robber in the monkey mask lightly kicked Sophia's foot. "You, gather them all up and put them in this bag." A black drawstring bag dropped near her head.

She didn't move. Her lungs had simply forgotten how to work, and it made her lightheaded. If it wasn't for the fact that her whole body was trembling with fear, she would have thought she was paralyzed.

"Did you not hear me?" the monkey-mask robber asked, his voice rough.

"You're scaring her," the man next to Sophia said. "I'll gather them up. Please leave her be."

With her cheek pressed against the cool tile floor, Sophia watched as the thief placed a foot on the man's back, causing him to wince. "Who do you think you are? A hero? I don't need heroes here. Maybe I want her to be scared. Maybe I want you to be scared, too. What do I need to do to make you scared?"

Sophia did not want to find out what he was willing to do to ramp up everyone's fear. She forced herself to move and pushed up. "I'll do it. I'm sorry."

The monkey robber stepped away from the nice man. "Ah, now that's what I like to hear."

Still shaking, Sophia began stuffing the bag with wallets and jewelry just like the teller was filling the bank robbers' duffel bag with cash.

"We'd like to thank you for your cooperation, ladies and gentlemen," the giraffe said, zipping up the duffel bag and sliding the strap over his shoulder.

"Let's move," the lion said. "Cops will be here any minute."

Sophia felt someone behind her. The man in the monkey mask snatched the drawstring bag away from her. He brushed his gloved hand against her cheek. "Until we meet again, sweetheart."

Sophia felt sick and terrified. The only time she wanted to see him again was when he was in handcuffs and on his way to jail.

He glanced back at her. The grinning monkey mask made her skin crawl. As he slung the bag over his shoulder, a thought struck Sophia like a bolt of lightning. He had their wallets—wallets filled with credit cards they could cancel and cash, at least in her case, that couldn't pay for more than a large coffee. However, her wallet also held her driver's license. The one she got about three weeks ago. The one with her new address on it.

She dropped to her knees. What if he truly meant he planned to see her again? The thought struck fear in her heart. Arms wrapped around her, causing her to flinch slightly.

"You're okay. It's over. They're gone. They can't hurt us." The man who had tried to protect her may have been a stranger, but he made her feel safe and she needed that right now. She allowed herself to lean into him.

Rising to their feet, she said what she was thinking, her voice trembling like the rest of her. "They have our wallets, our IDs."

He placed gentle hands on her shoulders. "I know. We'll tell the cops everything. I'm sure all they want is the cash and the credit cards. Maybe they'll get caught because they use our credit cards somewhere. This could be a good thing."

"But he said—" Her fear had to be palpable. She could feel it coming off her like heat.

"Listen, that jerk clearly enjoys being scary. He just wanted you to be afraid. Don't give him the satisfaction."

"You're not afraid?"

The man shook his head. "Something tells me that Monkey Man wouldn't act so tough without a mask on and a gun in his hand." The sound of sirens blared outside. The police were here a little too late. "Hopefully the police catch them quickly."

He stepped back and his hands slid down her arms and held her hands.

"I wish I felt the same way." She tightened

her grip on his hands. "Thank you for helping me."

"Of course."

She let him go and felt less steady as soon as she broke contact. "I don't even know your name."

One side of his mouth smiled. "Evan," he said, holding out his hand in greeting.

She shook it. "Sophia. Nice to meet you, Evan."

"Nice to meet you, too. Although, I wish we had met any other way than this."

Sophia felt herself smile. "Me, too."

The police entered the bank and Sophia was placed in a cubicle to wait for a detective. She texted Fallon that she was alive and well but wouldn't be coming back to work. She couldn't think straight and wasn't sure how long she'd be stuck answering questions.

When she sat back in her chair and craned her neck just a bit to the left, she could see Evan sitting in the cubicle across from hers. He was giving his statement to someone and was using his hands to emphasize whatever point he was making.

"Miss Reed?" A female detective walked in and sat behind the banker's desk. Sophia nodded and the detective continued. "My name is Detective Gibson. I am going to ask you some questions and then we're going to get you on your way. I'm sure you didn't plan to spend your day at the bank."

Sophia answered all of the detective's questions. Told her everything she could think of about the robbers, even though there didn't seem like much to tell. She couldn't see their faces, they wore gloves and she was still in quite a bit of shock.

"You didn't notice any distinguishing marks, tattoos, jewelry, anything on any of the men?"

Sophia closed her eyes and searched her memory for something. She shook her head. "No. I'm sorry. All I remember is their masks and their voices."

The detective slid a business card across the desk. "Don't apologize. You've been through one heck of a traumatic event. Once the shock wears off, if something comes to you, anything, give me a call, okay?"

Sophia took the card and promised to do so. Evan exited his cubicle at the same time. Seeing him immediately relieved some of her anxiety, and she seemed to bring a small smile to his face at the same time.

"All done?" he asked.

"Yeah. You?"

He ran a hand through his dark hair. "Yeah, I really should go back to work, but I feel like I'm going to be useless."

"I already texted my business partner that I'm not coming back today. I want to go home, but I'm also terrified to go home."

Concern etched his face. He reached out and touched her arm. "I don't blame you for feeling like that. But I'm going trust the police will do their job and find these guys before they can do any more harm."

She wanted to believe that. "Since neither one of us wants to go to work, maybe we should grab a drink and pretend we didn't meet during a bank robbery."

"That would be great...except the bank robbers stole all our money and credit cards," he answered with a laugh.

Sophia cringed. "I forgot about that."

"We could go find a nice park bench and start contacting credit card companies together," Evan offered.

It was probably the strangest first-date idea ever, but it sounded perfect. "Let's do it."

Spring was Sophia's favorite time of year,

especially in Charlotte. The smell of the flowering trees and the feel of the sun on her skin were rejuvenating.

"What did people do before the internet and before all the credit card companies had apps?" Evan asked, slipping his phone into the inside pocket of his suit coat.

Sophia finished reporting the last of her stolen credit cards via the app on her phone. "They had to call the number on the back of their card, I guess."

Evan's brows furrowed. "How do you call the number on the back of a card that was stolen?"

"That's a very good question," Sophia replied with a chuckle.

"Well, I'm glad that I was robbed today and not twenty years ago." He shook his head. "Not that I wanted to be robbed. I definitely didn't want you to be robbed."

Sophia's heart beat a little faster as the memory reemerged. "That was the scariest thing that's ever happened to me. I really don't think I can sleep at home tonight. I am definitely begging my *yaya* for at least one night in her guest bed."

"Your *yaya*?"

"It's what people call their Greek grandmother." Sophia opened her photo app and pulled up her favorite picture of Yaya Iris. "My *yaya* is eighty-one and the coolest woman I know. I owe my excellent fashion sense to her as well as my love of butterscotch candy."

The grin on Evan's face grew wider. "You love butterscotch candy? I don't think I have ever met anyone under the age of eighty who loves butterscotch candy."

Sophia swatted his arm playfully. "Yaya always has a bowl of all the classics on the sofa table in her living room. She's got the peppermints, the cinnamon discs, the raspberry ones with the stuff that oozes out of the center and, of course, lemon drops."

"Lemon drops. I love those. First they're sweet and then you get that sugar layer off and you're hit by that sour." Evan pursed his lips like he'd eaten one.

He was adorable. Kind, funny and completely adorable. Somehow, on one of the worst days of her life, Sophia had managed to also meet the perfect guy.

As she stared into his warm chocolate-brown eyes, she wished he was puckering up for another reason.

"Are you okay?" he asked, snapping her out of her fantasy of kissing a man she'd known for all of a couple of hours.

Sophia laughed at herself. "I'm fine. I'm just really glad we met, and I hope this isn't the last time I get to talk to you."

He took her phone out of her hand and started tapping away.

"What are you doing?" She tried to grab her phone back, but he leaned away and kept typing.

When he was finished, he held it out for her. "I added myself to your contacts."

Sophia scrolled through until she found him. "Evan the Hot Guy from the Bank? That's the name you put in my phone?"

"I figured that would be the easiest way for you to remember me."

As if she could ever forget.

They spent the afternoon getting to know one another. Evan had grown up in a small rural town in North Carolina. Went to Chapel Hill on a full-ride scholarship. His father passed away when he was in college and his mother retired to Florida. He called her twice a week to check in. Sophia loved that. She could tell a lot about a man by the way he treated his mother. He also had a younger brother who lived with him.

As for work, he was actually an employee of Wharton Bank—not at the branch they had been at today but at the corporate office. He was an information analyst. Sophia wasn't exactly sure what that was, but at least he had a good job and a plan to climb that corporate ladder. Those were two things the last guy she met on an internet dating site was severely lacking.

Sophia told him about growing up in one of the suburbs of Charlotte. She probably shared too much information about her free-spirited parents, who sold the family house and bought an RV when her dad retired. They had been traveling the United States ever since. He asked question after question, though, as if her life story truly interested him.

"So what do you do for a living?" he asked as the sun began to drop behind the city skyline.

Sophia opened her mouth to answer, but before she could tell him all about her business, Evan got a call.

"I'm so sorry. I have got to take this," he said. He stood up and walked a couple of feet away.

Sophia tried to use that time to collect her

thoughts. Was this really happening? She was the last person to believe in love at first sight, but there was something about this guy. He seemed to be so genuine, so down-to-earth.

He ended his call and strolled back to the bench where she was waiting for him. His face showed his chagrin.

"As much as I don't want to go, I need to pick my brother up from work. Something happened…" He didn't finish that sentence and Sophia could tell he didn't want to.

The disappointment hit Sophia harder than she expected. "I totally get it. I should probably let my *yaya* know that I'm coming over. It was really nice meeting you, Evan."

"Next time, we'll get that drink. Maybe I'll throw in dinner, too."

Sophia's heart fluttered. The possibility of a real date made her giddy. "I would love that."

Yaya was more than happy to let Sophia stay the night. The two of them had some dinner, Sophia gave Yaya her account of the day and they ended the evening with some chamomile tea.

"For someone who asked to stay here because she is afraid masked men are going to show up at her door, you keep smiling down at your phone like you've learned they've been captured."

Sophia glanced up from her phone. "Sorry, Yaya." She quickly typed good-night to Evan the Hot Guy from the Bank. "I really appreciate you letting me stay here. I am freaked out, but I might also be kind of sort of falling for this guy I met today."

Yaya was intrigued and scooted closer to her on the couch. "You met a man today?"

It sounded strange given the circumstances. "I did. And I think I really like him."

Yaya's painted-on eyebrow quirked up. "Why did you leave this part of the story out when you were telling me about your day?"

Sophia took a sip of tea and curled her legs under her. "I don't know... Because it's silly to think two people could meet this way, isn't it?"

"Sweetheart, I'm over eighty years old. I have heard sillier things than that."

Even though Sophia planned weddings and other major events for a living, she tended to be a bit skeptical when it came to love. Maybe it was because things never seemed to work out for her. Some men were intimidated by her independence. Too many wanted a woman who was ready to give up her career for a family. Others had no desire to settle down into a serious relationship at all.

Mr. Right didn't seem to exist in Sophia's world. Until today.

Good night. Tell your yaya that she inspired me to order an old-fashioned candy mix online today. Of course, I couldn't actually purchase it because my credit card is on lockdown, but as soon as I get that new card, those lemon drops are all mine. I'll save you the butterscotch.

"That must be him." Yaya laughed. "You most definitely like him. If you could see the way he makes you smile, you wouldn't doubt it for a second."

YAYA WASN'T THE only one who thought Sophia was falling hard. Fallon caught on real quick the next day at work.

"Ian picked up the pennies for the Westbergs' wishing well and Cassie got confirmation from the Chalet that we can have their private room as early as four on Friday. I also— Who in the world are you texting with?"

Sophia set her phone down and focused her

attention on her business partner. "What? I heard everything you said. Westberg pennies. Chalet four o'clock. Perfect."

"No, no, no." Fallon came marching around to the other side of Sophia's desk. "Do not pretend I am not seeing what I am seeing. You never smile that hard at your phone. Ever. Who are you talking to on there?"

Sophia grabbed her phone and pressed it to her chest. "No one."

"Liar. Since when are you seeing someone? Is it that guy you've been talking to from that dating site? I thought that didn't work out."

That absolutely had not worked out. "I perhaps met someone yesterday during the bank robbery, and the traumatic event kind of brought us together."

Fallon's eyes went wide. "Are you serious? You met a guy during the bank robbery? How does that even happen?"

"I know it sounds weird, but I really like him." Sophia felt like she was carbonated, filled with little happy bubbles. She hadn't felt this good in a long time.

"Well, you are going to tell me everything after our meeting."

The Wharton wedding was the biggest event Sophia and Fallon had ever planned.

Doing business with them meant Engaging Events would finally earn its place on the map. All of Sophia's and Fallon's hard work would finally pay off.

"I promise. I will tell you everything you want to know."

"You aren't going to mention what happened yesterday, right?"

Sophia shook her head. She felt a chill down her spine as the memory of having a gun pointed at her flashed through her mind. She had no intention of rehashing the robbery with the woman whose family owned the bank.

"Good," Fallon said with a nod. "Miss Wharton is going to sign with us and we're going to be planning events for every bigwig in Charlotte."

Sophia forced a smile. Hopefully, that was true.

Fallon left the office, and Sophia sent one last text before her meeting. She and Evan had been debating why certain emojis even existed.

Meeting in a few minutes. Do not spam me with any more emojis. I admit I may not be able to rationalize why there is an oil drum emoji.

He answered back just before she put her phone on Do Not Disturb.

Finally! I stumped you! Although I am still not sure it makes complete sense for there to be a merman. We may need to discuss that one again.

There was a knock at her door. Cassie, their assistant, poked her head in. "Miss Wharton and her fiancé are here."

Sophia smoothed down her dark hair. "Send them in," she said, getting to her feet.

The door swung open and a petite blonde walked in with her phone to her ear and a scowl on her face. She wore a black power suit with a crisp white blouse underneath. Her black Prada pumps and matching clutch cost more than Sophia's entire summer wardrobe. "We're meeting with the wedding planner right now. I understand that it needs to be done by today, but you're the one who set up this appointment for us. I'll call you when we're done."

This was not going to be an easy one. Miss Wharton was a woman who knew exactly what she wanted—she didn't accept excuses, and her taste was impeccable. Fallon was right behind her and followed in by the man who had held the door. He was grinning from ear to ear until their eyes met. Sophia's legs gave out almost immediately and she fell into her chair.

Evan.

CHAPTER TWO

One hour earlier...

EVAN ANDERSON THOUGHT he had it all figured out. He had brokered the deal of a lifetime. He was on the brink of getting everything he thought he wanted. All he had to do was stick to the plan.

Then the bank was robbed. He met Sophia. And his world flipped upside down. Now he wasn't sure about anything.

"May I go in?" he asked Jamie's administrative assistant, Riley.

Riley was twenty-three years old, and Evan knew he was hopeful that he could pay dues as an assistant and move up the ladder quickly if he learned everything he could from his boss. Unfortunately for him, Jamie tended to go through assistants like the seasons. Riley was okay for spring, but he was unlikely to make it through the summer.

"She might be on a call, but I'm sure she'll be fine with you going in."

This was why Riley wasn't going to make it. Evan went in anyway, knowing Jamie wouldn't be as pleased as her assistant assumed. She didn't like to be interrupted when she was on the phone. The look on her face confirmed that to be true. She glanced at her watch as she continued to chastise whoever was on the other end of the line.

Evan was a little early. They didn't have to meet with the wedding planner for an hour, but things had changed after yesterday's events. Evan had been changed by a woman who fancied butterscotch candy and had the most beautiful green eyes.

He took a seat and waited for Jamie to finish her call, pulling out his phone and scrolling through the messages he'd exchanged with Sophia. They had been chatting via text since they left the park. Neither one of them could sleep after the day they'd had, so they kept each other company. She was so witty. He really liked that about her.

He liked a lot of things about her. More than he should. He had made a deal with his friend, but maybe that wasn't the only solution to their problems. They were two intelligent people—surely they could come up with another plan before things went too far.

He texted Sophia a wind chime emoji.

Why would anyone ever need to text someone a wind chime? Am I the only person who thinks most of these emojis are completely pointless?

He waited for her response. Jamie was laying into someone about the bank robbery yesterday. It was the second robbery at a Wharton Bank in months, and she didn't appreciate it happening on her watch. His phone chimed.

This feels like a challenge...

It hadn't been, but he loved that she saw it that way. She continued.

I bet I can come up with a reason to send any emoji. For example, I would send my neighbor the wind chime one if the noise from her wind chime was annoying me. The emoji makes the text less confrontational.

He could feel his smile widen. She was hilarious. Game on. He scanned his emoji options. He sent her the green blob that looked like something they'd have on the wall in a high school science room.

I don't even know what this is.

"Why are you early?" Jamie asked. She had set her cell phone on the desk, put the caller on speakerphone and must have muted herself.

"I need to talk to you when you're off the phone."

"I could be on the phone until it's time to go. The calendar invite I sent you was for a specific time for a reason. You need to come back when it's your time."

He gave her a stern look. "Don't talk to me like I'm one of your employees."

"Technically, you are one of my employees," she tried with a shrug.

Evan cocked his head to the side, waiting for her to try again.

"Fine," she said with an exasperated sigh. "I'm sorry. It's been a stressful morning." She held up a finger to stop him from responding and unmuted herself on her call. "I don't care what else he has to do today—we need to meet this afternoon whether he likes it or not."

Evan and Jamie had met in college. They'd tried dating for a hot minute and realized they were much better off as friends. Then both of them had lost their fathers, and they'd bonded over tragedy. Jamie had been his best friend ever since, which was one of the reasons he was willing to go along with this plan of hers.

Jamie ended her call and rubbed her temples. "Useless. Everyone is useless. We have a robbery in one of our branches and I've got people acting like their two o'clock dentist appointment is more important than talking about how to make our customers feel safe."

"I'm sorry there's a lot on your plate. Maybe we should cancel this meeting with the wedding planner. Who needs that kind of distraction right now?"

Evan's phone chimed with a text.

According to my computer, that is a microbe. Obviously, germaphobes would use that on the regular.

"Why are you smiling at your phone like you're in love with it?"

He flipped it over and gave his full attention to his friend. "Sorry. I was just... Listen, I think we need to talk about what we're doing here. Maybe we should rethink this marriage idea."

"Don't do this to me, Ev. Not today. We have a plan. You know my uncle values three things—loyalty, intelligence and commitment. If I want to be in charge someday, we need to do this."

Jamie's uncle was the current CEO of Wharton Bank. Jamie was in line to succeed him. And she deserved it. No one was more intelligent than Jamie. She graduated summa cum laude from UNC Chapel Hill and was number one in her class when she got her MBA from Northwestern. As for loyalty, she had that in spades. Jamie would do anything for her family and they knew it. The last requirement her uncle Gordon had was that his successor needed to prove they were capable of commitment. The odd way he wanted proof of that was the reason Jamie and Evan were meeting with a wedding planner this morning.

"I know he's making you feel like we have to do this, but maybe he'll come around and see that people can commit to things other than a spouse."

Jamie narrowed her eyes at him. "What is going on? Why are you suddenly acting like this is a bad idea?"

"I'm not. It's ju—"

"I thought you were on board. You know that Patrick is champing at the bit to prove that we're not really together."

Patrick Wharton was the real reason they were doing this. Patrick was Jamie's cousin and also wanted their uncle's job.

"I know. I—"

"If he catches one whiff of doubt on you, we're done for. No promotion for me. No dream job for you. Patrick most definitely will not hire you as the head of Risk Management. He will give that job to the guy he trusts the most in the world instead of the guy *I* trust most in the world. Think about how that job will help you with Zeke."

The job was a huge incentive for Evan going along with the plan. Marrying Jamie meant that she'd meet all of her uncle's conditions and would be the likely choice to succeed him. When she was CEO, she could give Evan the job he wanted. He could skip several steps and go right to the top. That kind of money would make it much easier to take care of his brother.

Evan's 22-year-old brother had Down syndrome and had moved in with him after their mother had moved to Florida about three years ago. Zeke didn't want to leave North Carolina and hadn't graduated from high school until last year because of his special needs. These days, he was part of a program that allowed him to work full-time and provided supervision when he wasn't at work and Evan was.

Evan scrubbed his face with his hand. "I know, I know. Taking care of Zeke is the most important thing to me. I'm just a little discombobulated after what happened yesterday. You aren't the only one wrestling with the impact of the robbery. I was there, remember? Someone pointed a gun at me."

Jamie's expression softened. "I know, and I am so sorry about that. I can't imagine what that was like. I'm also really glad you're all right. If something had happened to you, at my bank nonetheless, I never would have gotten over it."

"Thankfully, we don't have to think about that. Being in a situation like that makes you think about what's important, though."

"Am I not important? Are our careers not important?" She was back to being defensive.

Evan had no right to throw a wrench into the plan at the last minute like this. He knew that, but he hadn't expected to meet someone like Sophia. Could she be as awesome as she seemed? Maybe he was kidding himself.

Historically, Evan had terrible luck with love. After his last girlfriend cheated on him, he decided that a fake marriage to his best friend would not only be good for his career but his heart, as well.

"I'm not backing out. I'm the one who put the idea on the table," he said, taking a different approach. "We're meeting with the wedding planner today. This is going from idea to reality. I want to make sure you're sure. Are you willing to give up any chance of meeting someone you could really fall in love with?"

Am I willing to give that up? That was the real question. If he married Jamie to help her take over the bank, he would not be able to fall in love with Sophia…or anyone. He meant anyone.

Jamie swept blond hair out of her face. "You know I don't have time to fall in love. When and where am I going to meet someone anyway? All I have time for is work. Plus, we only have to stay together as long as my uncle is alive. The man is seventy-five. He's not going to live forever."

"Okay, that's a morbid thought."

Jamie sighed. "You know what I mean. You aren't going to be chained to me forever." She stood up and walked around to his side of the desk. She sat on the arm of his chair and threw her arm over his shoulders. "I'm going to guess this sudden worry for my love life is more about being worried about *your* love life."

Evan rolled his eyes. "You know I don't have a love life."

His phone chimed with another text. He had to fight the urge to look at it, knowing it was probably from Sophia.

Jamie reached for his phone. "Who are you texting with?"

Evan was quick to snatch his phone away and downplay what was happening. There was no way to describe what was going on anyway.

"No one. Mind your business," he said playfully.

Jamie's phone rang and she stood up with a huff. "I need you, Ev. Please tell me I can count on you."

"You can count on me. Always."

Jamie's lips curled into a slight smile. "Thank you. Now get out of here so I can get some work done before we have to go."

She pointed to the door as she answered her phone. Evan pulled himself up and left the office. Gripping his phone tightly, he tried to muster up the will not to look at Sophia's last text and to stop whatever this was that he was doing.

He made it all the way to the elevator before he gave in.

"I'M GOING TO need you to step up when it comes to planning this wedding," Jamie said as they exited her car outside the office of Engaging Events. "Hopefully you won't have to do too much. That's why we're here to sign the contract—the wedding planner should do most of the work. I'm saying whatever the wedding planner needs us to do, I need you to do it."

Her phone rang in her purse.

"Awesome. So, you're cool with a camo theme and whiskey shots instead of a champagne toast?"

"Ha ha. You're a real comedian." Jamie tried to act unamused but couldn't hide her smile. Evan's sense of humor was her favorite thing about him and one of the big reasons they stayed friends after the dating idea failed. She pulled out her phone and was again back to doing business.

His own phone chimed with a text.

Meeting in a few minutes. Do not spam me with any more emojis. I admit I may not be able to rationalize why there is an oil drum emoji.

Finally! He knew he'd get Sophia to admit defeat eventually. He texted her back as they entered the building.

"Welcome to Engaging Events," a young woman said once they were inside. "My name is Cassie. Can I get you anything? Coffee, water?"

Jamie paid no attention, too focused on her call. Evan slipped his phone in his pocket. "We're good, thank you."

"Miss Wharton, we're so excited you're here," another woman with beautifully braided hair said, trying to engage Jamie without noticing she was on a call.

"Always working," Evan said, stepping in between. "I wonder sometimes if she's already married...to her phone."

The woman laughed and held out her hand. "Fallon Best. I'm the co-owner of Engaging Events."

He shook her hand. "Evan Anderson. I'm the lucky guy getting married."

"Does she need a minute?" Fallon asked.

"She has this amazing ability to multitask, and we're on a tight schedule. The sooner we can get started, the better."

"Okay, well, let's introduce you to my partner. Cassie, can you let her know our clients are here?" Fallon turned back to Evan. "We are thrilled you have chosen to work with us. We understand that the Wharton family could have hired anyone, and you won't regret choosing us."

Evan needed to get used to the way the

world saw the Whartons. Growing up in a working-class family, he wasn't accustomed to people fawning all over him.

"She's ready for you," Cassie said.

Jamie seemed to hear that and headed for the office. Evan grabbed the door and held it for her and Fallon. This was going to be interesting. He had a feeling they weren't going to be used to a bride who wanted the groom to make all the decisions. He smirked, thinking about throwing out the camo idea just to see their expressions.

But as he followed Fallon into the room, his eyes landed directly on the one person he did not want to talk about his wedding with—Sophia Reed.

Evan felt all the blood drain from his face as Sophia fell into her chair. He swallowed hard, trying to figure out how to do damage control.

Jamie ended her call and dropped her phone in her purse. She sat down across from Sophia. "We are on a very tight schedule. I'm Jamie Wharton, this is my fiancé, Evan Anderson, and we are *thrilled* you are *thrilled* to have our business. Now that we have that out of the way, what do you need from us to get started?"

Sophia didn't, maybe couldn't, take her eyes off Evan. He slid into the chair next to Jamie. His mouth was dry and words failed him.

When Sophia didn't speak, her partner took over. "Well, like I said earlier, my name is Fallon Best. This is my partner, Sophia Reed. Sophia will be the one in charge of your wedding. Right, Sophia?"

Evan wanted to explain, to tell her exactly what was going on here, but Jamie would never go for telling the wedding planner the truth. The way Sophia looked at him made Evan want to crawl under a rock. He had led her on and that was unforgivable. The least he could do was fess up to knowing who she was.

"What a small world." He spoke to Jamie even though he held Sophia's stare. "Sophia and I met yesterday. She was at the bank during the robbery."

Sophia's eyes widened just a bit. Jamie immediately tensed. "Oh. Well, please know that everyone at Wharton Bank is so sorry about what you experienced yesterday."

Sophia took a deep breath and it was as if she'd somehow rebooted herself. Her gaze shifted from Evan to Jamie. "Thank you. It was very scary. I'll admit, I plan to bank online for a bit because of it."

"We take security matters very seriously," Jamie assured her. "We are doing our best to make customers feel safe again when they go walking through our doors."

Evan felt a bit guilty about shifting some of the awkwardness onto Jamie, but it had to be done.

"I appreciate that," Sophia said. "Now, back to the business at hand. The first place to start is always the date. Then we need to talk about the budget and what level of service you want from us."

Jamie didn't hesitate to let it be known that she didn't want to lift a finger in the process.

"So full-service it is." Sophia jotted that down on the notepad in front of her.

"Obviously, if you need us to okay something or have questions, you can always contact Evan. He's the one you should call." Jamie reached over and grabbed Evan's hand. "He's very excited about the whole thing. Aren't you, sweetheart?"

He didn't realize they were going to try so hard to sell themselves as a couple. His embarrassment heated his face. "It's going to be fun, I'm sure."

"Well, isn't that sweet?" Sophia said with a hint of there's-nothing-sweet-about-it in her tone. "It's not often we get a groom so involved in the process, but it seems you've got yourself one hands-on, committed guy. That's very special."

Evan let go of Jamie's hand and scratched the back of his neck.

Jamie patted his knee. "I'm very lucky. Not everyone gets to marry her best friend. We're both lucky."

"Best friends?" Sophia's voice went up an octave. "So lucky. So very lucky. Luckiest."

Fallon's laugh gave away her nervousness. "So, dates. Have you two thought of a date?"

"My uncle has graciously offered his property on Lake Norman for the wedding and reception. We were thinking Fourth of July weekend."

"Fourth of July next year?"

"No, this year," Jamie corrected her. "We'd like to get married this year. As quickly as possible."

"So soon?" Sophia's glare fixated back on Evan as she tucked strands of dark hair behind her ear.

Fallon jumped in. "The Fourth of July is on a Sunday this year. Were you thinking about the fourth or the third?"

"The third is perfect."

When Sophia didn't respond, Fallon continued, "The fact that you are using a private residence makes a date like that a little easier. Two months means we will need to make decisions quickly in order to lock down what we need that day. We'll do our best, of course, to find vendors who can provide whatever your heart desires given your time restraints."

"Great," Jamie said, oblivious to the tension in the room. "Moving on to the budget. We aren't trying to rival the royals or anything. We'd like to keep things around three hundred thousand, but we can go up to half a million if needed."

Evan's eyeballs almost popped out of his head. The Whartons were rich, but never in a million years did he think she would want to waste so much on a fake wedding. "I thought we were planning a small wedding—just family and close friends. Do we really want to spend that much?"

Jamie threw her head back in laughter. "Honey, we will have no problem spending that much even on a small wedding. I am the only female Wharton in my generation. Ever since my father passed away, my uncle has been promising to throw me the wedding of my dreams. Trust me, I even talked him down to get to this number. He wanted to spend three times this much."

"Oh, now it makes so much more sense," Sophia said, nodding her head. Evan got the feeling she wasn't talking about the budget. He knew how this looked. He wanted so badly to explain he was in no way taking advantage of Jamie. He was not some gold digger.

"I'm also wondering, how many of these meetings will we both need to attend?" Jamie asked. "I am not someone who has a lot of time for meetings."

Sophia stopped glowering in Evan's direction. "We can contact you in a variety of ways. We typically communicate via phone or email. Whatever you prefer. If you, for example, *love* texting, we can be available via text."

Evan shifted uncomfortably in his seat. He wanted to tell her he did love texting her, but that this was way more complicated than she could ever imagine.

Jamie snickered. "Evan loves texting recently," she said, thinking it was an inside joke and having no idea who had really been on the other end of the line.

"Email works best," he said, shifting as far away from the texting conversation as he could.

"We'll also draw up some ideas and create an online inspiration board that you'll have access to. We want to make this as easy for the *bride* as possible." Sophia's emphasis made it clear she had no intentions of making anything easy for Evan. Not that he deserved easy. He had gotten himself into this mess. He would have to claw his way out.

Jamie's phone rang. She seemed to fight the urge to answer it. "All of that sounds wonderful. I look forward to hearing some of your ideas. Is there anything you specifically need me for, or if I left you with my fiancé, would that be fine?"

"You're going to leave me here?"

"There are pressing matters I need to attend to, *sweetheart*," she said through gritted teeth. "I am sure you can call an Uber to get you back to the office."

"We just need to discuss our fees and sign the contract. Are you comfortable with Evan handling that part?" Sophia asked.

Jamie stood up and started fishing for her phone, which had stopped ringing but chimed with a voice mail. "He's perfectly capable of signing his name. I'll talk to you later, Ev?"

"Later, schnookums." Two could play at the terms-of-endearment game.

Jamie's eyes flashed, but she managed a smirk. She was out the door before Evan could say anything else. He checked his watch. She'd given this meeting a whopping seven minutes of her time.

"Fallon, I think I can handle the rest of this meeting," Sophia said. "You're free to go work on whatever else you have going on."

Evan's heart thumped hard in his chest. As soon as Fallon left the room, he knew there was no way for him to properly explain what happened.

Would she forgive him? The loss stung

worse than expected. It had been silly for him to entertain the idea of letting this woman into his life—his out-of-control life.

Yet, even now, sitting across from her, all he wanted to do was confess everything and beg her to go to lunch with him. He wanted to press his palm against her cheek and lower his face to hers. What he wouldn't give to kiss those lips just once.

"Sophia…"

CHAPTER THREE

ONCE THEY WERE alone in her office, Sophia pulled out a manila folder from her drawer and grabbed a pen. Her face felt warm as he stared at her from the other side of the desk. She couldn't meet his gaze. She was too angry to look at him.

"Sophia…"

"Our contract is pretty standard," she said, opening the folder and jotting down the wedding date. "I'm marking down that you are interested in full-service support."

"Sophia, I feel like I need to explain," Evan said.

That was hilarious given the fact that there was absolutely nothing he could say that would explain why he had been chatting her up for the last twenty hours like he was anything but a soon-to-be married man.

"I think what we're going to do is both agree that yesterday we experienced a traumatic event. I was feeling very vulnerable, and it was nice to talk to someone who understood. I clearly mistook your friendliness to mean you were unattached. I have been set straight."

Evan wrung his hands. "I still feel like I should apologize. I was flirtatious. It was… misleading."

Misleading? Yeah, it was misleading. She tried not to let it show that her blood boiled. He clearly didn't think he'd be outed as engaged so quickly. As bad as she felt for herself, she felt worse for Jamie Wharton. Sophia had the sinking feeling that he wasn't marrying her for the right reasons.

"Let's move forward, okay?" She pushed the folder in his direction. "Full-service wedding planning includes an overall concept and design, planning, managing, coordination with all the vendors, and the hundreds of other little details that have to be ironed out before you and your soon-to-be wife take off for your honeymoon, which we can also help plan if you'd like."

Evan sat forward in his chair. "Wow. That sounds like a lot of work."

"Which is why full-service wedding planning costs more than the rest." She pointed to the number on the contract. "We have a team who does everything from sending out invitations and managing RSVPs to pinning the boutonnieres on the groomsmen. On this page—" she flipped to the list of duties "—you can see all of the things included in this package."

Evan glanced it over. He seemed impressed. "You do all this?"

"We do."

"I'm sure Jamie will appreciate that she won't have to worry about a thing." He signed his name and pushed the papers back toward her. "Is there anything else you need from me?"

If only she could answer that the way she wanted. Sophia had so many questions for him. Like, was he really some kind of sociopath? How could someone who seemed so kind and genuine be nothing more than a shallow flirt getting married to his supposed best friend? His extremely rich best friend. Jamie's wealth probably answered that question.

Her faith in men had been once again shattered just when she thought it had been restored. The robbers weren't the only bad guys in the bank yesterday.

She did her best to maintain her composure. "Perhaps we can schedule a time to walk the property where you plan to have the ceremony and reception so I can begin putting together the dream wedding."

"Yes, let's do that. I was going to take off a half day not this coming Monday but the next to take my brother to the doctor. I could probably do any time after one thirty."

"Let's plan on two, just to be safe." She wanted to ask about his brother but resisted. That didn't stop the questions from filling her head. Why did he have to go to the doctor with his brother? Was his brother sick? Was it related to why he'd had to disappear so quickly yesterday?

"Great. It's in my calendar," he said, holding up his phone. "Should I pick you up here or…"

Sophia's shoulders tensed. There was no way she was driving with Evan anywhere. Being in a car with him would be a big mistake. "We should drive separately and meet there."

"Right. Well, it's gated, so you'll have to

wait for me to get there. I guess I better be on time. My brother always complains that I'm late for everything."

The questions were back but she stopped herself from asking any of them. "I'll try to remember not to worry if you're a few minutes late," she said.

"You would have worried?" His expression was hopeful.

"*Worry* is a nice way of saying *be annoyed*," she said to burst his bubble. "That's it for today. I'll see you not this coming Monday but the next."

"Right. Next Monday."

Evan held her gaze just long enough to make her pulse quicken and her anxiety bubble over. Oh, the thoughts she'd had before she knew who he really was. Her wishful thinking and foolishness had caused her to imagine a scenario where the two of them would have been much more than wedding planner and client.

He buttoned his suit coat as he stood up. Today he wore a navy suit, striped shirt, no tie. He had clearly wanted to come across as classy but easygoing. *Likable.* That was his shtick. Evan was the ultimate Mr. Nice Guy.

His charm had obviously gotten him this far, but it was likely all he had going for him.

"Again, I am so sorry for not being more up-front yesterday. I—"

Sophia wrinkled her nose. "We've moved on, Mr. Anderson."

Evan let out a resigned sigh and gave her a sharp nod. "Have a good day."

Her professionalism demanded she return the nicety, but her hurt feelings kept her mute. She walked him out and stood by the door, watching him head for the corner and pull out his phone to call for a ride.

"Are you okay?" Fallon asked, coming up behind her.

Sophia wrapped her arms around herself and turned toward her friend. "I'm fine. We just signed our biggest wedding yet. I'm better than fine."

Fallon didn't look so sure. "Cassie, if anyone calls, can you take a message? Sophia and I have a few things to discuss."

Sophia followed her partner back to her office. "I really am fine."

Fallon shut the door. They never spoke about personal matters in front of their assistant. Right now, however, Sophia didn't want to talk about personal matters with anyone.

"What happened in that meeting?" Fallon asked.

Sophia was so embarrassed. On top of that, she couldn't even explain to herself how she had fallen into another trap with a guy who'd had every intention of breaking her heart from the moment they met.

"Well, let's see, the biggest wedding of our careers needs to be planned in two months instead of the two years it needs to be perfect. The bride seems completely uninterested in planning her own wedding, which she wants to happen in two months. Did I mention that she wants this wedding in two months?"

"Okay, the turnaround on this is going to be tough, but we can do it with that kind of a budget. Money makes things happen a lot faster. You seemed upset about something before they even mentioned the date, though."

Sophia rubbed her temples—she could feel the migraine coming. "It was obviously a shock to see the guy from the bank walk into my office."

"Small world indeed. But you looked like you had seen a ghost."

"I must have PTSD or something," Sophia tried. She avoided eye contact, knowing that she was about to give herself away.

It took another couple seconds, but Fallon managed to put two and two together. When Sophia mustered the courage to look, Fallon's expression had turned worrisome.

"Please tell me that the guy who had you smiling so hard this morning is not the same man who walked out of our office a few seconds ago."

Sophia covered her face, which was flushed with the heat of her embarrassment. "I should have known better than to believe someone good could come my way."

"He didn't mention he was engaged yesterday? You guys didn't talk about what you do for a living?"

Sophia stopped to think about it. They had talked about him working for Wharton Bank. Hadn't she told him she worked as an event planner?

"He definitely did not tell me he was engaged. He told me he worked for Wharton Bank, and I didn't want to jinx us by mentioning we were planning the Wharton wedding. I wonder what his reaction would have been if I had said that."

Fallon bit down on her bottom lip. "Are you okay to take the lead on this? Do you want to—"

"I'm *fine*," Sophia assured her. "I'm going to look at this as a blessing. Thank goodness I found out he was engaged today and not three months from now when I could have truly caught feelings."

Convincing Fallon and herself that was true wouldn't be hard because there was no way what she had been experiencing were real feelings for Evan. That was impossible. Love at first sight was a bunch of baloney.

"Jamie Wharton is marrying someone who will probably cheat on her before they're even married," Fallon pointed out.

"We are not in the business of giving people advice on who or who not to marry. We are here to plan their wedding day. Period."

Fallon threw her hands up. "Okay, you're right. We don't discriminate…even against lying, cheating bozos who don't deserve people like Jamie Wharton—or you. He doesn't deserve you, either."

Sophia knew that to be true. She deserved a

faithful man. A man who valued her strengths and loved her in spite of her weaknesses. An honest guy with true intentions. That kind of man had to exist. They must.

She sat behind her desk. "I am going to start my to-do list for Miss Wharton, and then we can work on finalizing the plans for the anniversary party on Friday."

Fallon left her to it. Sophia could handle this job. This wedding was going to put Engaging Events on the map. Her phone chimed with a text.

I feel like I need to say I'm sorry one more time. Is there an emoji for that?

Sophia didn't reply. Instead, she opened up his contact and changed his name from Evan the Hot Guy from the Bank to Jamie Wharton's Fiancé.

YAYA OFFERED TO let her stay a second night, but Sophia had to face her fears and go home. The robbers were not going to show up at her house. They were probably too busy counting all their stolen money.

That didn't stop every bump in the night

from making her hold her breath for a few seconds. *Houses creak*, she told herself. *Wind rustles things outside. No one is coming to kill you.*

Every time she closed her eyes, she saw the man in the monkey mask making good on his insinuation that they would meet again. Her pulse raced, her muscles tightened. Every breath was a struggle.

It was useless. She got out of bed and sat on the couch. Thank goodness for television. It helped block out the noises and distracted her from her paranoid thoughts. The nightly news replayed after all the late-night talk shows were over.

"Tonight, we're sharing some new information about that bank robbery yesterday," the newscaster said, getting Sophia's attention right away. "Police confirmed today that it appears the robbery at Wharton Bank and Trust on Fourth Street was connected to another robbery here in North Carolina. Let's go to Diane Redfern, who's been gathering information all day."

Sophia sat up straight and the sick feeling in the pit of her stomach returned. Diane was full of information. Three months ago a group of men in animal masks robbed a Wharton Bank two and half hours away in Raleigh. The two cities' police departments were working together to solve the crimes and were asking anyone with any information to come forward.

Picking up her phone, she clicked on her text messages. But it was the middle of the night. No one she knew was awake right now. She scrolled through her texts anyway until she got to the one from Evan. She hadn't replied to him all day and he must have understood that to mean he should leave her alone.

Of course, he was a client. She had to be careful not to be rude. Ignoring his texts would be rude. Would it be rude to text him at one in the morning? Perhaps she should reply. He wouldn't text back until morning and there wouldn't be the possibility of them getting into a conversation.

She typed out a quick text. No apologies needed.

Her finger hovered over the send button. It was a harmless reply. He would probably think it was odd that she sent it while he was sleeping, but who cared?

She pressed Send. Three little dots appeared

on his side a second later. Sophia's shoulders tensed, her heart pounding. He was awake and they were about to have a conversation.

Is this how you get all that work done? You don't sleep?

Since he was well aware of the effect the bank robbery had on her, she figured she might as well be honest.

Back home. Couldn't sleep. Saw on the news that yesterday's robbery was tied to another in Raleigh.

She watched as the three dots reappeared as he typed out his reply. They disappeared but no text came through. Suddenly, her phone was ringing. Jamie Wharton's Fiancé was calling. She stared at it for a few seconds, the shock preventing her motor skills from working properly.

"Hello?"

"I figured it was easier to talk than text." His voice was soft and warm like velvet. She had to remind herself he was a client.

"Oh" was all she could muster.

"I didn't hear that about Raleigh. Did that happen today?"

"No, they robbed a bank there three months ago. Same guys most likely. They wore the animal masks." An image of the man in the monkey mask flashed before her eyes and took her breath away. The hairs on her arm stood up.

"Well, that's good news," Evan said much to her surprise.

She pulled the blanket off the back of the couch and threw it over her legs. "How is it good news that they're serial robbers?"

"Because it means they'll probably try again, and the bolder they get, the more likely they are to mess up and get caught. It also means they're on the move. You don't have to worry about them coming to your house. They're probably long gone and planning their next robbery somewhere else. You're safe."

Immediately, his words had a calming effect. She was safe. They weren't going to come looking for her. "You have no idea how much I needed to hear that."

"I do know. I could feel your fear the other day."

"It was the way he said 'Until we meet

again.' It—" She wriggled as a tingle ran up her spine. She'd never been so scared and she hated it. Sophia prided herself on being self-reliant and confident. This criminal had stripped some of that confidence away from her, made her feel vulnerable in a way she wasn't prepared for.

"Hey, I get it. I hate that he did that to you." She could feel his anger and it was strangely comforting. "I hate that he singled you out. I want the cops to catch these guys more than anything. I believe they will."

"I hope so. I will definitely sleep better when they are behind bars. Maybe I need to buy a baseball bat or something."

"For protection?" he said with a slight chuckle.

"Well, I'm not comfortable with weapons, but I could handle a bat. I played softball when I was younger." For one season, and she struck out every time at bat, but she wouldn't bother to mention that part.

"Maybe an alarm system would do more good. I know a guy. He'd give you a good deal," Evan offered.

That was…kind of him. She shook off the warm feelings. He was engaged. Marrying one of the wealthiest women in Charlotte. Sophia was far from wealthy. She didn't have the money to buy a home alarm system no matter what "deal" he could get her.

"I'll figure it out. Thank you, though."

"Of course you will," he said softly.

She would. Her confidence grew with the encouragement. He had a way of doing that, making her feel better simply with his words.

"So… I guess we should go to bed." She smacked her forehead with the palm of her hand. Why did this have to be so awkward?

"Try to get some sleep tonight. Based on the list of responsibilities I signed off on today, you have a busy day ahead of you tomorrow…and pretty much every day until the wedding."

All the warm fuzzies vanished with the word *wedding*. *His* wedding. Evan was not someone she could think of as anything more than a client. He was getting married.

"That is true. I should let you go. I apologize for sending a text so late. I hope I didn't wake you. I was trying to try to catch up on some things I didn't get to during the day since I couldn't sleep."

"You didn't wake me." He sounded sad,

and it made her curious. "I have too much on my mind to sleep."

Sophia fought the urge to ask him what was wrong. He was not her friend. He was her client. "Well, good night, Mr. Anderson."

"You know you can call me Evan," he said.

"I know," she replied. Her chest tightened. She could never enjoy the luxury of casualness with him again. "I'll be in touch during business hours."

Evan paused. "Of course. Good night, Sophia."

She ended the call and tossed her phone to the other side of the couch. She never should have texted him. Why did he have to feel so right when she knew he was wrong?

CHAPTER FOUR

"CAN I HAVE peanut butter and jelly?" Zeke asked as they walked into the dimly lit Chalet.

"I'm not sure they're going to be serving PB and J at this thing, bud. I think it's going to be kind of fancy. Remember we talked about being fancy?"

Zeke tugged at the tie around his neck. "I remember. I can take this off when it's over?"

"As soon as it's over," Evan promised.

"Well, if it isn't the Anderson brothers!" a voice boomed. Kristopher Hamilton was a six-foot-five beast of a man. "Where is Jamie? Don't tell me you left the poor woman at home."

"This is a boys' night out. Right, Zeke?"

"Boys' night out and we get to be fancy." He held up his tie in case Kris had missed it. "Can I have some champagne?"

"We'll see about that," Evan said. "Maybe a sip when we toast the Hamiltons."

Kris and Evan had met in Miss Grayson's first-grade class. They bonded over their love of superheroes and soccer, and their massive crush on Miss Grayson.

"My mom is going to be disappointed you didn't bring Jamie. She wanted to hear all about the wedding plans."

"Ha!" Evan couldn't help but laugh. "Trust me, she'll get more information from me. Jamie put me in charge. Well, me and the wedding planner."

The wedding planner. The thought of Sophia caused an ache in his chest. Since their late-night chat, she'd communicated with him only via text and only about the wedding.

"Interesting. The only thing I was allowed to have an opinion on when Beth and I got married was... Actually, I don't think she asked my opinion about anything," Kris said with a laugh.

"Well, Jamie is not your typical bride. My opinions have been given full rein."

Kris shook his head. "Can you believe your brother and Jamie are getting married, Z-Man?"

"Jamie and Evan are having a wedding," Zeke said. That was what Evan had drilled into his brother's head over the last few weeks. That was all he needed to know.

Kris slapped Evan on the back. "Yeah, he is. I know you guys have been friends for a long time, but I'm not going to lie, I'm shocked things turned romantic. I didn't see that coming at all."

No surprise there. Anyone who knew them knew there had been nothing romantic about his relationship with Jamie. This was the toughest hurdle to overcome—convincing everyone they were truly in love so her uncle wouldn't question the legitimacy of their marriage.

"Sometimes love works in mysterious ways," Evan said with a shrug. "Honestly, it took us both by surprise, too."

Kris chuckled. "It must have, because I still remember you telling me about that disastrous date you two had back in college."

He wasn't wrong. *A disaster* was a good way to describe it. Evan and Jamie knew right away they were more like brother and sister than boyfriend and girlfriend. Definitely not husband and wife.

"Hopefully we'll be as happy as your parents have been for the last forty years."

"You and me both, friend." Kris threw his arm around Zeke's shoulders. "You ready to go to a fancy party?"

"Yeah!" Zeke fist-pumped the air.

Kris led them back to the private room where the anniversary party was being held. Mr. and Mrs. Hamilton planned to renew their vows before dinner, and they were standing by the door to greet their guests as they arrived.

"Evan Anderson! My word, you get more handsome every time I see you," Joyce Hamilton said, opening her arms for a hug.

"I fear the day you don't say that, you know." Evan hugged the woman who had been like a second mother to him growing up. "Thank you for inviting us. You two are a true inspiration. Forty years of wedded bliss is a real accomplishment these days."

"Forty years with the right woman is easy, my boy," Gary Hamilton said, shaking Evan's hand and pulling him in for a quick hug.

"Zeke, you look very handsome tonight," Mrs. Hamilton said, giving him a fist bump.

"We're being fancy tonight for you. I have a tie."

"I see that. That's a very nice tie, too." She

smiled at him. Evan had always appreciated the kindness the Hamiltons had shown his brother. Craning her neck to see if there was anyone coming up behind him, Joyce asked, "Where is the future Mrs. Anderson tonight? I have so many questions about the wedding."

As much as he hated to disappoint her, Evan knew it was best that he brought his brother as his date tonight. Too many people here knew him well, and he didn't feel like acting all night. He just wanted to be himself. "She had to work late tonight, but she sends her good wishes and promises to come with me the next time we're invited to a Hamilton family gathering."

"I'm going to hold you to that," she said with a wink.

More guests arrived, giving Evan the perfect out. He and Kris brought Zeke over to the bar to grab a drink. Kris's wife was there, looking in desperate need of a rescue from the conversation she was stuck in with one of Gary's brothers.

"Beth, honey, look who's here," Kris said, helping her out.

She apologized but ended her conversation with Uncle Harold before wrapping Evan up in a warm embrace. "Thank goodness you're here. I could not handle hearing about Harold's battles with IBS one second longer," she said into his ear.

"Happy to be of service."

"Z-Man! How are you, buddy?"

"I'm fancy tonight." Zeke showed off his tie for the hundredth time since they'd arrived.

Beth eyed Evan warily. "Where's your fiancée?"

He hoped this was the last time he'd have to give an excuse. "She's very sorry. The bank robbery the other day has made things difficult for her at work. It's been somewhat of a PR nightmare."

Beth swept her strawberry blond bangs from her eyes. "Difficult for her? How about you? You were there."

"I'm fine. It was no big—" He stopped as soon as his gaze landed on the woman speaking to the Hamiltons.

Sophia, dressed in the palest yellow, held a leather folio as she pointed to the back of the room. Her dark hair was pulled back into a ponytail tied at the base of her neck. When her eyes locked with his, she seemed to freeze just as he had. She was so beautiful that she took his breath away. He managed to raise his hand a give her a little wave hello.

She didn't return the gesture. After what felt like hours but was probably less than a few seconds, she regained her composure and finished talking to Joyce and Gary.

"Who are you waving at?" Beth asked, glancing over her shoulder. "The party planner? Do you know the party planner?"

Know her? He wished he could know her, know her the way Kris had been able to get to know Beth when they first met. What he wouldn't give to be able to spend every night picking her brain and learning everything there was to know about her.

"That's my wedding planner." His reply was somber, wanting her to be anything but that.

"Sophia? Isn't she fabulous?" Beth asked, oblivious to the heartache he was feeling. "She planned my sister's wedding last summer. I'm the one who recommended her to Joyce and Gary. She's the best."

"Only the best for a Wharton wedding." He couldn't stop staring even though he tried. Sophia led the Hamiltons to the area in the back, presumably where they were going to renew their vows. Pastor Williams from their church stood under an arch of white and pink flowers.

"May I have everyone's attention," the pastor called out. "I need everyone to take their seats so we can begin our celebration."

Evan and Zeke followed Kris and Beth to their table. Although Pastor Williams had basically asked for all eyes on him, Evan couldn't help but follow Sophia's every move.

He spent most of the evening watching her work. She was a party-planning ninja. Always one step ahead of the action and capable of drifting unnoticed into the background so the Hamiltons were the center of attention at all times.

It was as if she was a conductor of an orchestra, carefully directing all of the activities without overshadowing the stars of the show. It was impressive, which was unsurprising given all she had done since he had met her was impress him with her courage, her intellect and her humor.

She was the consummate professional with impeccable style. The yellow dress she wore accentuated her slim waist and showed off her long legs but wasn't too revealing.

The more he stared, the more Sophia seemed to ignore him. When the video slideshow began after dinner, Evan noticed her slipping out the door.

"Hey, buddy, I'm going to run to the bathroom," he whispered to Zeke. "You stay here with Kris, okay?"

Zeke gave him a thumbs-up. He got up, hoping to catch up to Sophia just to say hello. Nothing more. He had expected more of a chase, so when he darted into the hallway, he practically ran her over. He placed both hands on her waist to steady her. Their bodies so close, he could smell the perfume on her neck and feel the warmth that radiated off her skin.

"Sorry about that," he said, letting her go and stepping back.

Sophia's startled expression made him want to reach for her again. He kept his distance, knowing it was selfish to want to be close to her so badly.

"You," she said in a breath.

"Small world, huh? The Hamiltons are like family. I grew up with their son, Kris."

She didn't respond. The hand pressed to her chest slid down to her waist where one of his had been a moment before.

"It's a wonderful party," he continued, unsure how else to respond to her silence. "You're doing a fantastic job. I've never seen Joyce so happy. She'll be talking about this for years to come."

Her eyes narrowed and her jaw tensed. "Your fiancée wasn't able to join you tonight?" she asked with a sharpness that almost made him flinch.

The overwhelming desire to confess that Jamie was only his fake fiancée was so strong. He had to fight it with everything he had. "It's a boys' night out tonight. Just me and my brother."

He hadn't mentioned that Zeke had Down syndrome when they spoke about him that first day. He wondered how she felt about him omitting another bit of information. He would have told her had their time not been cut short. Evan was always up-front about Zeke because some people were uncomfortable around people with disabilities, and Zeke was always going to be part of his life. It usually didn't take long for Zeke to win people over once they got to know him—Sophia wouldn't really get to know him, though.

"Well, I need to get back to work."

"Right," he said. "I was headed to the men's room."

"Have a good night, Mr. Anderson."

Ugh. He hated that she kept things so formal. "You, too."

Neither one of them moved. Evan still couldn't take his eyes off her. Her cheeks were tinted the slightest pink. Was she embarrassed or heated by anger?

"I need you to…" She motioned for him to move.

"Right. Sorry." He sidestepped out of her way and she did everything possible not to brush against him as she passed by.

She hated his guts. He probably deserved it. Why did his timing have to be so bad?

He stood by the door for a few minutes instead of going to the restroom. The slideshow was over when he returned, and guests were mingling.

"Evan, come over here," Joyce called. Sophia stood next to her and stiffened as soon as he changed directions to come their way.

Zeke sat next to Joyce, and Beth sat on the other side of her mother-in-law.

"I told Joyce that Sophia was planning your wedding," Beth said.

"I need details. Sophia, dear, you have to give me some details. Evan, give her permission to tell me everything."

Sophia tried to paste on a smile, but her discomfort was clear. "I'm sure Mr. Anderson can tell you all about it. Miss Wharton has put him in charge of making most of the decisions."

"Evan and Jamie are having a wedding," Zeke added.

Evan smiled at his brother's enthusiasm. "Yes, we are, bud. There's not much to tell just yet, Joyce. We're getting married Fourth of July weekend at her uncle's estate. That's about all that's been decided so far. We're in the early stages of planning."

"The Wharton Family Estate?" Joyce flushed. "I get to visit the Wharton Family Estate? Are you kidding me? That place has been featured in *Southern Living* more times than I can count!"

"Sophia and I are going there next week to scope it out," Evan offered up as a juicy detail. "I'll have much more information for you after we do that."

"I guess I'll have to be patient," Joyce said. She looked up at Sophia. "Do your best work for this one. He's a gem. He deserves the perfect wedding day."

Joyce's high opinion of him was appreciated, but her words clearly made Sophia all the more uncomfortable.

"I always strive to do my best, Mrs. Hamilton. I'm sure Mr. Anderson and Miss Wharton's wedding will be very memorable."

"I'm sure it will." Joyce reached for Evan's hand. "Your father would be so proud of the man you've become. I don't think he could have ever imagined you would one day marry into one of the most prominent families in the whole state."

"I'm still trying to picture you and Jamie as a couple," Beth mused. "What was it that you told Kris after your first date with her? Kissing your aunt Nell would have been more romantic?"

"Aunt Nell has a mustache, but she's not a man," Zeke shared.

Everyone at the table tried not to laugh and failed. There were probably a few things Evan wished he could take back saying now that they were going through with this fake marriage. The chemistry between him and Jamie had been so lacking, it was embarrassing.

"Not all relationships are love at first sight. Some of them need time to bloom," he retorted. Insta-love wasn't the norm. No one could deny that.

He glanced at Sophia and immediately he wanted to deny it. The sparks he felt when he was around her were like none he'd ever experienced. Their connection had been immediate. As soon as she got in line behind him at the bank, he had felt it.

"I'm going to check in with the restaurant manager. Enjoy the rest of your evening, everyone," Sophia said, making her escape.

Evan hated that she had to think he was in love with Jamie. Even if the marriage lasted only a few years, he'd be hard-pressed to earn her trust back. By then, she'd surely be married to someone else, as well.

"She's pretty," Zeke said. Evan nodded. His brother wasn't blind.

Evan watched as she once again slipped out of the room. All he wanted to do was go home and brood for a bit, but Kris had other ideas. He dragged Evan over to the bar for some drinks and some laughs. It lightened his mood a bit. At the end of the night, he and Zeke were the last nonfamily members remaining.

Sophia returned with a couple employees and began breaking down the flower arch and collecting all the decorations and centerpieces. He found himself watching her again. When she caught him staring, he tried to look away, but he was probably ridiculously obvious.

"Do you two need a ride home?" Beth asked Evan, nodding her head as if that would make him answer her question affirmatively. "I saw all those drinks my husband kept handing you all night."

He waved her off. "I didn't drive. You two live in the suburbs and in the opposite direction than we're going. Zeke loves rideshares. Don't worry about us."

"Thanks for coming tonight. It meant a lot to my mom and dad," Kris said.

"Wouldn't have missed it for the world. Next bash is on me. Or maybe I should say the Whartons." He laughed, but it wasn't as funny to him as it should have been.

"Evan and Jamie are having a wedding," Zeke said. "We get to be fancy again and I get to have more champagne!"

"Whoa, buddy. One glass of champagne during your toast," Evan said. "We don't want to get ridiculous."

He glanced around the room, searching for Sophia, but she was gone. The disappointment he felt was more intense than he'd expected. He needed to get over this obsession.

The Anderson brothers walked out with the Hamilton crew, who had to wait for the valet to retrieve their cars. They said their goodbyes and stepped outside. Evan requested a car with his ridesharing app.

The temperature had dropped and there was a slight chill in the air. Evan noticed Sophia rubbing her arms with her hands to stay warm.

An internal battle began. If he went over to her and offered her his jacket, which was the gentlemanly thing to do, she would likely refuse. Things would get awkward because he'd have to insist. Was making her miserable worse than leaving her cold?

She glanced at her phone, and whatever she saw didn't make her happy. Her gaze then fell in his direction and his heart leaped when she didn't cringe. He couldn't stand it. He had to give her his jacket.

"Come on, Zeke. I need to talk to the wedding planner."

"She's pretty."

"Yeah, but let's keep that thought in our head, okay?" They approached Sophia. "Are you waiting for a ride?" Evan asked, slipping out of his suit coat.

She sucked in a breath and wasn't able to hide that she was freezing to death out there. "Yeah. Ian packed the company van and noticed there was no gas. He and Olive went to get some while I finished up here. I guess the closest gas station wasn't so close." She leaned forward and searched for her ride in both directions.

"Here," he said, placing the jacket over her shoulders, figuring she couldn't say no if he didn't even ask.

"No, no. I'm fine. My ride is almost here."

Evan put his hands up, refusing to take the jacket back. "A few minutes is an eternity when you're cold."

"Thank you," she said, resigned.

"Sophia, this is my brother, Zeke. Zeke, this is Sophia."

"Hi," Zeke said before firmly pressing his

lips together. He did that when he had to keep thoughts in his head.

"Hi, Zeke. It's nice to meet you."

Evan bounced a little on the balls of his feet, shoving his hands in his pockets. "Zeke and I had a great time at the party. It was really well planned out. You are very good at what you do."

She didn't look at him but instead searched the street for her ride. "Thanks."

"So you guys plan other events besides weddings?"

This question made her turn her head his way. "We're event planners. While weddings make up a large portion of our business, we do other events, as well—parties, fundraisers, corporate retreats."

"Wow, that's cool. I didn't think about how many different ways your skills could come in handy." Her job was so much more interesting that his. "What's the biggest event you've had to plan?"

"The biggest event in terms of size was a fundraiser for the Charlotte Children's Hospital. The biggest in terms of status is pretty obvious."

"What's that?" he asked, his eyebrows pinching together.

"Honestly?" The way she looked at him made it clear he should know the answer to that question.

"My wedding?"

"Evan and Jamie are having a wedding," Zeke repeated.

She nodded. "The Wharton wedding is the most significant event we've ever been hired to plan. It will make or break our company for sure." She shrugged out of his suit coat and handed it back to him. "My ride is here."

Evan didn't want to say good-night. He stepped to the curb and opened the door for her.

She let out a sigh. "I wish you weren't so nice. You make it so much harder because you're so nice."

He didn't mean to make things hard for her, but he was selfishly happy to hear that she thought he was nice.

"You're pretty," Zeke blurted out.

She smiled faintly. "Thank you. It was nice meeting you, Zeke."

"Good night, Sophia," Evan said, unable to hide his own smile.

She climbed into the van. "Good night, Mr. Anderson," she replied, pulling the door closed.

The formality stung as it always did. He watched her drive away and slipped back into his jacket that had wrapped around her in a way he'd never be able to.

His wedding had the potential to help her business like no other event could. How ironic that she was the reason he wanted to cancel the stupid thing. Not only would this fake marriage give Jamie what she wanted and Evan the resources to take care of Zeke for the rest of his life, but it would also help Sophia's business. Now there wasn't any way he could back out.

His phone rang in his pocket. It was Jamie. "Hey, we're just leaving the Hamiltons' anniversary party."

Jamie's voice was full of frustration. "We have a *huge* problem."

CHAPTER FIVE

SOPHIA CHECKED THE time on her phone again. It was almost two thirty. Evan had clearly said they were supposed to meet at the Wharton Estate at two o'clock. He had warned her he was often late, but this was excessive.

Sitting in her car outside the gated entrance, her patience waned. This was where he'd told her to meet him. The text she'd sent to tell him that she had arrived was still unread. Was he on his way? Had he been in an accident? Did something happen at the doctor's with Zeke? Maybe he couldn't answer her text because he was being a responsible driver. She shouldn't worry.

That was easier said than done. Her imagination was running wild and tended to lean to the negative. Calling him was her only option. As soon as she pulled up his contact information, a black sedan pulled up behind her. Evan jumped out of the driver's seat and jogged up to her car.

Today he was dressed in a beige suit with a slate blue tie that complemented it nicely. He took off his aviator sunglasses as she rolled down the window.

"I am so sorry," he said. "I should have called, but I was on a call the whole way here. The doctor's appointment went longer than we planned. I know I said I have a tendency to be late, but I promise I am not usually this late."

She appreciated that he respected her time. She also wondered why the doctor's appointment had taken so long. She couldn't ask something like that, though. It was too personal.

"It's fine. I'm glad it wasn't an accident or something. You had me a little worried."

A grin spread across his face. "Worried or annoyed?"

"Worried," she admitted.

"That's sweet." Instantly, his expression changed to pained. "You can follow me up to the house," he said.

Confused by his sudden shift in emotion,

she waited for him to pull up to the gate and open it.

The tree-lined lane leading up to the main house set Sophia's imagination into over-drive. She could imagine the photographs of the wedding party that could be taken here before the guests arrived as well as the lights that could be strung from tree to tree, creating a fairy-tale atmosphere at night.

As they pulled into the enormous circle drive, Sophia took in the grandeur of the house. While not quite as large as the Biltmore in Asheville, the Whartons' house was still immense. The French-style chateau had a turreted front entrance and wrought iron accents. The exterior was a mix of neutral-colored brick, stone and stucco. One wing had a steep-pitched roof and a row of gabled dormers. The other had arched dormers that matched the windows on the first floor below them. Sophia counted four chimneys.

"We're supposed to check in with the house manager," Evan said once they both exited their vehicles.

"Is that the new term for a butler?" she asked, following him to the front door.

His smile lit up his whole face. "I think so."

The man radiated charm. She was drawn to it.

Sophia forced herself to focus on the intricately carved vines and arcs on the wrought iron front door instead of Evan's face. It didn't matter if she looked at him or not. He was like a magnet. She found herself wanting to lean into him.

"I should take some pictures out here before we go in," she said, digging her phone out of her purse.

Sophia left him on the stoop, needing to put space between them. She took some pictures of the circle drive and the view down the lane from the house. An older gentleman answered the door and greeted Evan. Sophia dashed back to be introduced.

"This is Sophia Reed. Our wedding planner," Evan said. "Sophia, this is Nelson, Mr. Wharton's house manager."

"Pleased to meet you, Miss Reed," Nelson said with a bow of his head. "Would you please come in?"

Nelson stepped back and the two of them entered into the rotunda foyer that made for quite a grand entrance. From the marble floors to the crystal chandelier, everything was exquisite.

"Mr. Wharton is on his way and wants to make sure you two meet with him before you leave," Nelson said. "He usually retires to the sunporch when he gets home. I'll show you where that is before you go out back."

Sophia felt like she was touring a museum instead of someone's home. She couldn't imagine living in a house where she was afraid to touch anything, and she was currently experiencing that fear as they made their way through the massive living room that, according to Nelson, had a hand-carved mahogany fireplace mantel.

The dining room looked like it could accommodate close to thirty people. Sophia couldn't seat thirty people in her entire house. The Wharton estate made her little bungalow seem as spacious as a dollhouse.

"How big is this place?" Sophia asked as they entered the gourmet kitchen.

"The main house is over twenty thousand square feet," Nelson answered. He seemed more than willing to share details about the estate. "There are nine bedrooms, nine full bathrooms and four half baths situated on ten acres of land. We also have a three-bedroom guesthouse on the property along with a pool and a separate pool house."

"We heard Patrick's staying here while his house is under construction. Is that right?" Evan asked.

"Mr. Wharton's nephew has moved into the guesthouse. He brought his dog, so staying here in the main house was not a viable option."

"He brought his dog but not his wife?"

Sophia was surprised to hear him digging for so much family gossip and that Nelson was so willing to give it.

"Ms. Eliza helped him get settled in, but I believe she has been staying with her mother in Raleigh the last week or so. They swear their house renovations will be finished before summer's end. We shall see," Nelson said, his tone skeptical.

"Oh, wow. That long, huh?" Evan sounded disappointed. "Jamie was hoping they'd be out of here before the wedding. She didn't want them to be bothered by the preparation. She already feels bad enough that her uncle has to deal with all of it."

"You tell that poor girl not to fret. Her

cousin knew about the wedding when he chose to come stay here. She shouldn't feel guilty about a thing. I haven't seen her uncle this excited in quite some time. He's thrilled about hosting this wedding." Nelson opened a set of French doors. "Here is the sunporch. This is where you will find Mr. Wharton when you are finished exploring the grounds."

"Thank you, Nelson," Evan said.

"Yes, thank you very much," Sophia added.

"You're welcome. Mr. Wharton wants nothing but the best for Miss Jamie, so please take your time and do whatever you need to in order to make her day spectacular."

"I will," Sophia promised, feeling like an even bigger jerk for wanting to stare at Evan's face earlier. That handsome face belonged to a man who was about to marry someone else. Someone who was beloved by her family and even the family's house manager. Sophia shouldn't be swooning over him. He was off-limits.

Evan placed his hand on the small of Sophia's back as he guided her to the door that led to the backyard. Heat radiated from that spot throughout Sophia's body. She moved swiftly to avoid the contact.

The Wharton estate was magnificent. The grounds were impeccably maintained. Mounds of hydrangeas, peonies and black-eyed Susans filled the flower beds around the house. Perennials in every color—yellows, blues, purples and pinks—filled in the gaps.

As if that wasn't impressive enough, there was a massive flower garden on the east side of the property. They wouldn't have to do much to dress things up for the ceremony and reception. The natural backdrop was better than anything Sophia and Fallon could come up with.

"I've been here a few times over the years for some big events. There are usually people everywhere. I don't want the wedding to be that big."

"Have you or Miss Wharton thought about where you want to have the ceremony?"

He sighed loudly, his hand raking through his hair. "Can you please call her Jamie? I have no idea who you're talking about when you call her Miss Wharton. Just like when you call me Mr. Anderson—I look around for my dad, who is dead, so that's weird."

Sophia pressed her lips together. Evan was the guy she imagined as her perfect mate.

Mr. Anderson was Jamie Wharton's perfect mate. Evan was a sweet, funny guy who she fantasized about kissing all day long. Mr. Anderson was only supposed to kiss Jamie Wharton.

"I would simply like to keep things professional," she explained. "This is a professional relationship and you are my clients."

He touched her hand, which sent an electrical current up her arm. "I get it, Sophia. I promise that things between us will remain one hundred percent professional even if you call us by our first names."

Her breathing was slightly uneven. She took a step away from him and took some pictures of the massive lawn leading to the waterfront. "Fine. Whatever you prefer. Have you or Jamie thought about where you want the ceremony?"

"We haven't talked about the wedding at all. If you ask me, this place is too big. How do you have an intimate wedding with only family and close friends when you have this much room to work with?" He spun in a circle with his arms out. "Don't get me wrong. It's beautiful here and I appreciate that her uncle wants to let us use his estate. It's just a bit too much for me. I don't want a thousand witnesses."

His answer was so intriguing. Number one, they hadn't talked about the wedding at all? Secondly, who called wedding guests witnesses? Was it a crime or a wedding ceremony that would be taking place here?

"Well, one way we could make it feel smaller is by creating smaller spaces within all these acres of land. The ceremony could easily be held in the garden." There was a towering white trellis at one end of the flower garden that could be used as the backdrop for the bride and groom. Guests could be seated in front and along the paver walkways leading to that spot.

Sophia walked him over to the trellis to show him what she was imagining. He nodded his head as she described her vision. She led him over to the lawn next.

"Right here, we could set up the reception. We could get a big tent. That would clearly define the space for you. We could set up areas on the lawn for different purposes—dancing, drinks, photo booth. Perhaps with the wedding being close to the Fourth of July, we could do a carnival theme and have games. At the end of the night, we could bring everyone down to the waterfront for a spectacular fireworks display."

"Those are really good ideas," he said when she finished. "I love the carnival idea. Reminds me of the neighborhood Fourth of July events I went to as a kid. My dad would give me five bucks to spend and I'd waste it all on the dart game trying to pop the balloons so I could take home some dollar-store framed picture of a white tiger."

Sophia laughed. "You didn't play the ring toss game so you could score a stuffed animal that felt like it was filled with chunks of Styrofoam?"

His killer smile was back. "Maybe I should have. I guess I thought of the dart game as dangerous because I got to throw sharp objects at things. But I'm pretty sure the carnival workers dulled those dart tips on purpose."

"If we go with this theme, I will make sure you get sharp-tipped darts, Mr. Danger," Sophia promised.

"Perfect." He inhaled deeply and kept his gaze fixed on her. She wanted to look away, but his warm brown eyes held her in place. "Do you want to walk down to the lake? Maybe it will inspire some more ideas."

Ideas for *his* wedding. He made it so difficult to keep that reality at the forefront of her mind. "Sounds like a plan," she replied, letting him lead the way.

A long pier led to the large covered dock, which protected an enormous speedboat. A wooden porch swing hung from one end of the roof.

"What a view," Sophia said, taking it all in.

"It's good to be a Wharton." He sat down on the swing and patted the spot next to him.

He would be a Wharton by marriage soon enough. Sophia resisted the temptation to sit next to him. "I'm going to get a few pictures of the estate from this vantage point," she said.

She couldn't wait to plan this wedding and get it over with so she would never have to talk to, see or think about Evan Anderson ever again. Staying focused on the task at hand was the only strategy she had for getting through this.

"It looks like your mind is whirling with a thousand more ideas." He was right beside her, staring up at the house, trying to see what she saw.

"A million ideas is more like it," she lied.

"You're amazing like that."

The compliment did nothing to help the way he always quickened her pulse when he was close. Sophia had everything she needed. Leaving was the best solution to her problem. Being attracted to the groom was definitely a problem.

"Well, I think I have everything I need. I'm sure I can find my way back to my car." She started to move past him, but he touched her arm.

"Wait."

"I really must—"

"Mr. Wharton wanted to meet with both of us when we were finished. I don't know if he's home yet."

Sophia swallowed hard. If she couldn't escape, she would need to put some space between them. A walk would help. "Perhaps we should head up to the house, then."

With a sharp nod, Evan led the way. As they stepped onto the pier, a huge rottweiler came bounding across the lawn. It was running full speed down the hill and toward them. Evan stood helplessly in the dog's path, and it didn't stop when it got to him. Sophia felt like she was watching the attack in slow motion. Evan had nowhere to go. He put his hands out and shouted, "Stop! Heel! Sit! No!"

None of the commands had any effect. Sophia wasn't sure if the dog was coming for Evan or wanted in the water and Evan was simply in its way. The animal jumped and took Evan right into the lake with it.

Evan surfaced and swam to shore alongside the dog. Sophia covered her mouth, unable to hold back the laughter. She ran down the pier to meet him on land.

The dog arrived first and proceeded to shake the water off all over Sophia. She screamed and tried to get out of the way.

"That would be Patrick's dog. Can you guess why Old Man Wharton didn't want it in the main house?" Evan asked, wiping water from his face.

Sophia held her arms out. "We're a mess. Mr. Wharton isn't going to let either of us inside the house like this."

He strode out of the water and shook his head like the dog. Sophia jumped back to prevent herself from getting any wetter. He tugged off one of his shoes, tipping it over and letting the water pour out.

"Stop laughing," he demanded with a grin.

It was all too much for both of them. Neither one could stop their fits of giggles. "There are lots of towels in the pool house. We can dry off in there."

Sophia was once again impressed. Whereas the main house was historic and over the top, the pool house had a very fresh, modern design. Three sets of black-framed French doors looked out to the pool. In the great room, there was a billiards table, a big-screen television, a fully stocked bar and plenty of seating to relax on. There were also two luxury bathrooms with showers, a laundry area and a linen closet full of towels.

She gently blotted the water from her face with the ultraplush towel. The private bathroom was all white and gray with marble counters and shower walls. There wasn't one water spot on the glass doors. It was so clean in there, it was hard to believe anyone ever used it.

Sophia checked her reflection in the mirror and fixed the collar of her shirt. Her black pants and white-and-black-striped shirt were damp but not unwearable like Evan's suit. She had no idea what he was going to do.

"Is everything okay?" she called out as she

made her way to the great room and sat on the couch.

Evan appeared, wearing nothing but a towel wrapped around his waist. He used another towel to dry his dark hair. "It's a good thing my phone is water resistant. I had to call Jamie so she could call Nelson to bring me some clothes."

Sophia's mouth had dropped open. She turned her head, fixing her gaze on the television that she wished she had turned on before he came out.

She jumped to her feet. "Why don't I run up to the house and see if I can help get you some clothes."

"You're more likely to get lost in that house than you are to find Nelson," Evan said with a chuckle. "He'll be here in a minute."

Sophia's eyes were drawn back to where he stood in nothing but a towel. She could feel the heat on her cheeks. "Okay," she practically whispered.

"I wish I would have known I was going for a swim. I would have worn a swimsuit instead of a business suit."

His attempt at humor couldn't overpower

the effect his lack of clothing was having on her. His phone rang.

"Did you get ahold of him?" he asked. "Seriously? I'm sure I would look ridiculous in something your uncle wears, but the man has to own one T-shirt, right?"

And pants. The man had to own some pants that Evan could put on. But even a shirt would be a major improvement.

He grumbled some more and ended the call. "Nelson is having some trouble finding me something to wear. My shirts are in the dryer. I guess we could wait for them. I don't suppose it's a good idea to put dry-clean-only suit pants in there, would it?"

Sophia shook her head and let out a sardonic laugh. Ruining a suit that nice would be criminal. "No. No, do not put any part of the suit you were wearing in the dryer."

Evan's bare chest heaved with a sigh. "Okay. This is great. I didn't even work today. I put that suit on because I knew I'd be seeing Mr. Wharton. Now I'll be seeing him wearing Lord knows what."

"I'm sorry." She knew how intimidated she felt about having to meet with Mr. Wharton.

"Well—" he glanced around the room

"—you want to play pool until Nelson finds me some dry clothes?" He tossed his phone on the couch and breezed past her to grab two pool cues off the rack on the wall, not waiting for her to answer.

"We can't play pool," she said as he thrust the cue in her direction.

"Why not?"

"You're in a towel."

Incredulous, he asserted, "I can play in a towel."

She took the cue from him and placed it on the table. "I am not playing pool."

"Oh, you're bad at pool," he joked.

"I'm not bad. I'm just not going to play pool with you."

He gently poked her in the arm with his pool cue. "Admit it—you think you'll lose. I bet you don't like to lose."

She checked her shirtsleeve to make sure there wasn't any blue chalk residue. "Don't poke me with that." She tried to sound angry, but she couldn't suppress the laugh that bubbled out of her.

He spun the cue like a baton in front of him. "Just admit it. It's okay to be bad at something."

She picked up her cue and poked him in the chest. "I would kick your butt."

"Oh, would you?" That sly smile spread across his face. "Then let's play."

"What is going on here?"

Sophia turned toward the unfamiliar voice. Standing in the doorway to the swimming pool was a man in a pretentious three-piece suit. He was around the same age as Sophia and Evan. His sandy-blond hair was slicked back, and he was holding a leash in his hands.

"Patrick."

"Since you're marrying my dear cousin, this isn't quite how I thought I would stumble upon you."

Sophia set her pool cue on the pool table and clasped her hands in front of her. Her face burned with embarrassment to be caught playfully flirting with an engaged man.

"We're waiting for Nelson to bring me some dry clothes. That beast you call your dog tackled me into the lake a few minutes ago."

Patrick stared hard at Sophia, the scrutiny only exacerbating the horror she felt. She wished for the ability to become invisible in that moment.

"This is Sophia Reed, our wedding planner. We're here to tour the grounds."

Patrick stepped into the room. "Your wedding planner," he said as if that was unbelievable.

"Why are you here? Jamie never leaves the office before six. You aren't as dedicated to the bank as she is, huh?"

Patrick puffed out his chest. Nelson knocked before entering the pool house.

"I found you some dry clothes, Mr. Anderson," he said, holding out the pile. "Mr. Wharton has arrived home and is anxious to speak with you and Miss Reed about the wedding planning."

"Oh, Uncle Gordon is home. Perfect," Patrick said. "I think I'll run up to the house and have a chat with him while you're getting decent."

Evan's jaw ticked. "Maybe you should find your dog and put that leash to good use first."

Patrick turned to leave. "Buster will find me, but I have some urgent concerns to share with my uncle that really can't wait."

Sophia didn't need Patrick to spell it out. Evan needed to get dressed quickly. Mr.

Wharton could not be left alone with Patrick for very long.

Evan clearly agreed as he darted back to the bathroom and was dressed in a minute. His anxiety was written all over his face.

"Let's go."

CHAPTER SIX

JAMIE WAS GOING to be so angry. Angrier than she had ever been. And she would have every right to be mad, because Evan had promised to keep up this charade and yet he'd allowed his selfishness to jeopardize everything.

Evan whipped off his towel and hurriedly pulled on the pants and shirt Nelson had handed him. There was no time to waste.

Why did Sophia have to be the kind of woman whom Evan had always dreamed about? Why did she make him want to throw it all away and risk everything? He couldn't do that, though. He had made a promise to Jamie and this wedding was too important to Sophia's business. Not to mention what would happen if the greater Charlotte area found out that the Wharton wedding had been called off because the groom fell in love with the wedding planner. Her career would be ruined.

"Let's go," he said as he jogged toward the

exit. He needed to make sure Jamie's uncle understood that there had been an unfortunate mishap and that he and Sophia had been making the best of a bad situation and nothing else. No matter what spin Patrick put on it to raise doubts.

Patrick's stay at the estate had been troubling Jamie since she found out that her cousin had moved into the guesthouse the other night. She had called Evan in a panic the night of the Hamiltons' anniversary party. Her mother had spilled the beans that Patrick and his wife had to temporarily move out of their house because they were having renovations done. Renovations Patrick had never mentioned before.

"Perhaps I should go and you can talk to Mr. Wharton on your own. I feel like my presence just makes things…worse," Sophia said, hesitating.

How could he explain why it was troublesome for Patrick to have access to Gordon that Jamie would not without explaining this whole mess? Jamie was sure Patrick's plan was to influence their uncle into choosing him as his successor. That would be a terrible mistake.

"Nelson made it very clear that he wants to speak to both of us. I'm sure he wants to meet you since you're planning his niece's wedding. He probably wants to hear what ideas you've come up with now that you've seen the property. He will no doubt have some opinions of his own to share, as well."

Sophia appeared less than pleased to have to stay. He didn't blame her. Evan had put her in this position—ever since the day of the robbery, he couldn't help himself from wanting to get to know her. He'd foolishly thought he could start something... But it could never be.

"Come on, let's go," he said, racing out of the pool house. The less time Patrick had alone with Gordon, the better.

Evan tried not to think about how ridiculous he appeared. Nelson had lent him a white undershirt and a pair of black pants that were one size too big. His feet were bare and his hair was a mess. Not exactly how he wanted to present himself to the man who had been like a father to Jamie since her dad passed away.

He reached the sunporch and waited for Sophia to catch up. She looked as anxious as she had that day at the bank. Her face was flushed and she swallowed hard when she joined him outside the door.

"It's going to be fine," he assured her. "Just be your amazing self."

"Please don't compliment me right now. That is not helping."

He gave her a sharp nod. He needed to tone it down or Gordon and Patrick would see right through him. The way he felt about this woman was like nothing he'd ever felt before—and it was how they expected him to feel about Jamie.

"I just thought it was interesting," Patrick could be heard saying as they entered the sunporch. He and his uncle were seated on the two rattan wingback chairs at one end of the porch. Gordon held a glass of sweet tea in his hand.

Gordon Wharton was in his midseventies but always boasted about not feeling a day over forty. He was a handsome older man with pronounced cheekbones, white hair and a white beard. His most striking feature was his crystal-blue eyes.

"Wow, Patrick usually finds everything to be dreadfully boring. What was so interesting?" Evan asked, confronting the situation head-on. He knew Patrick had rushed over here in order to sow doubt about Evan's relationship with Jamie.

"Evan, finally. Patrick claimed you were indisposed at the moment," Gordon said. "I heard you decided to take a swim in the lake without your swim trunks."

"It wasn't my intention to jump in. Patrick's dog made that decision for me. It was almost like someone commanded the animal to attack me. Weird, isn't it?"

Patrick chuckled. "Is that paranoia I hear? I certainly didn't sic my dog on you. The maid accidentally let him out when she came to clean the guesthouse. Good ole Buster must have thought you were an intruder. He's very protective of family, a true Wharton," he said, winking at his uncle. "We're a protective bunch. Right, Uncle?"

"Evan will be family soon enough," Gordon replied, allowing Evan to relax a bit. "You need to keep that dog under control or it will have to go to Raleigh with Eliza."

Patrick's jaw tightened. He surely didn't appreciate being scolded in front of Evan. "I apologize for my dog's poor manners. I feel bad. I know you're on a tight budget. Feel free to send me your dry-cleaning bill. It's the least I can do."

"That's not necessary, but thank you for the offer." Evan had been dealing with wealthy people like Patrick ever since he became friends with Jamie. No, Evan didn't come from money like Patrick did, and he had a brother to look after, but that didn't mean he didn't have money in the bank. Patrick's snobbery was another big motivator to help Jamie.

Gordon shifted the conversation. "Enough about the dog and Evan's swim in the lake. I want to hear about the wedding. This must be the wedding planner."

"Sophia Reed," she introduced herself. "It's very nice to meet you, Mr. Wharton. Your estate is absolutely beautiful. I couldn't be more excited that you're having the wedding here."

Gordon coolly appraised her, looking her up and down. "You came highly recommended, and my usual event planner had too much going on over the Fourth this year."

"Their loss is my gain. I appreciate the chance to make Miss Wharton and Mr. Anderson's day a memorable one."

"I'm an old man who has been to many

weddings. I hope you can do something to make this one unique. I want to spare no expense for this momentous occasion. Jamie is my youngest brother's only child and my only niece. I was thrilled when she announced her engagement. I want her wedding day to be special because it's the only one she's ever going to have. Isn't that right, Evan?"

His gaze shifted to Evan. Those ice-cold eyes were intimidating. Evan feared that they could see through his lies. "I don't think many people get married with the intention of doing it more than once."

It wasn't a lie and yet it insinuated that he and Jamie were going to stay married. He swallowed, waiting for Gordon and his lie-detecting eyeballs to respond.

"I suspect you're right about that," he said before taking a sip of his sweet tea. He motioned toward the pitcher of tea on the coffee table in front of him. "Can I offer you two a drink?"

"Thank you," Sophia replied. "That would be nice."

Evan quickly poured her a glass. With the drink in her hand, he could see that she had a slight tremor. She was more nervous than she needed to be and that was all Evan's fault.

"Please, take a seat," Gordon insisted.

Evan sat down on the loveseat. Instead of sitting next to him, Sophia chose to sit on the other side of the room on a chaise. It was the smart thing to do given the scrutiny they were under. There was no telling what faux pas he'd commit if she was too close.

Gordon jumped right in and began picking that brain of hers. As Evan expected, she presented herself as competent and professional. She shared her preliminary ideas and was sure to rave about the estate whenever she could.

Everything Evan had done to put the plan in jeopardy, Sophia saved with her amazingness. Gordon was completely sold. He loved all of her ideas. So did Evan.

"It was lovely to meet you, Mr. Wharton," she said, setting her glass down. "But I am going to head back to my office and get started on some idea boards to share with Miss Wharton."

Sophia stood up and Evan followed. "Let me walk you out," he said.

She shook her head. "I think I can find my

way. You enjoy your time with your soon-to-be family, Mr. Anderson. I will be in touch."

The formality was back. Something told him that given the events of the day, it would be sticking around.

JAMIE CAME DOWN to Evan's floor to pick him up for lunch the next day. She glanced around the work area to make sure no one else was close enough to overhear. "Good work. Whatever you and the wedding planner said to Uncle Gordon has him head over heels about this wedding. Patrick hasn't poisoned him against us *yet*."

That was a relief. It wasn't unreasonable for Jamie to worry about Patrick's influence. He had graduated from a decent business school, had been loyal to Gordon and, unlike Jamie, was married. He had assumed that made him the only one who met their uncle's requirements. No one had been more unhappy to hear about Jamie and Evan's engagement than Patrick.

"I didn't do much, but I'm glad that he's on board with Jevan."

The crease between her eyebrows deepened. "What in the world is Jevan?"

"It's our couple name. Jamie and Evan—Jevan."

She pinched the bridge of her nose and shook her head slowly. "I can't with you."

Evan grinned. His goofy sense of humor was one of the reasons she loved him, but it was also a major reason she loved him only as a friend.

"I guess I better call Sophia and let her know we aren't going to use hashtag Jevan on all our wedding social media."

Her eyes went wide. "Please tell me you're kidding."

He chuckled as they started for the elevators. "I am positive that if I had suggested it, Sophia would have convinced me it was a bad idea. She's full of only fantastic ideas. She's the one who really sold it to your uncle, too."

"Well, we hired the right person, then." She checked her phone. "Don't forget, we're having brunch at the estate on Sunday the sixth. I need Zeke to be on his best behavior and for you to be the greatest fiancé of all time."

"Oh, no pressure."

"You and I are living under constant pressure until we get what we want. We can't let our guard down even for a minute."

Something told him that Jamie would probably characterize flirting with the wedding planner while wearing nothing but a towel as letting his guard down. Clearly, he needed to be more vigilant.

"You can count on me and Zeke. He's all about telling people that we're having a wedding. I don't think he knows what that means, but he says it…a lot… So we're good. He's not going to give anything away."

"Good," she said as her phone rang. She answered it. "This is Jamie…This morning? Where?…Okay, I'm heading to my office right now." She ended the call and cursed under her breath.

"What's wrong?"

"Same guys robbed another branch in Belmont. Police are on the scene now. This is exactly what I didn't need today." She was busy searching her contacts. "I've gotta go. Rain check on lunch?"

"Go."

Jamie pressed the up button by the bank of elevators to take her back to her office on the twentieth floor. Evan returned to his desk and called her favorite restaurant and scheduled a delivery. She still had to eat, and she was way too distracted to take care of herself.

He wondered if Sophia had heard about the newest robbery. She had been such a wreck after learning theirs was not the first that he worried she would be stressed when she found out there'd been another.

Deciding she should hear it from him rather than the news, he called her cell phone. He was immediately sent to voice mail. He tried texting her, asking her to call him when she had a chance.

After an hour with no call and no reply to his text, he called again. Voice mail. He texted.

Really important that I talk to you.

She replied a few minutes later.

Feel free to email me and I will get back to you as soon as I can.

He wasn't going to email her this information. He wanted to talk to her, reassure her that everything would be okay. He called her office.

"Engaging Events. This is Cassie, how may I help you?"

"Hi, Cassie. This is Evan Anderson. I need

to talk to Sophia. Is she in with another client? I can't seem to get her on her cell phone."

"Oh, that's weird. She's free for another hour. Let me put you through." Cassie put him on hold. Instead of transferring the call, she came back on the line a minute later. "Um, Mr. Anderson, she asked me to ask you to please email her any questions or concerns you had right now. She will get back to you quickly. She promises."

Sophia was avoiding him. When he had tried to call her after he left the Wharton Estate, she had declined his call then, as well.

"Thanks, Cassie." He hung up and emailed her one sentence—CALL ME.

Within minutes, she replied.

Dear Mr. Anderson,
I would prefer that our main mode of communication be email. That way we both have a clear record of what we discussed and I can reference back if I am ever unsure of what you want from me.
Thank you.
Sophia Reed

Evan felt like a heel. How many times had he made her feel unsure of what he wanted from her? What *did* he want from her? Oftentimes, it was a lot more than he had a right to ask for. She was protecting herself, making sure that he respected the boundaries that existed. Something he hadn't done yesterday. He had crossed a line once again and she was not having any of it.

He sent her a message about the newest bank robbery but let her know he didn't have too many details. He just wanted her to be aware so it didn't come as a surprise when she turned on the news tonight.

Sophia chose not to reply, and it drove Evan mad. Was she okay? Did this stress her out? Would she be able to sleep tonight? Would she go to her *yaya's*? There were so many questions with no answers, because he was simply her client...not her friend.

A day turned into a week turned into two weeks. Still no word from Sophia other than an email to both him and Jamie regarding her idea boards. She had manipulated the pictures she took at the estate to appear like their actual wedding day. Jamie was too busy managing the press releases regarding the string of bank robberies to give her feedback.

Late one afternoon, Evan's cell phone rang.

The number was unfamiliar, but he answered it anyway.

"Mr. Anderson, this is Detective Thatcher from the Charlotte Police Department."

Detective Thatcher was the one who had interviewed him after the bank robbery. A tiny glimmer of hope flickered. Maybe the third robbery was the charm and they had caught the guys terrorizing the area. "Yes, Detective. Good news, I hope."

"I wish I could say we had something positive to share, Mr. Anderson. Unfortunately, I'm calling because we felt we should make you aware that one of the tellers from the robbery has reported a home invasion. We can't say for sure that the two crimes are connected, but with your connections to Wharton Bank, I felt you in particular should be made aware."

Evan rested both elbows on his desk and manhandled his hair with his free hand. There was a giant knot in his stomach. "It could all be coincidence, though, right? Maybe that person is just having a run of some very bad luck lately?"

"Absolutely. Like I said, there's no evidence

that the two crimes are connected. But because the bank robbers took your identification, it is possible that they are using that information to further victimize witnesses."

Sophia immediately came to mind. "Are you contacting everyone? Everyone who was at the bank when it was robbed?"

"Detective Gibson and I are calling everyone who was in the bank."

Evan quickly thanked the detective and got off the phone. He found Sophia's number in his contacts and prayed she would pick up when he called. It went straight to voice mail.

He ended the call and dropped his phone on the desk. She wouldn't answer him. He rubbed his eyes. He shouldn't worry. She had people who could be there for her. She had friends and family who could reassure her that everything would be fine. He didn't need to fill that role. More important, she didn't want him to fill that role.

Evan attempted to go back to work. His ability to focus, however, was nonexistent. Sophia had to know by now. There weren't that many people in the bank that day. As much as he knew he shouldn't, he texted her.

Did the detective get ahold of you?

She wouldn't be able to ignore that if she hadn't spoken to anyone yet. He got no reply. The silence from her was too much to handle. Evan couldn't function until he knew she was okay. There was only one solution. He grabbed his things and left work.

Engaging Events wasn't too far from his office. He called for a car and was there in less than fifteen minutes. There was no plan. He had no idea what he was going to say. He only knew he had to see her.

"Mr. Anderson," Cassie said, looking a bit confused. She flipped the pages of the desk calendar in front of her. "Did I forget to make note of an appointment?"

"No, I don't have an appointment today. I was wondering if I could talk to Sophia, though."

"Let me see if she's available."

Just as Cassie stood up, Sophia's door opened and she came out, her eyes cast down at the open portfolio in her hands. "Cassie, what happened to the samples we had from—" She looked up and her mouth fell open.

A couple of heartbeats later, she snapped

her mouth shut and retreated back into her office, only to return with her phone in hand. She scrolled through something. When she looked satisfied with what she saw, she narrowed her eyes at him. "What are you doing here?"

CHAPTER SEVEN

SOPHIA'S FIRST THOUGHT—and fear—on seeing Evan was that she had accidentally sent the text she'd written and deleted. After she'd gotten off the phone with Detective Gibson, she had begun a text to Evan that let him know she was scared out of her mind and she needed him to tell her everything was going to be okay because he was the only one who made it feel like that was true. After she had finished typing, she'd realized that there was no way she could say that to him.

He was her client. He was getting married. She couldn't ask him to provide her with the comfort she desperately needed.

It wasn't there, so she must have deleted it. Why was he here, then? Could he read her mind now?

Evan cautiously stepped forward. "I wanted to make sure you were okay. I assume you got the call from the detective?"

Sophia attempted to put on a brave face and sound unaffected. Her racing heart and rattled nerves didn't help her accomplish that task. "I did."

"The detective in charge of the bank robbery?" Cassie asked. Cassie was a sweet soul.

"Yeah. There was a new development." She had no idea how she kept her voice calm.

"Are you okay?" Evan asked.

"I'm fine."

He shook his head. "I think we all know that when people say they're *fine*, they're not."

"That's true. *Fine* is always code for *not-so-fine*," Cassie agreed. She had worked for Sophia and Fallon since they opened up their office a few years ago. She was a loyal and organized assistant, but Sophia and Fallon maintained appropriate employee/employer boundaries.

Sophia did not want to discuss her personal problems with her employee. Or her client for that matter... But Evan was giving her no choice. "I am perfectly fine. The detective was simply letting me know that it's possible the robbers are coming after the people who were at the bank."

"They are not coming after us," Evan said,

moving in her direction but stopping before he got too close. "One person was a victim of a break-in. They aren't sure it was even related."

Cassie pressed her hand to her chest. "Oh, my gosh, Sophia. That is so scary! They know where you live, right?"

They did know where she lived. Her stomach rolled. She heard the words the man in the monkey mask had said before he left— *Until we meet again, sweetheart.*

"No one is going to come to your house," Evan asserted. "I don't want you to be scared."

"I'm not scared." The lie made her voice sound weird. "It's going to be fine," she said to Cassie. "What time is my next appointment? I'm sure there's not enough time to fit Mr. Anderson in right now."

She needed Cassie to get the hint, but the poor woman was too rattled by the recent developments to catch on. "You don't have anything until four."

"Perfect," Evan said. "Sounds like there's plenty of time for us to chat about a few things." He walked past her and into her office.

Frustrated but clearly defeated, Sophia followed him in and shut the door. She walked around her desk and sat down.

"I really think it would be best if you let me get back to work."

"I just want to make sure you're okay. And I want to help if you're not." Instead of leaving, he sat down across from her.

"I'm okay. You can go back to your job, your life, your future wife. You don't have to worry about me."

Her words seemed to pack quite a punch. He looked visibly wounded. "I know I'm probably overstepping—"

"Not *probably*," she interrupted. "You are. You always are. You seem like a very nice guy. It was that nice-guyness that caused our misunderstanding after the robbery. I'm trying to do my job and help you plan the perfect wedding day. Your constant attention makes me question if I did in fact misunderstand that first day."

He rested his elbows on his knees and dropped his head. She was in the right to call him out. He was still acting like someone interested in more than a working relationship.

"As much as I need this wedding to help build my business, I have no interest in being a part of an extramarital relationship. If that is what you are thinking, I will have to terminate our contract. I am praying that you are simply the extremely nice guy I thought you were when we first met and that you will respect my feelings and back off."

He lifted his head. "I apologize. I never want you to feel like I am propositioning you for something like that. I respect you. I truly can't help that I'm worried about you. I was there when you were traumatized by those jerks, and I feel protective of you as a result."

Sophia wanted to climb over her desk and into his arms. The sincerity in his words made him a million times more attractive than he already was. That was why it was so difficult not to spill her guts to him, not to tell him all about her fears and her paranoia, which were growing by the second. Letting him comfort her and make her feel safe would be so easy.

"I don't need you to protect me," she said instead. "I am capable of protecting myself."

He nodded. "Of course you are. I didn't mean to imply…"

"Of course you didn't. You are a nice guy, Evan. Go be a nice guy to your soon-to-be wife. Her banks keep getting robbed. She must be very stressed. I'm sure she needs someone to be there to support her."

He breathed loudly through his nose. "I'm sorry to have bothered you. I'll see you at our next appointment, I guess."

He stood up and seemed to want to say something else but chose not to. His sad expression broke her heart. He wasn't a bad guy. She could tell. It was why it didn't make sense that he would be disloyal to someone he'd asked to marry him.

"Have a good day, Mr. Anderson," she said as he opened her office door.

He paused with his hand on the doorknob. "You, too, Sophia."

Fallon was standing outside her door when he left. Sophia closed her eyes and took a deep breath. There was no way her partner was going to let this one go.

Fallon came inside and closed the door. "Why was Evan Anderson here without an appointment?"

"He had a couple questions," she explained. It wasn't a lie.

Fallon folded her arms across her chest. "You would tell me if there was a reason I needed to be the point person on this account, right?"

"Of course. Everything is fine. I would never jeopardize our company's reputation. I have everything under control."

"If he's being inappropriate or—"

Sophia jumped to his defense. "He's not being inappropriate. He's being nice. He knows that I am a little bit afraid of these bank robbers coming to my house, and we found out today that it's possible they broke into someone's house. Someone who was a witness at the bank."

Fallon fell into the chair on the other side of the desk. "Oh, Sophia. I'm sorry. I didn't realize this was about the bank again."

Sophia held up a hand to stop her. "Don't apologize. I get why you're worried about the dynamics between me and Evan. I just want you to know that if I ever thought that my relationship with him could compromise this account, I would turn it over to you in a heartbeat."

Of course, she had told Evan she would terminate the contract. She hadn't thought about simply turning it over to Fallon. More than anything, the company needed to make sure that the Wharton family was happy with their work. If things got uncomfortable again, Sophia would have to turn it over to her partner.

Fallon looked chagrined. "I know you would. You wouldn't risk everything we've worked for over some guy. That's not your character. I'm sorry I had to even bring it up."

Sophia again asked her not to apologize. She deserved the doubt, though. Evan Anderson was the worst kind of temptation. But Sophia would resist, and she would make sure he kept his priorities straight. Fallon would never have to worry about Sophia and Evan again.

SOPHIA DIDN'T EVEN bother attempting to sleep at her house. There was no way she could rest there, knowing that the robbers had her address. She called her grandmother and offered to bring her dinner in exchange for a few nights in her guest room. That should buy her enough time to get a home security system.

On her way to Yaya's, she picked up food at her grandmother's favorite Greek restaurant. Demetri's had the best moussaka in town. Yaya often compared it to her mother's recipe, which was the greatest of compliments. Sophia's great-grandmother had been an excellent cook.

"I hope you're hungry," Sophia said as she entered the house. Yaya sprang up from her chair.

"I am always hungry when you bring me dinner. This is why I love when you come over. Cooking dinner for one is not my favorite."

She had the dining room table all set for dinner. Sophia set the bags of food down. "I got some baklava for dessert because I am eating all my feelings tonight. Please don't judge."

Yaya placed a hand on Sophia's cheek. "Oh, *paidi mou*. I will never judge you, you know that. We will eat until our bellies are so full we cannot even sit."

Her understanding was one of her best qualities. They dug into the food and didn't stop until it was all gone, including the baklava.

Sophia licked some of the sticky honey off her fingers. "That hit the spot."

"Did you eat all the feelings away or do you need to talk about them with me? I have these big ears for a reason, you know." Yaya tugged on her earlobes.

Sophia didn't even know if she wanted to dive in and face the feelings she'd been having all day. One thing was certain, it was better if she didn't mention anything about Evan. If she talked about him, her grandmother would see right through her.

"It's been a bad-news day. The detective from the bank robbery called me this afternoon and said that it's possible the robbers are now breaking into people's homes. People who were at the bank. They took our IDs and know where we live."

Yaya's eyes were wide with surprise. "You think these bad men might come to your house and rob you there, as well?"

Sophia thought about what Evan had said, hoping it would ease Yaya's mind as well as her own. "I don't know. There's no evidence that the two crimes are related, but they wanted to warn us to be vigilant."

"They say that, but you are not so sure they are unrelated." Yaya could read her so well.

"One of the men said something to me that makes me afraid that they could look for me."

Yaya moved her chair closer and took Sophia's hand in hers. "What did he say?"

Shaking her head, Sophia repeated the monkey man's words. Yaya gasped.

"It was a strange thing to say, don't you think?" Sophia asked. "Why would he ever see me again? It felt like a threat."

Yaya squeezed Sophia's hand. "You can stay here as long as you need to. I don't want anyone to hurt you. You can stay with me until those men are caught. I told your parents I would look after you. I know you just bought your house, but if you wanted to move in with me, I wouldn't complain."

Sophia pressed her lips together so she wouldn't laugh out loud. Her grandmother would love nothing more than to have everyone in her family move in with her. In Greek families, it wasn't unusual for multiple generations to live under one roof. Because of her grandmother's age, it was more likely for the older generation to move in with the younger, not the other way around. Yaya had imagined she would move in with Sophia's mother, her daughter. She had been heartbroken when Sophia's parents decided to travel once her father retired. It wasn't surprising that she would want to be with Sophia more permanently.

"I appreciate that, but I love my new house. I came here tonight because your house feels safer until I can get an alarm system."

"I'm sorry you're feeling scared. Your uncle Gus can help you with the house alarm. He knows people."

The comment made her think about how Evan had offered the same thing. "I'll give him a call."

Yaya gave Sophia's hand a pat and let go. "Now, are you going to watch my favorite television show with me tonight or are you going to be smiling at your phone again like last time?"

Sophia shook her head. "I will not be on my phone tonight."

Yaya frowned. "What happened to the nice boy who caught your eye at the bank?"

"Forget about him. There is no chance of that one working out."

"Well, that's disappointing," Yaya said, getting up and clearing the table. "I was sure I had seen the sparks between you shooting out of the phone that night. I thought you had been blessed with something beautiful after experiencing something ugly."

So had Sophia. It was embarrassing that she had been so wrong.

"There is someone out there for you, *paidi mou*. You must believe that love is possible. If you stop looking for it, it could pass you by. Don't stop looking."

Sophia helped clean up. "I won't, Yaya. My eyes are wide open. I promise." She wouldn't stop looking. But she wasn't going to hold out hope that it would happen, either. She might plan weddings for a living, but that didn't mean she believed that being married was necessary. Sophia didn't need a man to make her life complete.

"When I met your *papou*, it was love at first sight," Yaya said, her hand pressed against her heart. "Arie Markopoulos stole my heart and I didn't want him to give it back. He had eyes that matched the color of the sea and hair black as night. The way he looked at me that first day was the way he looked at me every day after. It made me feel like I was the only woman in the world."

Sophia's grandparents had met when they were nineteen years old in the coastal town of Oia in Greece. Yaya had told the story of how they fell in love many times over the years. Theirs was a love story like no other. Sophia's mother often joked she was going to tell people that was how she'd met Sophia's dad, because it was so much better than saying they had met on a group date to a bowling alley.

"Not everyone finds a man like Papou. You were one lucky lady."

"The luckiest," she replied with a grin. "But you, my sweet girl, will find someone who makes you feel just as lucky. You may not find him on a beach in Greece, but that doesn't mean he won't love you as much as your *papou* loved me."

"I would be happy with someone who loved me half as much."

Yaya touched Sophia's face. "You need to believe you are worthy of all the love. Don't settle for half and don't be so scared to be loved fully."

"I'm not scared. I just don't think it's that easy. I have this tendency to find men who aren't capable of loving someone the way Papou loved you."

Yaya threw her hands up. "Then be patient!"

If only it were that easy. Sophia didn't have the energy to argue with her grandmother. She wanted to get lost in some medical drama that Yaya loved and fall into a worry-free slumber.

The television show did help take her mind off her problems for a bit. Wouldn't it be nice to live in a world where all your problems could be solved in less than an hour? Only in TV Land could someone be diagnosed with a deadly disease, treated and completely recovered all in one day.

Sophia decided to go to bed before the news. The nightly news tended to focus on the negative things going on in the city rather than the positives, and she did not need any extra negatives tonight.

She tossed and turned a bit while trying to get to sleep. She tried not to think about the robbers or Evan or the mess she felt she was in. Of course, her brain had other ideas. As she finally drifted to sleep, it was Evan's face that she saw. He was smiling at her like she was the only woman in the world.

A sound caught her attention. Glass smashing. Footsteps outside her door. Yaya's house was getting ransacked. Sophia tried to get out of bed but felt pinned to the mattress. Her heart pounded and her chest ached as she attempted to slow her breathing. After what felt like an eternity, there was a shadow under the door and the doorknob turned slowly. The door pushed open and all she saw was the monkey mask.

Sophia bolted upright, her forehead damp with sweat. Her chest heaved up and down. She lifted a shaky hand to push the hair from her face. The room was dark and the house was silent. There was no one in the room and the door was still closed. She picked up her phone and saw it was three in the morning.

It had been a nightmare. Not real. There was no one there. She was safe. Telling herself those things over and over helped to regulate her breathing and slow her heart rate.

She lay back down and threw her arm over her forehead. Wide awake, there was no chance she would be getting any more sleep tonight. Once she was calm, the urge to call Evan was strong. She rolled over. She was a terrible person. Evan belonged to someone else. He couldn't be the person she relied on when things were tough.

Would that stop her? She could only hope.

CHAPTER EIGHT

EVAN WAS COMPLETELY out of his element. Why in the wedding planning world were colors named things like tangerine and azalea? Couldn't people say *orange* and *pink* so a guy could figure it all out?

"The color palette is really important. It's usually one of the first things the couple decide on. It's going to drive everything from flowers to attire. Have you spoken to Miss Wharton about her preferences? I added her to our emails in hopes she would help you decide. We only have one month left to put everything together." Sophia's tone was a bit more exasperated than usual.

Jamie had been a combination of unable and unwilling to deal with any of the wedding plans this week because of the newest robbery. Sophia had sent multiple emails with questions that he needed to answer and he felt completely out of his element. The invitations were in the mail—they needed to finalize these other details or people were going to show up and Evan wasn't even sure there was going to be a tent.

Evan was overwhelmed and, frankly, uninspired to make a decision. "What do you think? Which color palette do you like best?"

"This isn't my wedding, Mr. Anderson. It's yours. Which one speaks to you?" She waved her hand in front of the presentation board behind her.

None of them spoke to him. How were colors supposed to speak to him? "It's Fourth of July… So maybe we should go with that red, white and blue one."

"Would you prefer the navy or the dusty blue?"

"Why would they name a color *dusty*? That does not make it sound appealing."

Sophia clearly did not want to engage in a discussion about the absurdity of color naming. "So navy?"

"Is that what you'd choose?"

She sighed. "It's not my wedding. It's yours. You need to choose what you like so that you are happy with it on the actual wedding day."

Evan could feel her irritation. She also

looked tired. It had been a few days since they learned about the break-in. He wondered if she had been sleeping okay.

Asking her personal questions would likely not be well received. She wanted answers to her questions. He didn't need to make this so complicated. He could pick out the color scheme for the wedding.

"Maybe red, white and blue is too on the nose. Jamie wouldn't like that. She would rather be more subtle. I think she would like that one with the pink instead of red." He pointed to the one labeled Navy and Blush. It included a gold accent. "It looks more sophisticated, which is how I think of her."

Instead of being happy that he'd finally gave her an answer, Sophia held her head in her hands. "*Sophisticated* and carnival games don't exactly go together. I'm going to have to rethink everything."

"No, I love the idea of the games. That makes it fun. That part is me. She's the sophisticated woman from the city and I'm the small-town, fun-loving guy. It will be a good balance."

Again, this didn't seem to make her any less distraught. She stood up and he thought he saw her wipe under her eye. "I need a minute. I'll be right back."

He turned in his seat and watched her as she made her way to the door. "Sophia..."

She left the room. Stunned and more so concerned, Evan didn't know what to do. He couldn't help but take the blame for how she felt. He assumed her mood had to do with him since he had a tendency to unintentionally push her buttons whenever they were together.

A couple of minutes later, she returned and took her place behind her desk. "Sorry. Let's talk about formalwear. I sent you three styles of tuxedos and I haven't heard back from you and your groomsman."

"Sophia, whatever I did—" Evan leaned forward "—I'm sorry. I am not trying to make things difficult for you today."

She shook her head. "You haven't done anything. It's me. I'm off my game today, but I promise I'm fine now."

"It's okay not to be fine. It happens to the best of us. Even me."

Sophia folded her hands in front of her. "I'm just tired. I've been having some trouble sleeping."

"You've been worried about the break-in?" That had to be it. It wasn't him. He didn't want her to be struggling, but he was happy he wasn't the cause of her misery.

She tucked her hair behind her ears. "It's been a rough couple days. I've been having these nightmares. It's getting annoying more than anything. I feel so out of sorts."

"I'm sorry. That's not good. Do you want to talk about it? Maybe talking will help you get it off your mind."

Sophia raised one eyebrow. "Did you get a counseling degree since the last time I saw you?"

He smirked, happy to see her sense of humor was back. "I am not a counselor, but I am a good listener." He tugged on his earlobe.

She laughed and the sound was magic.

"What's so funny? You don't think I can listen?"

"No," she said. "It's not that. It was the earlobe thing. My *yaya* did the same thing the other night."

"Did you talk to Yaya about these nightmares?"

Her face fell. "No. I didn't want to worry her. Being able to take care of me gives her some purpose. She likes thinking she's keeping me safe."

"Do you feel safe?"

She stopped as if she needed to think about it. "I know that no one's coming to look for me at my grandmother's house, but it doesn't stop the paranoia that just takes over the second I lie down to go to bed."

"I wish there was a way to help you with that. I never thought I would say this, but I really do wish I had a counseling degree."

That earned him a little smile. "I never thought I'd say this, but I kind of wish you did, too. I need someone to tell me how to get rid of these nightmares. I feel like my brain is in a fog."

Evan had noticed the darker circles under her eyes. She was still lovely. Her olive skin looked like it would feel soft and smooth. If he could take away some of her worry and fear, he would. Unfortunately, he'd had similar anxiety the last few days.

"I have to admit that I've been nervous, too. The detective who called me said something about being concerned that because of my connection to the Whartons, I may be a more likely target."

"I didn't think about that."

"I hadn't thought about it, either, until he said it. I mean, I take care of my brother. He's my responsibility. The last thing I want is to put him in danger."

"That's a heavy weight to carry," she said, leaning in. "How are you coping with it all? You definitely look more rested than me."

It was a fair question. He had been sleeping, but it was taking extreme measures to tire himself out. "I feel like I've spent the last few days training for a marathon. I run. Sometimes twice a day. I work, I run, I clean, I stay on my feet until I can't stand any longer."

"Well, at least you're being more productive than I am," she said with a slight smile. "I just lay in bed and binge-watch shows on my phone."

Evan wondered what kind of shows she watched. Wondered if they had similar interests. Did she like sitcoms like he did, or was she more into dramas? He felt an uncontainable desire to know more about her.

"What do you watch?"

Again, she smiled. Her cheeks flushed the slightest pink. "I'm slightly obsessed with nineties comedy shows. They're still so funny even after all this time."

His heart swelled, knowing they had something, even this small, in common. "I'm glad to hear you're watching something that makes you laugh." He pulled his phone out of his pocket. "Maybe we should call the detectives and see if there's any news. I don't know about you, but I don't want to worry about this if we don't have to."

"I guess." She shrugged. "The worst they could tell us is that they know nothing yet."

Evan dialed Detective Thatcher. Thankfully, he answered. Evan put it on speaker and let him know he and Sophia were both curious about the recent break-in and what they had learned about it.

"I'm glad you called, Mr. Anderson. We found out that the teller has been having some issues with a rebellious teenage son. It's been determined her son and his friends ransacked the house."

"So it wasn't related to the bank robbery at all?" he asked, holding his hand up for a high five. They were safe. She didn't have to stay up all night anymore.

"It doesn't appear so, sir."

"That is great news. I mean not for the teller, but… You know what I mean. Thank you." Evan ended the call and breathed a sigh of relief.

"Not related," Sophia said, looking about as elated as he felt.

"Not related. I think the only things these guys rob are banks. I don't think we need to be afraid they're going to show up on our doorsteps anymore."

Sophia leaned back in her chair, the most content expression on her face. "Yaya is going to be happy…and sad."

"Sad?"

"She won't like it that I'm going to want to go back to my own house." A full smile spread across Sophia's face. "I'm glad we talked about this stuff. Thank you for listening and for sharing how you felt, too."

This connection he felt was so intense—it was the best thing that had happened to him in a long time. He could fight it, but it wasn't going away. It grew stronger every time they were together.

"You're welcome."

She clicked a button on her keyboard. "Okay, let's get back to planning this wedding. We are running out of time, and now that my mind is free of distractions, I'm ready to work."

The wedding. The reason that building this connection was nothing but a dream. They had one month, and after that he would never see her again.

SUNDAY BRUNCH AT the Wharton Estate was going to be the first time Jamie and Evan would be together as a couple in front of her family. It made Evan nervous. As excited as they were about Jamie's engagement, her uncle Gordon did not get to where he was in life by being naïve. He was an intelligent man who knew his niece well. If she didn't appear in love, he would notice.

"Can I have peanut butter and jelly?" Zeke asked as they pulled up to the gate.

"Don't worry, Zeke, I told my uncle that PB and J is your favorite. He will definitely have that on the menu," Jamie said from the driver's seat.

Zeke celebrated by clapping and rocking back and forth in the back seat. Evan smiled at Jamie. She had always been so good to his brother. It mattered that the people in his life showed care and compassion toward Zeke. Evan wouldn't tolerate anything less.

"Will there be beef and cheese enchiladas?" Evan asked. "Those are *my* favorite. Did you tell your uncle to have those on the menu?"

Jamie rolled down the driver's-side window and punched in the code to open the gate. "Don't be weird. Please?"

"How is wanting my favorite food weird?"

She shot him an icy glare. "Best fiancé ever. That's what you need to be today. No slipups."

Her nerves were showing. They had to put on the show of a lifetime. They needed Gordon to believe that they were a committed couple even though their engagement had been rushed and Patrick most likely had been encouraging him to question it. Jamie had one objective—prove she was everything he wanted his successor to be.

"No slipups, friend. I promise." The gates opened. "What's going to happen the next time we come here, Z-Man?"

"Jamie and Evan are having a wedding!"

"That's right. How excited are we about the wedding?"

"It's going to be fancy and fun. And I get to have champagne."

"I think your lush lifestyle is rubbing off on him. All he wants to do is drink champagne at parties," Evan said to Jamie, who was worrying her bottom lip with her teeth.

He reached over and touched her shoulder. "We're going to do great. We're friends. We get along. This is easy."

She nodded. "Easy."

Brunch would be served outside on the patio. The table was beautifully decorated with fresh flowers and crystal candelabras. There was a platter of fresh fruit and a tower of mini muffins, frosted doughnuts and Danish. Glass carafes of a variety of juices and water were at both ends of the table.

Jamie's mother was already there. She was beautiful like her daughter, but Jamie had always looked more like her dad. Jamie was a Wharton through and through. Patrick's parents were also there. Gordon was seated at the head of the table—he was deep in conversation with Jamie's other uncle.

While Jamie and her mother and aunt caught up, Evan poured some orange juice into the glasses in front of him and his brother. Zeke was more interested in the pool than anything else.

"I want to swim."

"We didn't bring your suit, bud," Evan reminded him. "We're here to eat, not swim."

"Can I swim at the wedding?"

"I don't know. We'll see, okay?"

"I'll wear my swimsuit and a tie, then I can be fancy and swim."

Evan chuckled. That would be a look.

"Good morning, everyone," Patrick said as he and his wife joined them. Eliza had come in from Raleigh for the brunch.

As they took their seats, Evan noticed there was an extra place setting. He tried to figure out who was missing. All of Jamie's family members were here and accounted for.

"Is your mother joining us?" he asked Eliza, who shook her head.

Nelson appeared. "Miss Reed is here."

Sophia? Anxiety burst like a bomb inside Evan, scattering to every cell of his body. Why had Gordon invited their wedding planner to family brunch? Evan shot a look at Jamie, who seemed just as surprised as he felt.

Gordon actually rose from his seat and moved to greet her. "Fantastic that you could make it, Miss Reed. We're all anxious to hear how things are going and throw in our two cents."

Sophia was as beautiful as ever. She wore a floral dress and her hair was down. He wondered how she had slept the last couple of days—she seemed more refreshed than she had on Friday. At the same time, he could see her nerves in the way she gripped her handbag and her tight smile.

"Are you worried that Evan and I aren't capable of planning this wedding ourselves?" Jamie asked. "I don't remember having any input into Patrick and Eliza's wedding."

"Eliza's parents were the hosts of that particular shindig," Gordon responded, unfazed by her challenge. "This is a Wharton wedding."

Jamie's mom patted her hand. "Your uncle has been very generous. I think you can indulge him a bit, don't you?" Plainly, he was paying, so he could do whatever he wanted.

"Can I have a doughnut?" Zeke asked, reaching for the tower of baked goods.

Evan stopped him from being impolite. "Hold on a sec, Z-Man."

"I think Zeke has the right idea. Let's eat,"

Gordon said. "Nelson, have the staff bring out the rest of the food. Zeke, grab a doughnut, son."

Gordon didn't have to tell him twice. Zeke nabbed the big glazed doughnut on top. Evan stole a glance in Sophia's direction. She smiled at Zeke's eagerness.

"Tell the truth, has my cousin become a bridezilla or what?" Patrick asked Sophia.

Sophia didn't hesitate to come to Jamie's defense. "Your cousin is very easy to work with and as far from a bridezilla as one could be. Especially considering the time crunch we're under. I can't even tell you how gracious she's been."

"Pfft." Patrick shifted uncomfortably in his seat.

Evan smiled down at his plate. Leave it to Sophia to leave Patrick speechless. She was a force to be reckoned with.

Jamie's mom started asking her daughter questions about the theme and the colors. Thankfully, Evan had prepped her ahead of time so she could answer all the questions thrown her way.

The kitchen staff came outside with platter after platter of hot food. Pancakes and waffles in stacks, eggs of every type, and Evan's favorites—bacon and sausage patties. Jamie's aunt asked them to put the smoked salmon closest to her.

One of the servers set a plate in front of Zeke with the best-looking peanut butter and jelly sandwich on it. His eyes got as wide as saucers.

"That looks pretty good, bud."

Zeke grinned. "It looks delicious!"

"You're a big peanut butter and jelly fan, huh?" Sophia asked as she placed some scrambled eggs on her plate.

"It's my favorite," Zeke said before taking a huge bite.

"He also enjoys a good chicken nugget and never passes up pepperoni pizza. He has a very sophisticated palate."

Sophia's laugh washed away all the worry Evan had felt when she first arrived. It was nice to see her smiling. Hopefully her nightmares were a thing of the past.

"Are you talking about the wedding theme, Evan?" Jamie's mom asked. "I heard *sophisticated.* Can someone explain to me what 'sophisticated fun' means exactly?"

Sophia set her fork down and fielded that

question. "Like they'll be doing in their marriage, we're trying to meld their personalities together for the wedding. Miss Wharton is lovely and sophisticated while Mr. Anderson is a little playful. Together, they are sophisticated fun."

"Oh, I love that," Jamie's mom said with a happy sigh.

"Yeah, they're a real opposites-attract story," Patrick chimed in. "Evan was never really Jamie's type...until suddenly they were engaged."

"Suddenly?" Evan countered. "We have been the best of friends for a long time. It's not that unusual for people to fall in love when they have such a strong friendship."

Gordon raised his glass. "I think it's wonderful that there is a history between you two. There was no rushing into things. You know each other, so there will be no surprises when you start your life together."

Evan caught the slight dig there. Patrick and Eliza had gotten engaged after dating for only a month. Jamie always suspected his marriage was just as fake as theirs would be.

"There's nothing Jamie hates more than surprises," Evan said, giving his friend a wink.

"You can say that again."

"Well, that's too bad," Gordon said. "I had a little surprise planned for the happy couple after we ate."

"Uncle Gordon, you have done so much already. You do not need to do anything else for us." Jamie's worried gaze connected with Evan's.

Her uncle was generous, but he also liked to be in control. If he had a surprise for them, it was likely something that they would have preferred to have some say in and now wouldn't.

"I think we can trust your uncle to have our best interests at heart," Evan said in an attempt at calming Jamie and pleasing Gordon.

Patrick snickered. "Jamie may not like secrets, but Evan loves a good handout."

A rush of anger hit Evan so hard, he almost got out of his chair and leaped over the table to give Patrick a hand. To the face.

Instead of making a scene, he readjusted the napkin on his lap and popped a mini muffin in his mouth. He would not be baited into an argument in front of Jamie's entire family.

Jamie, on the other hand, had no qualms about giving it right back. "You would know all about handouts, wouldn't you? How's the guesthouse?"

"It's fantastic," Patrick said with a sneer. "But our dear uncle isn't footing the bill for my renovations."

"Is there a reason you two are acting like bickering children in front of guests?" Gordon asked.

Jamie's mother intervened and shifted the conversation. "You know I would love to hear about the changes you're making. How are those house renovations going, Eliza?"

The ladies began to discuss kitchen remodeling and paint colors. It gave Evan the time he needed to calm down. He could not let Patrick rattle him like that. He needed to keep his cool in order to impress Gordon.

Brunch ended and there was still enough food left over to feed another ten people and then some. Gordon invited everyone to the garden, where he wanted Sophia to explain her ideas for the ceremony.

Again, she was a rock star. Her vision was perfect, and everyone was impressed with her ideas.

"All right, time for the surprise," Gordon announced. Jamie and Evan exchanged worried looks. "I've asked Miss Reed to plan you a two-week honeymoon at my villa in Italy. You'll be leaving the morning after the wedding."

Jamie almost fell over but recovered quite quickly. "Uncle Gordon, I can't leave the country for two weeks. I have responsibilities."

"I have already asked your assistant to clear your schedule. Patrick and I will make sure that things are taken care of while you're gone. He's already shared some excellent ideas with me. You don't have to worry."

Evan knew Gordon wouldn't say something like that unless he was beginning to lean in Patrick's direction. The worst thing that could happen would be marrying Jamie for nothing. He could see that Jamie had picked up on the subtle snub, as well. She was practically vibrating.

"Uncle Gordon, we have a huge PR issue on our hands right now. I don't think the middle of this crisis is the best time for me to disappear. Evan and I appreciate the gesture, but we're happy to delay our honeymoon to a later date."

"Nonsense. You deserve this time with your husband."

Evan had no choice. He would have to be the one to give an excuse. "Sir, thank you for your generous offer. As much as I would love to visit Italy, I am the sole caretaker of my brother and I cannot leave him for two weeks. A trip like that would need to be something Jamie and I plan together."

"I assumed that when you and Jamie got married, you would be finding a more *appropriate* placement for your brother," Gordon said with a tilt of his head.

Evan felt the food in his stomach fight its way back up. Was he insinuating that Zeke should not live with them after they were married?

"The most appropriate place for my brother is with me. That has never been up for discussion."

"But you're starting a life together. Soon you'll be having a family of your own."

Evan clenched his fists. "Zeke will always be part of that family."

"Jamie and Evan are having a wedding. Not a family," Zeke said. "She is his friend. I am his family." His voice had a slight shake to it. He understood more of this conversation than Evan would have liked.

"The wedding will make them husband and wife. That's the start of a new family, young man," Gordon explained.

Zeke's eyes went wide. "Jamie is going to be your wife?"

CHAPTER NINE

SOPHIA WAS AS shocked as everyone else when Zeke began to have a meltdown over the news that a wedding meant his brother would be Jamie's husband and she his wife. Somehow, that hadn't been made clear to him before this.

"Excuse us a minute," Evan said, taking his brother by the hand and walking him out of the garden.

Jamie was rubbing her forehead. "We cannot go to Italy next month. I am sorry, Uncle Gordon," she said before storming off in another direction. Her mother followed after her.

"I think I could go for another mimosa," Patrick said. "Come on, Mom. Let me make you one. I make them the best." His mother took his arm, and his wife rolled her eyes but trailed behind them.

"I don't understand what is going on," Gordon said. "The man is going to have a wife to take care of—why would he still be responsible for his brother?"

"You wouldn't take me in if I couldn't live independently?" the other Mr. Wharton asked.

"As I recall, you couldn't wait for me to move out of Mom and Dad's house when I left for college."

"This is true. You were a bully. Always had to have your way."

"Well, maybe I owe you, then. If you ever need help, you can move into my guesthouse. That is if your son ever finishes his house and gets out of there."

The two old men laughed and headed back up to the house. Sophia was left in the garden by herself and wasn't sure what to do next. Maybe this was the perfect time to leave.

As she exited the garden, she saw Evan walking alone. He looked so sad, she couldn't stop herself from going to him.

"Were you able to calm him down?" she asked.

Evan glanced back over his shoulder. His brother was sitting on the swing on the dock. "He told me he doesn't want to talk to me for ten minutes, and if I talk to him before ten minutes is up, a new ten minutes will start up. He was very serious about it."

"I'm sure all this is kind of overwhelming for him. It probably is hard for him to imagine that things are changing."

"One thing that's not changing is where he belongs, which is with me." Evan punched his fist into his hand. "I can't believe that Gordon would stand there and insinuate that my brother would have to live with someone else just because we're getting married. Who thinks like that?"

His love for and protectiveness of his brother was admirable. "Not everyone is willing to be that selfless."

"If we were getting married, would you ask me to send my brother away?"

The thought of being married to Evan threw her for a second. Even in the hypothetical it was a dangerous thought, because it was more appealing than she could ever admit. "Absolutely not."

"My brother takes care of me and I take care of him. People think because he has Down syndrome that he can't contribute the same, but Zeke gives me more than I could ever give him."

Sophia's heart swelled. "I believe it. He seems pretty special."

Evan once again looked back at his brother, who was watching them. He turned his head as soon as Evan caught him staring. "He's the best. He's probably super jealous that I'm talking to you."

"Well, maybe he's not talking to you for ten minutes, but I bet he'll talk to me," she said, heading down to the waterfront.

"You let him know I only have eight minutes of the silent treatment left!" he called after her.

She smiled. "I'll remind him."

Zeke was rocking back and forth on the swing. He was dressed in khaki shorts and a blue plaid button-down with a red, white and blue comic book hero T-shirt peeking out from underneath. She loved his style. Zeke had a beautiful spirit. He also had a fun-loving side like his brother.

Sophia was more than happy to sit with him rather than go back up to the house with the rest of that crew. He would definitely be the best company.

"May I sit with you?" she asked.

Zeke patted the seat next to him but didn't speak.

"You're not not talking to me for ten minutes, are you?" she asked as she sat down.

He ducked his head, embarrassed. "No. Only Evan."

"You know your brother loves you a lot, right?"

Zeke shrugged his shoulders.

"Just because he's in love with Jamie doesn't mean that he loves you any less. It doesn't have to change anything. What they have is a different kind of love."

Zeke's brow furrowed. "Evan is not in love with Jamie. She is his friend. They are friends."

Interesting. It must really be confusing for him since they started out as friends. Surely the complexities of romantic love were a challenge for him to understand. Heck, she didn't understand them most of the time.

"Friends who are also in love. That's the best kind of person to be in love with. You want to fall in love with someone who is your friend."

"No. They don't even kiss!" Zeke threw his hands up.

"You've never seen them kiss?"

Zeke shook his head. That seemed a little odd. Maybe Evan was just careful around his brother. Maybe he didn't want to make his brother uncomfortable by being overly affectionate with a woman in front of him.

"He used to kiss Tanya. They used to kiss all the time."

Okay, that debunked her first theory. "I don't know, bud. All I know is I'm planning a wedding for them and you're going to get an awesome sister-in-law. It's not really bad news, is it?"

Zeke let out a heavy breath. "No."

"Don't be too mad at your brother. I'm sure he didn't realize that you were confused."

Zeke shook his head again. "I'm not confused. He is."

"My ten minutes is up," Evan said, joining them on the dock. "Can we be friends again?"

Zeke stood up and opened his arms for a hug. Evan didn't hesitate to wrap his brother up in an embrace. Sophia could feel the tears gathering in the corners of her eyes.

"We are family," Evan said. "Always. You and me forever, okay?"

"Forever," Zeke repeated.

"Don't listen to what Mr. Wharton says. He doesn't know anything about our family. We are Andersons and we stick together."

Zeke let his brother go. "We're best buds."

Evan was a bit choked up but managed to say, "Best buds."

Sophia had to look away. They were so heartwarming it was overwhelming. Everything that made Evan attractive when they first met paled in comparison with the way he treated his brother.

"Are you going to come back up to the house with us?" Evan asked.

Sophia wiped the wetness under her eyes and took a deep breath. She stood up and smiled at the reconciled brothers. "Lead the way."

"You handled the Wharton inquisition quite well," Evan said.

"They weren't so bad. I wasn't exactly sure what to expect when Mr. Wharton asked me to come. I imagined it would be a lot worse than getting to eat way too much food and answering a few questions."

"Gordon knows how to entertain, and his personal chef sure knows how to cook."

"They make the best peanut butter and jelly," Zeke added.

Sophia playfully nudged him with her shoulder. "You haven't had a peanut butter and jelly made by my grandma. She bakes her own pita bread and fills it with tons of peanut butter and homemade jam. They're amazing."

"Can she make me one?"

"She would probably love to make you one. She loves cooking for people. We have big family dinners every Sunday night. Between this brunch and tonight's dinner, I'll probably gain ten pounds."

"Is that why you didn't have seconds?" Evan asked.

"You have no idea how much I wanted to have one of those double-chocolate muffins and about ten more pieces of bacon. I love bacon. But Yaya would never forgive me if I didn't fill and clean my plate tonight."

"I love bacon, too," Evan said, pointing to his chest.

Sophia smiled. "Who doesn't? It's delicious."

Evan offered his arm when the ground became a bit uneven. Sophia had worn heels today, and she needed the help. She took his arm, touching his skin, which had been warmed by the sun. His personality was so much like the sun—bright and warm.

"Can your grandma make Evan bacon when she makes me a peanut butter and jelly?" Zeke asked.

Yeah, there was no way Yaya was ever meeting Evan or making him bacon. If she met him, she would know immediately that Sophia was smitten. Sophia didn't want her *yaya* to be disappointed in her for coveting someone else's husband.

"My grandma makes good bacon. She could make your brother a BLT when she makes your PB and J. Maybe I could bring them to the next wedding planning session," she offered.

"Why don't we come to Sunday dinner?" Zeke asked. "Is it fancy?"

Evan's face blanched, his shock morphing into embarrassment almost immediately. "Zeke, you don't invite yourself to someone else's dinner. That's rude, dude."

Jamie stepped off the patio. Sophia let go of Evan, hoping Jamie didn't notice. As she approached, Sophia prayed there would be no more talk of Sunday dinner.

"Zeke, buddy," Jamie said. "I am so sorry all of this is so confusing. You know that you belong with Evan, right? I promise that just because we're having a wedding doesn't mean anything is changing for you."

Sophia was struck by that promise. How could she say nothing would change? Things were bound to change after they got married. They would all be living together. Evan and Jamie would probably have kids someday. The thought made Sophia's heart hurt.

Stupid heart.

"Why do you want to be Evan's wife?" Zeke asked. "You think he's weird and he thinks you're—"

"Okay!" Evan interrupted. He put his hands on Zeke's shoulders and gave him a gentle push toward the patio. "Let's not focus on that right now. Let's go see if there are any doughnuts left."

"Evan thinks I'm what?" Jamie chased after them.

Sophia exhaled. This was the strangest couple she'd ever planned a wedding for. She watched the way Jamie and Evan interacted.

It was clear they were friends. They acted like they were already family, but something was a little off.

There was no affection between the two of them. They didn't hold hands. In fact, Evan never reached for her, nor she for him. There didn't seem to be any fireworks when they looked at one another. No sparks when they were close. They never kissed. Zeke's words hung heavy. It was like they were brother and sister instead of future husband and wife.

Maybe that was wishful thinking. Even if the two of them weren't madly in love, there was no chance that she and Evan could ever be anything. Dissecting their relationship was wrong. It was presumptuous of her to think she could know the intricacies of their relationship. She didn't know what they were like when they were alone. Not everyone was comfortable with public displays of affection.

Evan came up beside her and handed her something wrapped in a napkin. "There was one double-chocolate one left. You really should have it," he said. "It's mini. You'll still be able to eat everything your *yaya* makes."

"Thank you." Sophia reminded herself that

he was simply being nice. It wasn't anything more than that. Evan was nice to everyone.

A splash caught everyone's attention. Patrick's dog had jumped into the pool.

"Why is your dog swimming in my pool?" Gordon asked clearly perturbed.

"Buster! Get out of there!" Patrick shouted. "Who let the dog out?" He looked at his wife.

"Don't look at me, I've been here the whole time."

Patrick entered the pool area and continued calling for the dog.

"Did you?" Evan asked Jamie.

She shook her head and held her hand up like she was swearing in at court. "Not me."

Buster climbed up the steps and proceeded to shake, showering his owner with pool water. Evan covered his mouth as he laughed. Sophia knew he had to be enjoying the karma.

Patrick tried to grab the dog by his collar, but Buster wasn't having any of it. He wanted to play tag and Patrick and Eliza were it. Eliza tried to help her husband as Buster weaved in and out of the sunning beds.

"Well, this is more entertaining than I thought it would be," Evan said, unable to hold back his chuckle.

"How come the dog gets to swim, but I don't?" Zeke asked.

Evan threw his arm around his brother's shoulders. "Next time, buddy."

Eliza and Patrick seemed to have Buster cornered. It was quite a sight—Eliza in her designer dress and high heels and Patrick in his khakis and loafers crouched like they were hunters after their prey.

"Stay," Patrick commanded.

Buster tilted his head as if to think about it, and then immediately decided he didn't want to do that. The rottweiler bolted past Eliza, causing her to fall over. He ran toward the house and Sophia knew better than to get in his way. Everyone on the patio parted like the Red Sea and Buster made a mad dash for the brunch table, where he happily found a feast.

"No!" Gordon flailed his arms. "Get, you dirty mongrel!"

Buster paid no mind. He continued to wolf down everything leftover.

"This may be the best family brunch ever," Jamie discreetly said to Evan. They slyly high-fived.

Gordon demanded that his staff remove the

dog from the table as Patrick once again tried to get the dog to obey him.

Sophia watched the mayhem wide-eyed. She'd had many chaotic family dinners but this one took the cake. She shook her head as her phone rang in her handbag. She pulled it out to see her uncle was calling. Uncle Gus didn't call. The last time he called Sophia was the day her grandpa passed. A wave of fear took her breath away.

She answered the call. "Uncle Gus?"

She stepped away from the shenanigans for some privacy and plugged her other ear with her finger.

"Sophia, dinner is canceled."

Yaya did not cancel dinner. "What's the matter? Why is dinner canceled?"

He hesitated, which only ramped up her anxiety. "It's Yaya. We're at the hospital. She had an incident."

"An incident?" She began to walk toward the sunporch. Making a graceful exit might be challenging while she was having a panic attack. "What kind of incident?"

"She was complaining about not feeling herself, and then while she and your aunt were shopping for some last-minute ingredients, she fainted."

"Is she conscious now?"

"She came to, but they had already called an ambulance. I'm here with her now at the hospital. They're running some tests." He paused, his silence heavy. When he spoke again, his voice was raw with emotion. "Do you think I should call your mother now or wait until we know more?"

Yaya was in the hospital. Sophia's chest constricted, making it hard to breathe. Maybe she was the one having a heart attack. "Let's not call her until we know more. Which hospital are you at?"

"Memorial."

"I'm on my way." Sophia ended the call and looked for Jamie and Evan. Evan appeared at her side just as the tears started to fall.

Concern etched his face. "What's the matter?"

There was no containing the emotion. Hearing the worry and fear in her uncle's voice did not make her feel like things were going to be all right. Tears streamed down her face.

"It's my *yaya*," she choked out.

"What happened? Is she okay?"

Sophia shook her head. The words were stuck behind the lump in her throat.

Evan didn't hesitate to reach out. He took her by the hand. "How can I help?"

She shrugged. "I need to get to Memorial Hospital."

Jamie appeared. "What's going on? What happened?"

"Her grandmother is in the hospital. She needs to go."

"You can't drive yourself in this condition," Jamie said. "Why don't you let Evan take you to the hospital. I'll take Zeke home and then come get Evan."

Her kindness was overwhelming, but Sophia shook her head. "I can't ask you—"

"You did not ask me," Jamie interrupted. "We are offering. Please let us do this for you."

There was no way she could say no. She was in full panic mode anyway. Driving herself wouldn't have been smart. She was so thankful for Jamie and Evan.

"I'll explain to everyone else. You guys go," Jamie said.

Evan hadn't let go of her hand the entire

time. "Come on," he said, pulling her toward the house.

He grabbed some tissues on their way through the house. In the car, she felt safe letting it all out. Evan didn't try to get her to stop. He just held her hand and offered quiet comfort.

By the time they got to the hospital, she was taking slow, deep breaths and was calm enough to speak. "Thank you for getting me here. I probably would have gotten into a car accident if I had driven myself."

Those same brown eyes that had offered her such peace of mind that day at the bank were doing it again. "You do not have to thank me. This was the right thing to do. Let's find your *yaya* and make sure she's okay."

Sophia called her uncle Gus and was directed to the emergency room. Yaya did not want to be admitted even though the doctors were recommending that she stay for observation.

"Oh, boy," Evan said, looking down at his phone.

"What?" Sophia couldn't take any more bad news today.

"Nothing. Jamie dropped Zeke off at our

place, but she heard Patrick saying something about strategizing for a meeting that's tomorrow, so now she thinks she needs to head back to the estate. I'm going to have to call for a ride."

"No, don't do that. If you don't mind waiting for me to explain to my stubborn *yaya* that she needs to listen to the doctors, I can drive you home." It was the least she could do since he had helped her out.

"It's not a big deal. I don't want you to feel like you have to rush your time with your grandma."

Selfishly, his presence provided her with so much comfort, she wasn't ready for him to leave, either. She took him by the hand. "Please. Stay."

She didn't have to ask twice.

"I DON'T NEED to spend the night here. We have family dinner. I need to get home and make sure your wife is not adding too much garlic to the tzatziki sauce. You know how heavy-handed she is with the garlic. It's too much. I need to be home to help."

Sophia was so relieved to hear her voice, she didn't even care that she was fighting over her medical treatment. "Yaya," she said as she pushed back the curtain to the room. Seeing her usually vibrant grandmother wearing a hospital gown in a stark white room was almost too much. The tears were back. She hurried to her grandmother's bedside and wrapped her in a hug. "You can't do this to me."

"Oh, *paidi mou*. It's going to be fine. My blood sugar was low. I was too busy planning how I was going to feed you all and forgot to feed myself. We should go home so we all can eat."

Sophia couldn't care less about food. She wanted her *yaya* to be well, so they could eat together for years to come.

"Mom, they need to make sure it wasn't something more serious, and that takes time," Gus said. "A little time, not forever. You can be completely in charge of dinner next week."

Sophia agreed with her uncle. "You need to listen to what Uncle Gus and the doctors are telling you. They think you need to stay— they don't want to send you home where something worse could happen."

Yaya took Sophia's hand and gave her palm a kiss before pressing it to her cheek. "I am fine. They said it wasn't a heart attack. My heart was probably racing because of the low blood sugar. No need to worry."

Evan cleared his throat and caught Yaya's attention. "Who is this? Did he come with you or is he here to convince me to stay, as well? If you are from the hospital, you can go." She flicked her wrist to shoo him away.

"He's with me, Yaya. This is…my friend Evan." As soon as his name left her lips, his face broke into the most beautiful smile.

"I get to stay if I'm with her, right?"

Yaya smiled at Sophia and waggled her eyebrows. "You have been holding out on me."

Sophia dipped her chin and scowled at her grandmother. "Evan drove me here because I was so worried about you, I couldn't see straight. Do you see what you do to me? Can't you just do what you're told this one time?"

"I am fit as a fiddle. I want to go home. I also want to get to know your friend better. Evan, darling, thank you so much for watching out for my Sophia. She is very special."

"That she is," Evan replied.

"How did you two meet?"

Sophia did not need her grandmother thinking this was a potential suitor. She was about to explain he was her client when he answered.

"We met a few weeks ago at the bank robbery, actually."

Yaya's eyes went wide with surprise. One side of her mouth quirked up; she was quite pleased. "The robbery. You must be the friend on the phone. Sophia said you were very kind to her that day."

Great. Now it was better that she didn't find out he was a client, because Yaya knew exactly how Sophia had felt about Evan the day they met.

"She was very brave that day."

"That's my granddaughter. She takes after me."

Evan turned on that charm of his. "That's what she told me. She adores you, and I can see why. You're beautiful and tough. I like that."

"Oh, I like you," Yaya said, falling fast. Like grandmother, like granddaughter.

The doctor returned and Yaya was ready to fight. "I don't want to stay. You cannot make me stay," she asserted.

"No, ma'am. We cannot make you stay.

Like I said, it's in your best interest to stay and let us watch how things go tonight, but if you want to sign yourself out, I cannot stop you. So far, all the tests have come back negative for anything major."

"Because I am fine. How many times do I have to tell you all?"

There was no convincing her to stay. She would walk home if they didn't take her. The doctor sent a nurse in to finish with the paperwork and encouraged her to come back if any of the symptoms she'd been experiencing earlier in the day reemerged.

"If you are going home, you are not lifting a finger the rest of the day," Sophia told her *yaya*.

"It's Sunday dinner. I can't trust your aunt to handle it."

Uncle Gus shook his head. "You don't need to host a houseful of people tonight, Mom."

"Nonsense. I have five pounds of fresh lamb marinating in my refrigerator. We are having Sunday dinner."

"I already started calling the family, Mom. I told Nicholas and Maria they didn't have to come," Uncle Gus said. Sophia's cousin and his wife had three rambunctious children. It was probably best there would be a few less littles running around Yaya's house tonight.

Yaya, of course, was devastated at the thought. "Who's going to eat all the food we're making? Don't you dare call anyone else. Evan, you must join us for dinner."

Sophia froze. Evan seemed taken aback. "That's very kind of you, but I take care of my younger brother and he would be mad if I ditched him for dinner."

"Bring him, too! We have plenty of food now that Nicholas and his family of bottom-less pits aren't coming. Please—it will make me happy. You want to make an old woman happy, don't you?"

Sophia wanted the ground to open up and swallow her. There was no way he would turn down her invitation when she posed it that way.

"Well, we did hear you make an amazing peanut butter and jelly pita."

"Did you?" Yaya had the totally wrong idea about this "friendship." She was going to fall in love with Evan and be disappointed when she learned he was engaged to be married. "It's settled, then! You and your brother will come, and we will have our family dinner."

CHAPTER TEN

"I'M SORRY. YOU do not have to come to dinner if you don't want to," Sophia said as she drove Evan home to pick up Zeke. "Don't be bullied by my *yaya*."

Evan wasn't sure if she was offering him an out because she felt bad or if she was hoping he'd bow out without her having to ask him to.

He thought about how she had taken his hand and asked him to stay when they first got to the hospital. It was like the sky opened up and the angels all sang. He wanted her to want him to be there. He wouldn't force himself into her space, though.

"Do you want me to cancel? I don't want you to feel uncomfortable."

"I'm not uncomfortable," she said, tightening her grip on the steering wheel.

She was a terrible liar. As much as he wanted to be with her, Evan didn't want to make things hard for her. He had to play his part and help Jamie get what she deserved. And he would do whatever he had to so he could give Zeke everything he needed. Getting married would also help Sophia. Taking care of those three people was the most important thing in the world to him.

"You could tell her that I wasn't feeling well."

"She won't buy it."

"Okay… What if you tell her I forgot I had other plans?"

Sophia shook her head. "She'll know I'm lying. She always knows when I'm lying. You're going to have to come to dinner. You and Zeke are coming to Sunday dinner. This is probably a bad idea, but it's happening."

Evan knew it was wrong to be so happy, but it was a relief that she was letting him in. They couldn't be more than this, but he was selfish enough to take whatever he could get.

When they got to his house, Evan and Sophia went inside to get Zeke. Dirty dishes were piled by the sink, couch pillows were thrown on the ground, a pyramid of soda cans stood on the kitchen table. He had completely forgotten what a mess their place was at the moment. Evan scurried around, attempting to put a few things back where they belonged.

"Sunday is usually our clean-up day. We haven't gotten around to it yet, though. Obviously." He placed the pillows back on the couch. "Zeke is probably in his room." He left her in the living room and went to find his brother.

"Dude, what's up with the tower of soda cans on the kitchen table?"

Zeke sat on his bed with his headphones on. He tugged one side off his ear. "I was cleaning my room and decided it looked cool to put all the cans in a pyramid. You didn't think it looked cool?"

"It was cool, but Sophia is here."

His brother jumped up and took his headphones off. "Did she think my pyramid was cool?"

"I didn't ask her. Listen, buddy, she wants us to come to her grandma's for dinner. It's not fancy, but we have to be on our best behavior, okay?"

Zeke was thrilled about the dinner invite. His wish had come true. He had taken such a liking to Sophia, but that was no surprise.

It was impossible not to fall head over heels for someone like her.

"Thank you for inviting me to dinner," he said to Sophia when they joined her back in the living room.

"My grandma is very excited to have you."

"Can I have peanut butter and jelly?" he asked as he put on his shoes.

"You sure can, but I'm warning you now, my grandma is going to ask you to try some other things. Like all the things. She's a Greek grandma. Making sure everyone eats is her obsession."

"Good thing I like to eat. Your *yaya* can stuff me to the gills," Evan said, knowing it wouldn't be as easy to get Zeke out of his comfort zone. If he liked the pita PB and J, though, he would probably eat a dozen of them. Hopefully that would appease Yaya.

"You'll win her over. I don't doubt that. I'm sure everyone will love you."

He had to remind himself that Sophia's family could fall in love with him and it wouldn't change the fact that he couldn't be more to them. They got in the car and headed to Yaya's.

"Anything else we should know about your

family so I can make that good impression?" Evan asked when they parked outside the house.

"They're very loud. And they tend to talk at the same time, so it's hard to follow what's being said."

"Gotcha."

Sophia pressed the palm of her hand to her forehead. "There's one other thing you should be prepared for." She seemed anxious. "My aunts and my *yaya* obviously don't know that you're my client."

"Meaning they don't know that you're planning my wedding."

She nodded. "It could lead to some uncomfortable comments. They may have questions. Basically, I'm thirty years old and, in a Greek family, that makes me a spinster. I should have been married to a nice Greek man about ten years ago. They can't wait to plan my wedding."

Sophia's wedding… Someday her family would plan her wedding to some other guy. Maybe Greek, maybe not. She would be happy and loved. That mattered more than the way imagining it hurt his heart.

What if Evan had met Sophia ten years

ago? Five? One? Would she have laughed at his jokes and been charmed by him enough to accept a date? Would her family have accepted him even though he wasn't Greek? A thousand alternate realities flipped through his head like a slideshow. If they had met before he made this deal with Jamie, perhaps he and Sophia would be planning their real wedding instead of the make-believe one happening in a month.

"I can only imagine how amazing your wedding will be. Wedding planner weddings have to be the best, and I bet you'd give yourself a huge discount," he said, trying to keep things light.

Her forehead creased. "I would give myself a discount?"

"I would hope so. Do you have any idea how expensive full-service wedding planning costs these days?"

She shook her head and fought a smile. "I am aware."

He loved making her smile. It was becoming his favorite thing.

"They're here!" Evan heard a little boy yell as they approached the front door.

Oh, boy, the family was ready and waiting.

This was likely a terrible idea, but he couldn't help but be a little thrilled at the idea of getting to see this side of Sophia's life.

Sophia took a deep breath, seemingly preparing herself for what was to come. "I hope you're ready for this."

"We're ready to party, right, Z-Man?"

"Ready!" Zeke pumped his fist in the air. "Let's meet Yaya!"

Sophia opened the door and they stepped inside the home. There was a warmth that exuded from the space that had nothing to do with the temperature. Yaya's home was filled with color and family. She had pictures of everyone she loved everywhere. The open floor plan allowed everyone to be together.

She was seated on the couch with her great-grandchildren cuddling up to her. Two of Sophia's aunts were standing in front of the large dining room table set with a dozen place settings. Uncle Gus was in the kitchen sneaking a peek into one of the pots on the stove.

Sophia introduced Evan and Zeke to her cousins and the rest of the crew. She made it very clear that they were her friends, explaining that she met Evan during the bank robbery.

"Thanks to him, I didn't completely fall apart. He was so calm, and it sort of oozed off him and enveloped me during the scariest moment of my life. For that, I will always be grateful."

Her words were like a lightning strike to Evan's heart. Knowing that he had been able to give her that comfort was so gratifying. For the last few weeks, he'd felt like the villain who had tricked her into liking him. Hopefully the good would outweigh the bad.

"That is so sweet," her aunt Anna said.

"It sounds like fate brought you two together," her aunt Calista said. "He was there when you needed him."

"Let's not romanticize it," Sophia said. "Can I help with dinner?"

That was her way of ending all conversation about the potential for the two of them getting together. Sophia and her aunts and cousins retreated into the kitchen.

Was it fate that put her in his life? If it was, it was cruel. Why did he meet someone so amazing at the completely worst time for that to happen? Again, Evan's thoughts drifted to those scenarios of meeting her earlier. How things would have been different.

The little kids got up and began to run around. One of the boys chased his younger brother around the dining room table.

Sophia's grandmother pointed at Evan. "They've banished me from my own kitchen. If I can't be in there, I want to talk to you and your brother."

Zeke and Evan sat down in the living room with Yaya. Uncle Gus offered them both something to drink. Quickly, the space was filled with chatter and laughter. Sophia wasn't kidding about her family being loud. Children squealing, parents scolding, siblings gossiping, hungry teenagers asking for something to eat and being reminded they need to wait, family enjoying each other's company.

"Thank you for inviting us for dinner," Evan said.

"Thank you for being there for my granddaughter today. She worries about me, but she doesn't need to. It will take much more than some low blood sugar to take me down."

Evan admired her spirit. He could see why Sophia loved her so ardently. She was a listener. While her family socialized in the other rooms, Yaya wanted to know about the Anderson brothers. Zeke told her all about his job at the grocery store and his love of college basketball. She couldn't have known that the man could talk about Duke's and UNC's basketball teams for hours if given the chance.

"When Evan went to UNC, he brought me to all the home games. We cheered so much. Right, Evan?"

"We did. Those are some of my best memories of school."

"It's lovely you're so close. I always wished Sophia had a brother or sister growing up, but my daughter and her husband wanted a small family. My son-in-law is not a big fan of all this." She waved her hand around. "He finds it a little too loud and he's a private person, and in case you haven't noticed, no one here is afraid to ask you about your business."

Evan could hear the sadness that colored her tone. It bothered her that Sophia's parents chose to leave. Sophia had made it seem like they were simply free spirits who wanted to explore places they'd never been. Her grandmother made it sound like they ran away from the family.

"I think your family is wonderful," he said, giving her a grin. One of the children shrieked and his mother yelled at him to knock it off.

The boy's teenage sister complained that their mother didn't have to scream at him. Her father shouted not to talk to her mother that way. "Loud but wonderful."

She laughed, and the sound caught Sophia's attention. Evan gave her a thumbs-up to let her know it was going well. She abandoned her post in front of the stove, where she was in charge of stirring something in the big pot.

"Is everything all right over here?"

"Your friends are my new favorite people. We may have to invite them every Sunday," Yaya said.

Evan watched as Sophia struggled with her obvious mortification with that idea. "Would you like some more tea, Zeke?" she asked.

"No, thank you. Your grandma is nice. She hasn't yelled at me once."

Yaya's eyes widened. "Did you tell him I was going to yell at him?"

Sophia blushed. "No. I warned him you were going to feed him too much and that everyone here was very loud."

"And that Evan and Sophia are having a wedding."

Both Sophia and her grandmother's jaws dropped. Evan should have warned her that

Zeke had a way of changing the messages he was given.

Yaya was way too pleased. Sophia was flummoxed.

"He means Sophia didn't want anyone to think our friendship meant we were going to be planning a wedding," Evan tried to explain.

"What are we talking about over here?" Sophia's cousin Katherine came out of nowhere. "I thought I heard someone say something about a wedding."

"We're not talking about weddings," Sophia said, finding her voice. "We're talking about how Evan and I are friends. Friends don't get married."

"But you said we should marry our friends," Zeke said, his face scrunched up in confusion. "It's important. Remember?"

Evan didn't recall that part of their conversation. Maybe it came up during Sophia and Zeke's private chat on the dock swing.

Sophia did her best to right the sinking ship. "Right. I remember. Of course people should marry someone they think of as a friend. I'm saying Evan and I are friends who aren't getting married."

"What's that about getting married?" Sophia's aunt Calista joined the conversation.

"Relax, Mom. She's saying there's no wedding planning going on."

"We are planning a wedding," Zeke said, still confused and rightly so. Evan should never have put him in this situation.

"Hey, buddy," Evan said, holding his hand out to help his brother out of the chair he was in. "Let's go see if we can get some more tea."

"I don't want any more tea, thank you."

"Why don't you come help me get some more tea. I need your help."

"Fine," Zeke said with a huff.

Evan gave Sophia a sympathetic glance. She had her hands full and it was best if he and Zeke removed themselves from this discussion. He trusted she would smooth things over.

Dinner was just as chaotic as Evan imagined it would be. It was next to impossible to follow the flow of conversation as multiple people spoke at once and there were always three different topics being discussed at the same time. Thankfully, none of them were about weddings.

Sitting around the Markopouloses' dining

table was nothing like being at the Andersons'. Evan loved every minute of it, though. They were boisterous but clearly loved one another. All of them were kind to Zeke, who found out he really liked pita bread. He also tried some lamb kebabs, but did not try the yogurt sauce the rest of them were drowning their lamb in.

When dinner was finished, everyone helped clean up. Everything was a team effort. He liked that about Sophia's family. Once the kitchen was back in order, most of the family said their goodbyes.

Evan found Sophia alone in the kitchen and slipped a treat into her hand. She smiled down at the butterscotch candy.

"I found your grandma's candy dish. This was the last butterscotch. You're welcome."

She unwrapped it and popped it in her mouth. "Thank you."

"No lemon drops. I was a little disappointed." He held up a peppermint candy. "I had to go with this. At least it will help with the onion breath."

Her smile was better than any lemon drop. "I'm sorry about that. The kids always seem to take the lemon ones. I should have thought to grab you one earlier in the evening."

"I had a really good night. Thank you for letting me and Zeke come." Evan was so aware of their close physical proximity. The smell of her perfume was subtle but intoxicating. He longed to run the backs of his fingers across her cheek, to brush his lips against hers. She was like a magnet, pulling him in her direction.

"Thanks for being there when I needed someone today. You always seem to calm me down when I'm facing my scariest moments."

He ducked his head. Her gratitude made him swell with pride. If bringing her a little peace when she was in a dark place was the only role he could play in her life, he'd happily do it. He would do anything for her.

"You can call me anytime. We're friends now, right?" He prayed she'd say yes even though he knew that he was asking her to put aside her own feelings to let him have her in his life.

She thought about it a couple of seconds as they both listened to Zeke recounting his favorite college basketball moments to an ever-attentive Yaya.

"We're friends," she said.

Evan's heart thumped hard in his chest. It was like the darn thing wanted to bust out and jump into her arms. It was no surprise, given that her name was now written on it.

"Friends is good." Well, it had to be enough.

She nodded. "I can take you guys home whenever you're ready."

Evan's gaze fell back on his brother, who was happy to have found such a riveted audience. "I think Zeke may never want to leave."

Sophia giggled. "Trust me, Yaya wouldn't complain about that for a second." Her expression turned somber. "I think I better stay here tonight. I don't want her to be alone after her fainting spell today."

"You're a good granddaughter."

She was quick to retort. "You're a good brother." When Evan shook his head, she asked, "You don't think so?"

"No, I'm just sensitive when it comes to being praised about being his brother. Sometimes I feel like people give me extra credit for being a good brother because Zeke has special needs. As if Zeke's disability requires me to do more than any other brother would do. But Zeke makes it pretty easy to be good to him."

She nodded. "I can see that. I didn't mean it like you're some kind of martyr. I meant… I don't know. You're a good person and it's evident in the way you are with your brother. You're kind and patient. You're thoughtful. You pay attention. You're like that with everyone, not just Zeke. So I guess that's what I meant. You're a good person."

Was he? He wanted to be. For her. For Zeke. But he was a liar. He justified his dishonesty by saying it was for a good cause, but it was still deceitful. Didn't that make him the bad guy?

Sophia didn't know the real him. She didn't know how selfish he was. How he coveted her even though he would be pledging himself to someone else in a month. She wouldn't think he was such a good guy if she knew the truth.

CHAPTER ELEVEN

AFTER DROPPING THE Anderson brothers off at home, Sophia returned to Yaya's. She knew she was in a world of trouble. There were going to be questions she'd have to answer. Answers she wouldn't want to give.

"Can I pour you some hot tea?" Yaya asked first. This was probably the only easy question she would get.

"Yes, please. Thank you." Sophia sat down at the dining room table and enjoyed the silence for a few minutes.

"Evan and Zeke are absolutely lovely," Yaya said, setting the cup of tea down in front of Sophia. "I am glad they came to dinner."

And so it began. Sophia decided that there was no reason to lie about what was going on. She respected her grandmother too much to be dishonest.

"He's engaged. He's engaged to be married

to the niece of Gordon Wharton. I'm planning their wedding."

Yaya covered her mouth with her hand. "Oh, Sophia."

All the pity was there in her voice like Sophia had dreaded. She knew Yaya could see how she really felt.

"It's fine. We truly have become friends. He's nice."

"You're in love with him." Yaya didn't ask. She knew. "Oh, sweetheart. What are you going to do?"

Sophia shook her head. The lump in her throat was so big that no amount of tea could wash it down.

"Does he know how you feel?"

Sophia shook her head again. He was her client. She couldn't tell him she had feelings for him. It would jeopardize her career.

"How can you let him get married when he doesn't know how you feel and you haven't given him a chance to tell you how he feels?"

Sophia's eyes lifted. "How he feels? I think that's pretty clear. He's getting married. He's planning his wedding to his best friend."

"Are you serious?" Yaya's eyebrows pinched together.

"Yaya, you spent a few hours with the man. I don't think you can honestly say you know how he feels better than I do."

Yaya reached for Sophia's hand. "You forget that I see. I watch. And you are so blind sometimes."

Sophia didn't want to cry. She pressed her fingers against her eyelids. "You don't get it. It's easy to confuse his warm personality for some kind of special affection. It's just the way he is. It doesn't have anything to do with me."

"Is that what you tell yourself? Is that how you stomach planning his wedding to another woman?"

"It's the truth, Yaya. He doesn't have feelings for me. That would be silly. He's about to marry into one of the most powerful families in the entire country. She's been his friend for years. She loves him and she loves Zeke. They are getting married in a month." Those were the truths, and she couldn't ignore them just because of this stupid crush. She wasn't going to let herself project her feelings onto him.

"You're right, I don't know him very well… But I know people. I know when I see someone look at someone else like they are the single most important person in the world. The way your grandfather used to look at me."

Sophia pulled her hand away and stood up from the table. She wiped under her eyes. "I'm sorry, Yaya, but that's hurtful. That's the most hurtful thing you've ever said to me."

Yaya was startled. She placed a hand on her chest. "What? How is that hurtful?"

"Don't compare Evan to Papou. Don't compare us to you two. What you had was an epic love story. I don't have a love story. I have a job. My job is to help him get married the way he wants to the person he chose. Do you know how hard I have to work to push my own feelings aside so I can do my job?"

"Why would you do that? You have a right to your feelings."

"Because my feelings don't matter in this situation," Sophia said, exasperated.

Yaya was on her feet now. "Your feelings should always matter."

"I just mean they don't change the situation. Please don't ask me to have hope that they could." The tears came freely. She didn't have the energy to fight them anymore.

Yaya pulled her in for a hug. She didn't try

to convince her to give hope a chance. She simply let her cry because there was none.

JAMIE WHARTON WAS the epitome of classic beauty. Blonde, heart-shaped face, little nose, tiny waist. She was petite and perfect. Any wedding dress she tried on would look like it was made for her.

"This one is fine, right?" She ran her hands down over her hips.

Sophia had never worked with a bride less interested in the entire process. Jamie got no joy out of picking a dress—usually the most important decision of all.

Two weeks ago, she had instructed Sophia to order three dresses. There would be only one appointment, during which she would try on the dresses, choose one and have it fitted. Everything wedding related was a time suck, according to Jamie. The less time she could waste, the better.

"Do you want me to take some pictures so you can send them to your mom?" Sophia asked, thinking maybe a second opinion would help.

"No, no. My mother would be angry with me if she knew I was dress shopping without her, but if I had brought her, we would have been here for hours. I don't have hours."

Sophia had gotten the impression at brunch that Jamie and her mother had a good relationship. It was curious why she wouldn't want her mom here. Was time truly the only issue? Sophia wasn't here to judge. She was here to help the bride find a dress.

"You have two others to try on. Does this one feel like 'the one'?"

Jamie stared at herself in the mirror. The first dress had a simple design. Full satin skirt with a sleeveless lace bodice that had a very deep V. In the back, a line of buttons went from the waistband to the bottom of the skirt. It was stunning. Jamie should have felt like a princess.

"It's good," Jamie said with the shrug of one shoulder.

Good was never the word a bride used to describe the way her perfect wedding dress felt. Her lackluster response made Sophia feel like she had not done her job.

"*Good* doesn't scream *dream dress*." She motioned for someone to come over and help. "Maybe one of the others will really wow you."

"This is fine." She picked up her phone and

called someone. "Can you do a video call?" she asked.

"Sure." Evan's voice came over the speaker.

She'd called Evan? Sophia stood, shocked. Traditionally, the groom didn't see the bride until the day of the wedding or, these days, at a dress reveal photo shoot.

"How's this one? I think it's fine. Do you have any issues with it?"

"Ah, it looks nice."

Good and *nice*. They were going to buy a dress that inspired the two least colorful adjectives in the English language?

"Thank you. Say hi to Sophia and tell her it's okay if I buy this one without trying on the others." Jamie handed her the phone.

"Hi, Sophia." Evan sat at a desk and waved to the camera. "She's very efficient. Don't let her quick decision-making skills trick you into thinking she doesn't know what she wants. She always knows what she wants."

"I just wanted to make sure she's happy with it," Sophia explained.

"I'm happy that we can get this done before my four o'clock meeting." Jamie waved for the store associate. "It needs to be taken in a little bit and hemmed up. It's too long."

Sophia looked back at Evan on the phone. "And she looks gorgeous...not just nice. Never tell your bride she looks nice."

His smile was chagrined. "Got it. You look absolutely beautiful, Jamie!" he shouted so Jamie could hear him.

She held out her hand for the phone. "Thanks. Now, get back to work."

"Yes, ma'am. Bye. Bye, Sophia!" he called out before Jamie ended the video chat.

The two of them had a strange relationship. Sophia had worked with enough people to know all couples were different, but newlyweds, couples this close to their wedding day, were usually a bit more affectionate than Jamie and Evan.

Jamie stood still while the seamstress pinned the dress where it needed to be altered, but she stayed on her phone, checking emails. She was a driven person. Clearly, her work was her life. Sophia could relate.

"Take this away from me before I throw it through that mirror," she said, holding her phone out.

Sophia moved swiftly. "Is everything okay?"

"There hasn't been a bank robbery in three

weeks, and my uncle believes that he has Patrick to thank for that."

"How would he have done that?"

"He suggested we implement all of these new safety protocols at the branches. As if changes in a couple security measures over the last couple weeks has truly thwarted these criminals. Maybe they're still searching for their next target. Maybe it'll be months before they strike again. Who knows? All I know is it is highly unlikely that Patrick has saved the day with his insignificant security adjustments."

Sophia shared her skepticism. As much as she'd like to believe the robbers were gone, it was unlikely given how successful they'd been so far. Like Evan had said, they would get more brazen. They wouldn't stop until they got caught.

"I hope that when they do hit another bank, they mess up enough that they get caught this time."

Jamie looked at her through the mirror. "I hope that, too."

"I'm sorry work is so stressful right now. Wedding planning is stressful enough. Please trust that I'm here to take care of everything for you on that end."

"You're doing a great job, Sophia. I have not worried about this wedding at all. I know it's going to be incredible."

"That's good." More like a huge relief. Jamie didn't throw compliments around much. She was very to the point and always focused on business. Her only concerns were what was done, what had to be done and when the next thing on the list would get done.

"I was happy to hear your grandmother was okay on Sunday," Jamie said, catching Sophia off guard.

"Thank you. It ended up being something minor, but she's in her eighties, so it always makes me nervous when there's a medical issue. I apologize for making such a scene at your family's brunch."

Jamie laughed. "Please don't apologize. My family made an awful scene at brunch and my cousin's dog took a swim in the pool and ate the leftovers. You did not make a scene. You were reacting to some terrible news. Everyone was worried for you."

Sophia appreciated her kindness. It wasn't as obvious as Evan's, not the first quality one would notice about her. Jamie was ultrafocused, which could be misconstrued as self-absorbed, but she wasn't.

That made Sophia feel a million times worse for being in love with her fiancé. If Jamie was a horrible, coldhearted monster who cared only about money and power, Sophia could reason that Evan deserved better. Someone as warm and engaging as he was needed to be with a woman who was madly in love with him, who appreciated every silly, goofy inch of him.

Jamie wasn't a monster, though. She probably needed someone like Evan in her life. His warmth melted some of her cool. Maybe they balanced each other out. Sometimes opposites attracted.

"We didn't get to talk about my uncle's surprise. You know not to make any arrangements for us to go to Italy, right?"

"I gathered as much," Sophia replied. "His assistant called me about it last Friday. I hadn't had any time to even think about making plans yet."

"Good. I don't want you to waste your time on that. You have enough on your plate with this wedding. The honeymoon isn't really important to us."

"Why not?" The question flew out of her mouth before the filter in her brain could catch it.

"We're both busy," Jamie said, staring hard at her reflection in the mirror as the woman pinned the hem of her dress. "Well, I'm busy. Maybe I should have you plan the trip and Evan can take Zeke. Zeke could eat pizza every day. He'd be in heaven."

"I thought he was a PB and J kind of guy."

"He is. That's his favorite, but he loves pizza, too. Let me think about it. Maybe I'll surprise the boys with the trip. It can be my wedding present to Evan."

She was such a puzzle. Her wedding gift to her husband would be a vacation without her? It was sweet that she was thinking about Zeke. It was so evident that they were all close. She cared about them. She loved them. Something just didn't fit, though.

There was that lingering feeling that Jamie wasn't in love. But how could she not be in love with Evan? He seemed like he'd be romantic. Attentive. Affectionate.

Sophia thought about how he reached for

her when she needed comfort. How he offered his arm to steady her or placed his hand on the small of her back to guide her.

"So you and Evan have been friends for a long time, huh?"

"Since college. We hung out in the same group of friends. We got really close after we both lost our dads. It was nice to have someone who understood. He's good at knowing when I need to talk and when I don't."

That sounded like Evan. His empathy was one of his greatest strengths. "Is that what won you over eventually? His understanding?"

There was a shift in Jamie's expression. Sophia couldn't read it. Jamie seemed caught off guard maybe. "Um… I don't know if it was that. One day, we realized we should be together. I'm not sure if I can pinpoint exactly how we knew."

"Sometimes love comes as a surprise. When we aren't expecting it," Sophia offered.

"Right," Jamie said with a nod. "Exactly."

Sophia left it at that. She and Jamie had more in common than she ever expected. Sophia could relate to her on so many levels even though they came from quite different worlds. They both loved their jobs, they worked hard to be successful. They were close with their extended families. And then there was Evan. Love had come unexpectedly to both Sophia and Jamie. It came out of nowhere for the same guy.

But only one of them was going to spend the rest of her life with him. Sophia felt the pain of knowing it wouldn't be her.

"How does that look?" the seamstress asked, stepping behind Jamie and gently readjusting the train of the dress.

"What do you think, Sophia?" Jamie asked.

She was a vision. Evan would be blown away when she walked down the aisle. She would bring tears to his eyes and probably many others in the crowd of friends and family. She would be the perfect bride for the perfect groom.

In the fitting room, tears welled in Sophia's eyes. "Beautiful."

CHAPTER TWELVE

"Would it be rude to put Patrick farthest away from the bridal party?" Evan stretched to place a card with Patrick's name on the other side of the table.

Sophia had all the RSVPs in a stack and the drawing of the reception layout spread out on the conference table in front of them. When he'd shown up, Fallon and Cassie were packing up for the night. Sophia had agreed to meet him after he got done at work.

"I think you can put Patrick anywhere you want, but it is custom to keep family together."

Today was seating day. A big day for a wedding planner. Figuring out where everyone went was like putting together a puzzle. In every family, there were people who couldn't be seated next to certain other people. Friends who needed to be closest to the bar. Aging grandmothers who had to be close to the exits.

"Let's start with the easy stuff. Parents, siblings and other immediate family. Your mom and your brother will obviously be together. The question I have is, do you want them with other family members from your side or do you want them to be with Jamie's mom and uncle?"

"Let's put them at their own table. The Whartons make my mom nervous, and I don't want her to spend the whole evening uncomfortable."

"That is very thoughtful of you," she said, placing the cards with his mother's and brother's names at Table 3.

"Who else would you like to put with your mom? Are there aunts or uncles coming? Maybe a grandparent?"

Unlike Jamie and Sophia, Evan didn't have a huge extended family. All of his grandparents were gone. His dad had one brother, who lived in Arizona. He had sent his regrets. His mom had three sisters, but only one had said she was coming.

"My aunt Sheryl and uncle Lonnie are coming. They can sit with my mom. I would also put the Hamiltons there—Kris and Beth, and Joyce and Gary."

"Your families are that close?"

"Joyce was like a second mom when I was growing up. They would be the perfect ones to fill up that table."

Sophia nodded. "No wonder she seemed so fond of you that night."

"You did not like me that night."

Her expression softened. "I think the issue was that I had liked you too much earlier in the week."

His heart leaped a bit at that acknowledgment. He had liked her way too much, too... and still did. "I'm glad we're in a better place now. I'm happy we're friends."

Since friends were all they could be, he would call this feeling being happy. He was becoming a master at faking how he felt, which was good news since he was going to need to be an excellent actor in three weeks.

Sophia suddenly became overly focused on the stack of RSVPs. "Yeah, I'm happy, too."

That was a start. Maybe they could be friends. Friends who could be genuinely happy for each other. Friends who talked to each other on the phone sometimes. Friends who were just glad to know each other.

"Is there anyone else for your side of the family's parent table?" she asked.

He shook his head.

"Jamie mentioned the other day that you two became close after your fathers passed away. Tough thing to bond over."

Evan couldn't mask his shock. "Jamie talked about her dad?"

"We were talking about you, but she mentioned her dad. I'm sorry you both will be feeling that loss at the wedding. You know, sometimes people honor those that they've lost during the ceremony. Have you guys thought about doing something like that for your dads?"

"We haven't." If this was a real wedding, they both would have wanted their fathers' memories to be acknowledged. The lie made him hesitate. Would his decision to do this make his father proud? Would he understand that he was doing this to better things for Zeke and see that as noble instead of a con job?

"It's up to you two. Talk to Jamie about it. I don't want to add any sadness to your happy day, but I know sometimes things are bitter-sweet anyway because that important person isn't there."

"My dad would have been overwhelmed by the grandeur of this whole thing. He was a very simple guy."

Sophia gave him her full attention, her green eyes fixed on his face. "What did he do for a living?"

"He was a welder—he loved working with his hands. He drank cheap beer and loved a good baseball game on a Saturday afternoon. He never would have felt at home at the Wharton Estate. We had to buy the man a suit to bury him in because he didn't own a single one."

"My dad used to be a high school social studies teacher. He owned over a hundred ties. He pretty much never wore the same one twice during the school year. When he retired, he donated them all to Goodwill. He says he never wants to wear a tie ever again."

"I don't blame him," Evan laughed. "I can't wait to retire my ties, either. I do remember the first time I needed to wear a tie, though. I asked my dad to help me, but he had no clue. Instead of telling me he didn't know how to do it, he looked it up on the internet and watched how-to videos until he figured it out. That was the kind of person my dad was. He wasn't afraid to go outside his comfort zone if it meant he would be able to help me or Zeke."

"He sounds like he was a good man."

"He was."

Evan didn't realize how much he wanted to tell her about his family until after he met hers. "I could tell that your grandma misses having your parents around."

"Oh, for sure." Sophia's expression turned wistful. "She's not truly happy unless she's surrounded by family. It kills her that my parents decided to live on the road instead of here with her. I think that's part of the reason I settled down in Charlotte. I feel guilty that my parents left."

"Where else would you go?" The thought of Sophia living anywhere but here made his heart ache.

"I have no idea. I love it here. I love being near my family. Guilt may have been the initial reason for staying, but now I stay because it's my home."

Evan breathed a sigh of relief. He didn't

want her to go anywhere. Was it wrong that he planned to hire her every chance he got once he and Jamie were married? He wanted her, needed her in his life.

"My dad and I used to butt heads quite a bit when I was growing up. I worked my tail off at school because I did not want to end up like him, working overtime just to afford enough to put food on the table and a roof over my head. I was going to get a job in California for some big tech company. When he died, I changed all my plans. I knew I needed to be here for my mom and brother. I felt obligated, you know?"

She nodded. "I get it."

"But like you said, now in my life, I couldn't imagine doing anything different. I love having Zeke around. I love this city. I have no complaints. This is where I was supposed to be."

"It's funny how things have a way of working themselves out."

Would things work out for them? Would he be able to look back at this time someday and be okay with the fact that things weren't meant to be? Or was there a possibility that once the charade with Jamie was over, he and

Sophia might be able to explore what these feelings really meant?

He must have been staring at her a bit too intently. Her cheeks flushed and she looked away. "Okay, back to business. There's no one else for your mom's table, correct?"

"Correct. I don't think any of my cousins said they were coming." He'd reviewed the spreadsheet of names Sophia had shared with him last night. "We're a small bunch. Pretty much the opposite of your family."

"And to think you didn't even meet them all. That was the abbreviated version of Sunday dinner."

If only he could get invited over every week. Her family was so welcoming and made him feel part of her life. "I think I would need earplugs if I was ever in a house with everyone in your family or I might be hard of hearing by the end of the night."

"Ha ha," she said, fighting a smile. "I warned you."

"You did."

Sophia pulled out another card. "So what is your final decision on Patrick and Eliza's fate at your wedding? Are we putting them at the same table as Jamie's mom, aunt and uncles? Or is he banished to the back by the garbage cans?"

The image of Patrick by the garbage dump was too satisfying. "So tempting. So very tempting. But alas, I know that Jamie would say we have to go high because he only knows how to go low. He can sit with the rest of the family."

This was the way it went for the next hour. Sophia would ask him about someone and he would suggest a table for them. He looked at his watch. It was after six and there were still plenty of tables left. He had sent five texts to Jamie asking for some help with a group of random people who must have been put on the list by Gordon. She had yet to reply.

"Do you want to order some food?" he asked, stretching his arms over his head. He had been standing, bent over this reception layout, for too long. "Jamie isn't answering, and who knows if and when she will. The least I can do is buy you dinner to make it worth your time."

"I could eat."

"Then we should order. Do you have a favorite place around here that delivers?"

"There's an amazing barbecue place just

around the corner. We get stuff from there all the time."

She liked barbecue? Every time he thought she couldn't be more compatible with him, she was. "I love barbecue. Let's do it."

PULLED PORK FROM Cherry BBQ would be Evan's favorite from that day forward. Sophia knew how to pick a dinner place. Since the conference table was covered in the reception layout, they moved into Sophia's office and sat across from each other at her desk.

"What made you go into event planning?" he asked as he reached for a french fry.

"I've always been super organized. I love lists. I also get bored easily. I needed a job where things were fast-paced and every day was different but the same. Like, I do a lot of the same things when I plan any event, but every event is unique so there's always something new to keep it interesting. When I met with my high school career counselor, she suggested I look into it. I was sold as soon as I started researching it."

She wasn't kidding about her love of lists. Evan had never been sent so many color-coordinated lists in his life. "Well, it sounds like she knew what she was talking about. You are good at what you do."

"Thanks."

"Did you always know you wanted to be an information analyst?"

"I don't think most kids grow up thinking they want to be an analyst. I'm pretty sure I wanted to be a superhero when I was little, but they didn't offer that major at UNC."

Her laugh sounded better than the food tasted. "Oh, really? Shocking."

"Like I said before, I imagined working for a big tech company. Then I met Jamie, and she was part of this huge banking family. After my dad died, she's the one who talked me into the banking industry as a way to take care of my family. She knew her connections could help me."

"Wow. She's a good friend to have."

"She is. She comes from all this wealth, but she's more down-to-earth than you would think."

"I can see why you fell in love with her," Sophia said, poking at her brisket. His silence drew her attention. "Is everything okay?"

Evan tried to shake himself out of his head. The truth wasn't something he could give her. There was too much at stake. "Yeah, I'm good."

They ate without talking for a bit. He wondered what she thought of him. She had to have questioned his character when he'd come on so strong that first day they met.

"When I was little, I told everyone who asked that I wanted to be an ice-cream truck driver," Sophia confessed. "It was a big dream for me."

Evan almost spit up his soda. He coughed up what had gone down the wrong pipe. When he could breathe, he laughed. "An ice-cream truck driver? Seriously?"

"Tell me the sound of the ice-cream truck entering a neighborhood does not put joy into the heart of every little boy and girl who hears it."

"I love that you wanted to spread joy. It all makes perfect sense now."

Sophia had been the kind of person who wanted to make others happy ever since she was a little girl. Evan didn't think she even realized that wanting to make people happy was just as important as loving lists when it came to being a good event planner. She probably didn't see it as one of her strengths because it was simply her nature.

"Plus I had a slight obsession with those treats that were in a cone-shaped cup and had a gumball at the bottom."

"You weren't a Popsicle girl?"

"Come on, you have to be more adventurous than a Popsicle. Bubblegum surprise at the bottom? That's living large."

Evan shook his head and laughed. How could he disagree with such a rock-solid argument?

Their conversation continued, and this quickly turned into one of the best dates that wasn't a date that he'd ever been on.

"We should get back to work. Any word from Jamie?" she asked, closing up her take-out container.

Evan checked his phone. "Nothing yet. Is there anything else we could work on while we wait for her to get back to us?"

"Um…" Sophia spun in her chair and rolled herself over to her file cabinet. She pulled out a red file. "You could sign off on a couple things. I also need to tell the band what song you want for your first dance. They were asking in case it's something they aren't familiar with, so they'll have time to practice."

"We don't have to do a first dance, do we? Is that required?"

Sophia's eyes narrowed and her nose scrunched up. "Required? Nothing is *required*. This is your wedding, but it is fairly traditional for the bride and groom to dance their first dance at the reception as husband and wife."

"We could probably leave that out. I don't think Jamie would care. She's not that into dancing in front of a room full of people."

Sophia tilted her head. "You can't dance, can you?"

He tried to act offended. "What? I can dance."

She shook her head and a smile spread across her face. "You can't dance."

"I am a very good dancer. I could teach you how to Dougie, and I disco better than people who were actually alive during disco. No one can Y, M, C or A like I can."

Sophia stood up and walked around to his side of the desk. "You can't slow dance?"

Evan could feel the heat rising up his neck and onto his cheeks. He tried to hold his ground. "I can sway back and forth to a slow song, if that's what you mean."

Sophia held out her hand. "Stand up," she said. He took her hand and did as she asked. "You cannot sway back and forth on your wedding day in front of people who are friends with Gordon Wharton."

"That's why we should skip that part. Just make it a group dance right from the start."

She grabbed his other hand and placed it on her waist before resting hers on his shoulder. "I can teach you a very simple dance that anyone can do."

Evan wanted to pay attention to her words, but with their bodies this close it was next to impossible. He was like a teenager again, nervous and tongue-tied around a pretty girl.

"We're going to start out with a really easy first step. We're just going to go left, touch, right, touch, left, touch, right, touch." She led the way and he followed. "Super easy, right?"

"So far, so good," he managed to say. The hand on her hip felt like it was on fire. Could she feel that? Could she tell he was burning?

"You can also spin your bride as you go—that way you won't just be stepping side to side the whole song. You're the man, so you get to lead. The way you'll signal to Jamie that you guys are going to spin is by pushing with this hand and pulling with the other. Just enough to let her know that you'll be moving in this direction."

Sophia showed him how to do it. She guided them into a full circle and stopped.

"See? Still easy, right?"

"I think so." His eyes were locked on hers. She completely mesmerized him. The green in her eyes was flecked with gold he'd never noticed before. They were the prettiest eyes he'd ever had the pleasure of getting lost in.

"If you really want to impress your guests, you can twirl her. That's a little more complicated, and I suggest you two practice it before you do it in front of everyone. Let's just work on you leading for a minute, okay?"

Evan nodded. He didn't want to practice with Jamie, though. He wanted to save all of his dances for the woman in his arms.

"One important thing to remember is don't switch directions until after you touch. Then just pull here so I know where we're going." She showed him exactly how to do it. "Are you ready?"

"I guess. If I step on your foot, I apologize."

"You won't. You're leading. I'll go wherever you want me to go."

If only she meant those words in a completely different context. If things were different, if no one was counting on them, he would ask her to run away with him. Leave tonight and go somewhere they could be together forever.

"Ready?" she asked.

"Can we get some music? I feel like I need a beat that isn't made up in my head."

She let go of him and he regretted making the request. Sophia grabbed her phone off her desk and played a song he hadn't heard before.

She was back in his arms. "Okay, let's go."

He did as she told him. Step, touch, step, touch. He pulled her right and they glided across the floor of her office in a small circle. The song spoke of being better together. Of waking up with her smiling face next to him. Sophia grinned up at him as they moved together like it was meant to be.

Evan pulled her a little closer. Her smiling lips were inches from his. Step, touch, step, touch, spin, touch, step, touch. They were better together. There was nowhere else he wanted to be, nowhere else he wanted her to be other than here in his arms.

He stopped and, since he was leading, she did, too. Without thinking about the consequences—because right now, he was unable to think about anything except how much he felt for her—he let go of her hip and cupped her cheek. She inhaled sharply at the shock of it and before she could exhale, he pressed his lips to hers.

It was the first kiss of his dreams. It wasn't just sparks—this kiss caused an explosion of fireworks that could light up the entire Charlotte sky. His heart cartwheeled when he felt her kiss him back. It was a careful and controlled give-and-take that came so naturally it was as if their lips knew they belonged together, as well.

Sophia pulled away and pushed him back. The sheer horror on her face snapped him out of his bliss.

"You need to go. You need to go right now."

"Sophia—" Evan's stomach dropped as he realized what he'd done.

She retreated to her desk. He stepped toward her, but she put a hand out to stop him. "Please go. Now."

"I didn't mean—"

"You need to leave, Evan. You need to get out of here. Right now." She sounded on the verge of tears. "Please."

He had ruined everything for one moment of pure ecstasy. There was nothing he could say that would make this okay. He didn't want to cause her any more pain. He grabbed his coat off the back of the chair, and with his head hanging low, he walked away from the woman he had fallen head over heels in love with.

CHAPTER THIRTEEN

As soon as Sophia heard the door to the waiting room close, she touched her lips. Her traitorous lips. Her cheating, selfish, sinful lips. Tears welled in her eyes.

What had she done?

She had kissed a man who was about to marry his best friend. A best friend who had been nothing but kind to Sophia. She had betrayed the trust of that woman and it felt all kinds of wrong.

Sophia's career was over. Her business would never survive a scandal like this. Fallon would never forgive her. She'd have to move out of Charlotte and break Yaya's heart. There was no way she could work in this town again.

That wasn't the worst of it, though. The worst part was the broken heart in her chest. The one that a minute ago was rejoicing, jumping for joy at finally getting what it had wanted since she met Evan at the bank.

Maybe he wouldn't tell anyone. Maybe they could pretend this never happened. She snorted at her own ridiculous hope. There was no way this could be swept under the rug. The truth always came out, and she couldn't risk it coming out at the worst possible moment.

There was only one thing to do—Sophia had to tell Jamie what had happened. It was the right thing to do. She deserved to know that perhaps Evan wasn't ready to get married. They needed to confront this head-on if there was any chance for the two of them to at least salvage their friendship.

Jamie was a good person. She deserved to be with someone who wouldn't kiss the wedding planner while he was learning how to dance with his bride on their wedding day.

Sophia's mind was racing as her body trembled. That kiss had messed with her entire central nervous system. Yaya had been right. She was in love with him. That was the only explanation for her complete lack of self-control. She knew what was happening.

She'd sensed what he was going to do before he did it, and she hadn't stopped him.

She should have stopped him.

She shouldn't have kissed him back.

That kiss, though... Never in her life had she been kissed like that. Nothing had ever felt so right. So intimate. It was like he had reached inside her and kissed her soul to soul instead of mouth to mouth.

But it wasn't right, and she had to be honest about it. Even if it meant destroying everything that mattered to her.

SOPHIA QUESTIONED HER decision to come clean multiple times over night and then again as she waited for the receptionist to get off the phone. The anxiety of it all was enough to send Sophia over the edge.

"Do you have an appointment?" the older woman asked.

"Yes. Miss Wharton said I could come at eleven." Sophia thought she might throw up. She had texted Jamie first thing this morning, asking for a few minutes of her time. She'd said it was urgent. Jamie offered the only fifteen minutes she had between meetings. How was the poor woman going to head straight into a meeting after Sophia dropped this bomb on her?

"Let me check with her personal assistant, because there's no record of you on my list."

"We just made the appointment this morning."

"That's probably it," the woman said with a wink.

Sophia's phone chimed with a text. It was another one from Evan, apologizing for the hundredth time and begging her to call him when she was ready to talk. She didn't respond. She hadn't responded to any of his messages, because there was nothing to say. At least not to him.

Suddenly a wave of dread hit her. What if he had talked to Jamie already? What if she wasn't the one who was going to be dropping the bombs but the one who was walking into an ambush?

"Looks like you were right. You are welcome to go on up. Do you know where you're going?"

Possibly to her death. Sophia shook her head. She had no idea where Jamie's office was. The woman directed her to the elevators and gave her the floor number.

"Miss Wharton's office is in the northeast corner."

"Thank you," Sophia replied. *Dead woman walking,* she thought. There was no turning back now.

When she finally found Jamie's office, her redheaded assistant apologized and explained that this was only her second day on the job and she didn't realize she should have called down to the main desk to let them know Sophia was coming. She picked up her phone and called Jamie.

"Miss Reed is here." She nodded even though Jamie couldn't see her. "Okay, I'll tell her. She's ready for you. Go on in," she said, gesturing to the door with Jamie's name written on it.

"Thanks." Sophia's anxiety was at about a thirty-seven on a scale of one to ten. This was it. She wrapped her hand around the doorknob and took a deep breath. She deserved whatever she got. She needed to take it like a woman.

"Hey there," Jamie said, getting up from her chair. "You know you promised me that you had everything under control and I didn't have to worry about anything, right? Please tell me that hasn't changed, Sophia. I'm counting on you."

She motioned for Sophia to take a seat on one of the chairs in front of her desk. Jamie sat on the one next to it.

Sophia sat down and pressed a hand to her forehead. She wasn't feverish, but she felt like she was definitely going to throw up. Hopefully she could make it to the bathroom so she didn't ruin the woman's carpet as well as her wedding.

"Are you okay?" Jamie reached for her hand. "You are so pale."

Getting through this without crying would be a challenge. Sophia cleared her throat. "I am very sorry to have to come here today and interrupt your work. I just felt like I needed to be one hundred percent honest with you, and I couldn't wait any longer."

"Okay..." Jamie sat back. Her confused expression confirmed Evan hadn't come clean.

"I'm not even sure where to start. I guess from the beginning. You know that Evan and I met during the bank robbery."

Jamie nodded.

"Well, I need you to know that I had no idea who he was that day. We did not talk about what I did for a living. He did not mention he was engaged to be married to you."

Jamie uncrossed and recrossed her legs. "Okay…"

"We spent some time together after the robbery and after we were interviewed by the police. We just needed to unwind, and neither of us could focus on going back to work or our lives at that moment. We exchanged numbers. We talked. We continued to talk via text that whole night."

Jamie rubbed her jaw. "All right."

"When you both arrived in my office the next morning, I was shocked, to say the least, because I had misread what was going on so badly. I had thought he was flirting, but after you left, we cleared that all up. We had both experienced this traumatic event and we'd both felt very vulnerable. It was nice to talk to someone who understood."

"Did he acknowledge that he had come across as flirtatious?" she asked, leaning forward and interlocking her fingers.

"He did. He apologized and everything had been nothing but professional between us." Sophia wrung her hands. She fought the tears wanting to emerge.

"Had been." Jamie didn't miss a thing. She was just as smart as Evan said she was. "Had been until when?"

"Last night," Sophia choked out.

"What happened last night?"

The words came out in one long, run-on sentence. "I told him that I needed to know what song you were going to use for your first dance and he said he didn't know how to dance and, for some stupid reason, I offered to teach him a very simple dance and we were practicing and he seemed to be catching on and I thought everything was fine but he stopped and the next thing I knew, we were kissing."

Jamie dropped her head into her hands.

"It was one kiss and I don't know how it even happened, but I stopped it and he left immediately. I need you to know that it was never, never my intention for something like this to happen. I respect you so very much and I feel absolutely horrible about what happened. If I could go back—"

Jamie lifted her head. "Who have you told?"

This wasn't the question Sophia expected. "No one."

"No one? Not your grandmother? Not your best friend? Your business partner? No one?"

Sophia shook her head after each suggestion. "No one. You're the first person I've told. I felt like you had a right to know."

"Good. That's good." Jamie seemed… relieved? Sophia had just told her that she'd kissed her fiancé, and she had no other questions than who else knew about it. Maybe she was so shocked that she couldn't think about the true ramifications of what had happened.

"I want you to know that we will be refunding all the money you've paid thus far, and I will take care of canceling all the contracts. I'll pay all the cancellation fees. You won't have to do anything."

Jamie's eyes went wide. "Cancellation fees? Whoa, whoa, whoa. Nothing is being canceled. Do not cancel anything."

Did Jamie not understand what had been confessed here today? Sophia couldn't imagine why she wouldn't at least postpone things until she and Evan worked this out. "I won't do anything until you tell me to, of course…" Sophia added carefully. "But know that you will not be charged for anything."

"You haven't said anything to *anyone*?" Jamie clarified again.

"No one."

Her shoulders relaxed and relief colored her expression. "Then it's fine. Nothing's changed."

Nothing had changed? Everything had changed. Sophia felt like her entire world had been flipped upside down. Jamie, on the other hand, acted like everything was status quo. She seemed to be forgetting there was another person with a say in all of this. Maybe Evan didn't want to get married anymore. Jamie wasn't taking that possibility into consideration.

"Well, if you and Mr. Anderson decide to carry on, clearly I cannot be the one to manage your wedding."

"Who else is going to do it? We're getting married in a couple weeks. You can't leave us in the lurch like that."

I kissed your fiancé! she wanted to scream. Not only had she kissed him, but she had liked it. Loved it. She loved *him*. She was *in love* with him. Was Jamie? Wasn't this news even the slightest bit devastating?

"Miss Wharton, if for some reason you

don't want to fire us, I would have to ask Fallon to take over. I could easily bring her up to speed before the wedding."

"Great. If you think she can handle it, she can take over. Please don't tell her why. In fact, please never mention what happened last night to anyone. It is imperative that this stays between you and me."

"And Evan," Sophia added. Evan was the reason this was happening, but he didn't seem to be on Jamie's mind at all right now.

"Right." Jamie rubbed her forehead. Her expression was unreadable. She just looked tired. "And Evan."

"I need you to know that I do not intend to have anything to do with him ever again. I don't want you to think that there's anything going on here. This was…" She should never have started that sentence because she had no idea how to end it. There were no words for what had happened last night, what was going on between her and Evan.

"I appreciate that, Sophia. I don't think you're a bad person. I don't think any of this was your fault. As long as you do not speak to anyone about what happened, we're good. Please don't talk about it."

Sophia wasn't sure if she should be relieved or not. "I won't."

"Thank you." Jamie checked her watch. "I'm sorry, but I have a meeting that can't be postponed. I'm assuming you will give Fallon our contact information. From here on out, she should always call me first instead of Evan. I'll oversee things from now on."

"No problem."

She got up and shuffled some papers around. Her gaze lifted to Sophia for a moment. "Can you see yourself out?"

Sophia nodded and rose to her feet. She couldn't get out of there fast enough. Half of her still wondered if there wasn't a ticking time bomb waiting to go off. The other half felt sad that Jamie wasn't sad. Didn't she love Evan? Didn't she love herself?

Sophia's phone rang again. It was Evan. She wondered when Jamie would confront him about everything. She shouldn't be worried about it, but she was. Jamie was determined for the show to go on. Was Evan?

As soon as she walked through the doors of Engaging Events, Cassie cheered. "Yay, you're back. You've got three messages from

Mr. Anderson. He says it's urgent. He told me to tell you that you need to call him as soon as you got back."

"Well, Mr. Anderson is not in charge of my schedule. Thank you for the messages. I need to talk to Fallon. Is she busy?"

"No. She's in there by herself," Cassie said, glancing at Fallon's door.

Sophia knocked and waited for Fallon to tell her to come in. She had made Jamie Wharton a promise she wasn't going to be able to keep. Fallon was her business partner and friend. She had no intention of lying to her and putting her in the middle of this nightmare situation without all the facts. That was not the way this partnership worked.

"Did Cassie tell you Evan Anderson needs to talk to you?" Fallon asked. "Are you not getting calls on your cell?"

Sophia closed the door behind her. "We need to talk."

"I don't like the way that sounds."

"You're going to hate it even more in a few seconds." She sat down across from Fallon.

Her face fell. "Oh, great. Do you really need to ruin my day? I thought we were friends."

Sophia decided that ripping the Band-Aid

off was the only way to handle this. "I kissed Evan last night. Well, he kissed me, but I kissed him back."

Fallon blinked. And blinked again. "Are. You. Kidding me?"

Sophia shook her head. "I just got back from Jamie Wharton's office. I told her what happened."

Fallon groaned and her head fell back. "And we just lost the biggest event of our careers."

"No. She doesn't want to cancel, and she has no desire to fire us. In fact, she would have been fine with me staying on as event manager."

Fallon's head snapped up. "What?"

"She plans to still get married on the third."

"And what about him? Does Evan still want to get married? He kissed you. He must have feelings."

Sophia shook her head again. "He doesn't have feelings. I don't know what happened last night, but there is no way he's leaving Jamie freaking Wharton for me. He would have to lose his mind to do that."

"Love makes people lose their minds, Sophia."

"That's not what's going on here. My point is that you have to take over this event. I cannot be involved at all. I'll go over everything with you, and I'll be on call to answer any questions. I can handle all the behind-the-scenes stuff, but I can't be involved with Jamie and Evan, and I will not be at the wedding."

"If there's a wedding," Fallon corrected.

"There will be a wedding. We have to pray there's a wedding. If he cancels and Mr. Wharton finds out what happened, we're finished. We will never get another major event in Charlotte."

Fallon sighed. "He can't ruin us. It wasn't your fault."

Sophia didn't know where else to put the blame. She was the one who asked him to dance. She was the one who obviously couldn't hide her feelings. She wanted him to kiss her. She wanted him to want her. If this whole thing blew up in their faces, she had no one to blame but herself.

"Just promise me that you'll bite your tongue and pretend they are a happy couple. If this wedding happens, it needs to go off without a hitch."

"You planned it. *If* it happens, it's going to be spectacular." Fallon held out her hand. "Give me those messages. I'll return Mr. Anderson's calls and let him know that I am in charge of his special day now."

Sophia handed them over. Fallon pressed the speaker button on her landline. She dialed the number scribbled in Cassie's messy script.

It rang twice before he answered. "Hello? Sophia?"

"Hi, Mr. Anderson. This is Fallon Best. How are you doing today?"

He was quiet for a second. Fallon knew it was a loaded question. Sophia actually felt bad for him.

"Is Sophia available? I've been trying to get ahold of her all morning and she hasn't taken any of my calls. It's very urgent that I speak to her. I could come to the office, but Cassie said she wasn't in. Do you know when she's due in the office?"

"Mr. Anderson, Sophia will no longer be the event manager for your wedding. I am going to be taking over. We've already spoken to Miss Wharton and she is fine with the change."

Mentioning Jamie was another hard hit. Sophia could almost hear him reeling.

"Is she at home?"

"Who?" Fallon asked. Sophia scowled at her. She knew exactly whom he was asking about.

"Sophia," he said, sounding a bit frantic. "Is she at home? Is she at her grandmother's? Where is she, Fallon?"

"Well, Mr. Anderson, she had a meeting with your fiancée this morning. Perhaps you should ask her if she knows where she is. I'm sure you two have a lot to talk about anyway." Fallon paused for effect. "If there's anything you need from Engaging Events, please be sure to give me a call. Sophia will not be able to answer any of your questions going forward."

Without a word, Evan hung up.

"Now if we get fired, we both carry some blame," Fallon said.

CHAPTER FOURTEEN

Your house. Seven.

THAT WAS THE text Evan had received from Jamie at one o'clock today. That was it. No threats to do bodily harm. No name-calling.

Maybe Sophia quit without telling Jamie why. Would Jamie have accepted her resignation without questioning it? Probably.

Evan paced across his deck. The air was thick tonight. Summer was in full swing even though it was still technically spring. He took a long swig from his beer bottle. The smell of fresh-cut grass surrounded him. His neighbor had mowed tonight when he got home from work to beat the coming rain that had been predicted.

He had texted Jamie back to meet him here, outside. It was best that Zeke not be witness to what was about to go down. He wouldn't understand it, and Evan wasn't sure he could adequately explain it anyway.

The sound of a car door closing was the only warning he got that Jamie had arrived. She came around back and entered through the fence gate on the side of the house. She was silent as she approached. He tried to read her face, to figure out what she knew or didn't know.

"Hey," he said, testing the waters.

"Are you trying to ruin everything we've been doing with less than three weeks to go here?"

She knew.

"I wasn't trying to ruin anything. I didn't mean for any of this to happen," he said in defense. There was no plan here. He was flying by the seat of his pants.

Jamie's eyes filled with tears, something that did not happen very often. Anger was her go-to emotion, not sadness. She reserved sadness for the people and things she cared about the most.

"I trusted you, Evan. Everything I have worked my entire adult life for is on the line, and you promised me that you would help me."

"I know. When I made you that promise,

I meant it. I had no reason to believe that I wouldn't be able to follow through. There was no one in my life. How was I supposed to know I'd fall in love with someone? How could I have known she would walk into that bank and latch herself onto my heart? I can't explain it. I can't stop how I feel about her."

Jamie pressed the palms of her hands against the sides of her head. "Are you kidding me right now? The wedding planner? Of all the people in the world, are you seriously trying to tell me that you're in love with the wedding planner?"

"Yes." It was the truth. There was no reason to deny how he felt any longer.

Jamie dropped her hands to her hips, her gaze falling to the decking in front of her. "She doesn't feel the same way, Ev. She came to my office this morning and told me everything from the beginning. How you flirted with her and failed to mention that you were engaged. That you kissed her while she was trying to teach you how to dance with me on our wedding day. She swore to me that she wants nothing to do with you. That she will never have anything to do with you ever again."

Each revelation was a punch in the stomach. Sophia had gone to talk to Jamie before she even gave him a chance to explain, to come clean. If Sophia knew the truth, maybe she would understand and forgive him.

"I just need to talk to her."

Jamie's head lifted. "How's contacting her going so far?"

"Not great," he admitted.

"She doesn't want to talk to you. She doesn't want anything to do with you. She thinks I'm some pathetic fool who doesn't know my fiancé is a philandering jerk. I have to admit, I do feel more betrayed than I thought I would."

"Betrayed?"

"Not in the romantic sense," she clarified. "I'm hurt that I didn't even know you were having feelings for her in the first place. I'm your friend and you didn't talk to me about it."

Evan closed his eyes and lifted his face to the sky. "I didn't know how to tell you. With everything going on, I knew it would stress you out."

"And that I would tell you to get over it and keep your head in the game."

"Yeah, that, too."

"Wouldn't that have been better than this?"

Anything would be better than Sophia hating him and thinking he was a total creep. "I need to tell her the truth."

"Do you understand the gravity of what is going on in my life right now?" Her anger began to shine through. She was a mix of negative emotions and couldn't contain any of it. "My uncle thinks Patrick has saved the day and prevented all future bank robberies. If he had to choose someone to take over for him today, I don't know who he would choose. If you call off this wedding to live happily-ever-after with the wedding planner, I will have no chance. Zero! The company will go to Patrick and I will be stuck in his shadow the rest of my career. Not to mention you'll be fired on the spot. How do you plan to support Zeke when the entire business world thinks you left me at the altar? What will happen to Sophia and her company if word gets out that she had an affair with a groom? You would destroy all of us."

"What if we tell her and no one else? We go through with the wedding, but she knows the truth and can—"

"Can what, Evan? Wait for you? Have an affair with you while we pretend to be married? You're asking for nothing but trouble."

Evan threw his beer bottle as hard as he could against the fence along the side of the yard. It smashed into pieces. Everything she said, he already knew. All those things were the reasons he wasn't going to cross another line with Sophia. Everyone he loved would be hurt by his selfishness.

"I'm sorry," Jamie said, her voice more controlled. "I'm sorry this situation is no longer under our control. I'm sorry you met someone amazing right after we jumped all in on this plan. I love you and I want you to be happy. I don't begrudge you happiness, but none of us will be happy if we don't play our parts perfectly and see this through."

Evan rested his elbows on the deck railing and stared out into the backyard. A tear ran down his cheek. He sniffed and wiped it away. "You're right."

She came up beside him and placed a hand on his back. It was little comfort. "I really am sorry. I wish we hadn't done this. I wish we would have kept brainstorming. Maybe we could have come up with another plan, one that didn't include giving up your chance at love."

Evan shook his head. There had been no other solution to her problem. Her uncle and his controlling ways dictated how things had to be. If Jamie wanted to take over for him, she had to tick off all these ridiculous boxes. And better she did that with Evan than with someone who didn't truly care about her.

"I'm sorry I almost screwed everything up," he said.

"Thank goodness she came to me before she told anyone else." Jamie sighed. "She's a good person. Principled. Even knowing that telling me what happened could ruin her career if I had wanted it to, she did the right thing and came clean."

"This conversation is not going to make me feel better. I'll see you tomorrow?"

"Yeah." She glanced back at the sliding door. "Tell Zeke I said hi."

Jamie left the way she came, quietly walking around the house to her car. Evan stayed outside, looking up at the darkening sky. So apropos. A dark cloud hanging over his heart might as well hang over his head, too.

After he kissed Sophia, his world had shifted.

The consequences of wanting to be with her would be messy and hard, but together, he believed they could survive anything.

He went over to the fence and gathered up the shattered pieces of glass, setting them on the picnic table. Just a bunch of jagged shards. Kind of like his heart.

The sliding glass door opened. Zeke stepped out onto the deck. "Why are you outside?"

"I thought your favorite show was on. I didn't want to bother you."

Zeke put his arm around his brother's shoulders. "You don't bother me. You don't have to stay outside."

Evan threw an arm around Zeke, as well. "Thanks, buddy."

"You look sad."

"I'm a little sad."

Zeke hugged him tighter. "I'm sorry you're sad. I want you to be happy like me. Why are you sad?"

Explaining things meant admitting what he had done wrong. Zeke's admiration was a lot to live up to. He thought Evan was honest and trustworthy. He also had issues with people who lied. His black-and-white thinking made it difficult for him to understand that sometimes people told a lie for a good reason. Evan wasn't sure he could convince Zeke this was one of those times.

"I found out today that Sophia can't be at the wedding."

Zeke dropped his arm. "Are you pulling my leg, mister?"

"I wish I was."

"Why can't she come? She's the boss. She needs to be there."

"She's going to send someone else to be the boss."

"I am going to go to Yaya's and find out what's the matter."

As if he wasn't feeling guilty enough, he had to live with the fact that he had introduced Zeke to a wonderful family he could never be around again… And Evan had no good explanation for that.

"We can't go to Yaya's anymore. We can't see Sophia anymore."

Zeke raised his eyebrows and slightly tucked his chin. "She's our friend. We can see her whenever we want."

"You don't like it when I lie, so I'm going to tell you the truth, okay?"

"You always tell me the truth."

He used to. Zeke had always demanded it. Too bad Evan hadn't realized earlier that having to lie to Zeke about his relationship with Jamie was a big red flag that it was a bad idea.

"I did something that hurt Sophia's feelings and she doesn't want to be my friend anymore."

"You just need to apologize to her and she will still be your friend. Sophia is nice. If you say *sorry*, she will forgive you."

Evan rubbed the nape of his neck. The stress of the last twenty-four hours was taking a physical toll. "Not this time, buddy. The thing I did was bad. I shouldn't have done it and even if I say *sorry*, she won't be my friend again."

Zeke shook his head. "What did you do?"

"I don't want to tell you because I'm very embarrassed about it and I care about what you think about me. I want you to know that I am very sorry I messed things up, though."

"It's okay," Zeke said, patting Evan on the back. "I forgive you and Sophia will, too."

Evan envied his innocence and naivete. It allowed him to see the good in every situation. There would be no convincing his brother of the cold, hard truth. Zeke would have to learn the hard way.

A WEEK LATER, Zeke would have his first rude awakening. Their tuxedo fitting was the last major pre-wedding detail that needed to be checked off one of Sophia's famous lists.

Zeke was not happy when Fallon showed up to make sure everything was right. And he'd never been very good at hiding his disappointment.

"I need Sophia to fix my tie," he said when they brought him out to look at himself in the mirror.

"Here, I can help you," Fallon offered.

Zeke held his hand out with his palm facing her so she'd stop. "No, thank you. I need Sophia. Can you call her and tell her that Zeke needs her help? She will come for me."

Evan intervened before there was any more conversation about Sophia. "Let me do it, bud. Don't I always do a good job when we get fancy?"

"But she can call Sophia."

"You know what? We don't need to do the tie today. We're here to make sure the rest of the tux fits."

Fallon and the tailor looked them both over. "I think his jacket fits well, but the pants are too long," she said as she regarded Zeke. "Evan, you look great."

The tailor agreed and started to pin up Zeke's pant legs. Sophia had chosen the perfect look. Dark navy tux, white dress shirt, gold cuff links and blush tie. He looked like a million bucks, just as she had promised.

Evan went into the dressing room to change. When he came out, Fallon was there.

He handed her his bagged tux. "Sorry about my brother. He was sort of attached to Sophia. He didn't mean to be rude."

"It's fine," she assured him. "He wasn't rude. Sophia tends to make an impression."

Evan swallowed hard. "Is she...okay?" He had no right to ask. He also had no idea what excuse she had given Fallon for having to back out as the event manager.

"She's fine." Fallon smiled tightly before dashing away.

Fine was always code for *not fine*. Wasn't it? He hated himself for being the reason for her fineness, for not being able to fix it. It had been eating away at him all week.

When they finished with Zeke, it was clear

he was more than grumpy. The silent treatment was in full effect on the way home.

"You and I will have to get our hair cut before the wedding," Evan said. Zeke's hair was overgrown, shaggy around his ears.

Zeke readjusted his seat belt. He had nothing to say to that.

"Should we stop and get dinner? I could go for some chicken fingers. How about you?"

Zeke stared out the window without answering, his forehead resting against the glass.

"Or what about pizza? We could get extra pepperoni."

No response.

"Okay, I guess I don't have any good ideas. What would you like to eat? We can stop anywhere you want."

"I want Yaya's kebabs," he finally replied.

Stopped at a traffic light, Evan scrubbed his face with his hands. "You're killing me, buddy."

"Maybe you're killing me, buddy."

Evan lost his cool. "What do you want me to do? You want me to drive you to her grandmother's house and let you say your goodbyes? Do you need closure? What do you want?"

"Tell her you're sorry."

"She doesn't want to hear it."

"You didn't even try."

Zeke had no idea what he was saying. "I've been trying. I've called, I've texted. She won't talk to me, Zeke. She told Jamie she never wants to see me again. When someone says that, you have to respect it. I did the bad thing that made her feel bad. If I don't leave her alone, I'll be doing another bad thing. Don't you understand?"

Zeke was quiet as the light turned green. Evan stepped on the gas.

"I'm not hungry," Zeke said, turning back toward the window. "I want to go home."

Evan got in the right lane to turn onto the next street, which led to their house. At the last minute, he switched lanes and continued straight. He hoped he could remember exactly how to get to Yaya's house. If he knew Sophia like he thought he did, she would be at her grandmother's.

When Zeke recognized her car in the driveway, he perked right up. His smile lit up his whole face. "Sophia's here."

Evan parked the car across the street from the redbrick ranch. The shutters were the same shade of bright blue as the Greek flag. Blue and white petunias filled the flower beds in front.

"Go tell her you're sorry so we can all be friends again," Zeke said.

There was no chance he was knocking on the door. He was going to give Sophia the option to tell him to beat it. "I'm texting her we're here. If she wants to talk, she'll come out. If she doesn't want to come out, we're going home."

"She'll come out," Zeke said without any doubt.

He typed out the message but didn't hit Send. "If she doesn't come out, you can't give me a hard time. No more silent treatment, and no more asking Fallon to call Sophia. We have to accept her decision."

"She'll come out."

"I'm not going to send this text until we have a deal. I say *sorry* if she comes out. You don't give me a hard time if she doesn't."

Zeke tilted his head and thought about it for a second. "Deal."

Evan hit Send, and they waited. And they waited. And they waited.

"Maybe she didn't get your message. You should send her another one."

Evan shook his head and showed his brother the word *READ* under the blue text bubble. "She saw it, buddy."

Zeke slumped in his seat and crossed his arms over his chest. Once he tucked his chin, he was in full pout mode. "Why did you have to do such a bad thing?"

Evan glanced back at the house. She wasn't coming out. She never wanted to see him again. He'd known when he sent the message that this was how things would turn out, but it still hurt.

He started the engine and drove away.

CHAPTER FIFTEEN

"A FULL-SERVICE PACKAGE entails our involvement every step of the way from the engagement to the wedding to the honeymoon. We do it all."

The sweet couple seated across from her had stars in their eyes. They wanted it all. The bride-to-be was dressed head to toe in pink. Helping her choose the wedding colors would be a no-brainer. Her parents sat on her left, and even though her dad's watch was Cartier and her mom had diamonds on her fingers, ears, wrist and neck, they looked a bit sticker-shocked.

"Of course, we have day-of-the-wedding packages, as well," Sophia assured them. "We work with you about six weeks before the big day to make sure everything goes exactly the way you want."

There was a knock on Sophia's door, and Cassie poked her head in. "Sorry to interrupt, but I have Ms. Best on the line. As soon as you have a moment, could you come out here to take her call?"

Her clients may not have realized, but that was an odd request for Cassie to make. Panic set in. She excused herself for a minute while they looked over the continuum of services.

Once Sophia had closed the office door, Cassie picked up the phone. "Here she is, Fallon." She held out the receiver.

Sophia took the phone. "Hey, what's up?"

"Don't be mad…"

Don't be mad was never a good start to any conversation. It clearly meant you were about to be made mad, but your anger made them uncomfortable.

Fallon called because she was dying. Not literally dying…but close. She was sick. An unexpected illness usually wasn't a big deal. The two of them were an excellent team. If one had an emergency, the other stepped up.

It was a big deal this time, however, because it was the second of July. The day of the Wharton/Anderson wedding rehearsal. Fallon had thrown up in Mr. Wharton's rosebushes while they were setting up this morning.

"Are you okay? Did someone take you

home?" Sophia asked. Fallon had a full staff helping her with this event. Surely, someone had taken care of her.

"Ian drove me home. Please don't say anything when he submits a bill for a car wash and interior shampoo. His poor car may never be the same."

Sophia didn't want to think about what Fallon had done to Ian's car. "Well, don't worry. I've got this."

"Are you sure? Of all the days to get sick, this was not the one."

They were two days away from being done with the Wharton wedding. Two days away from never having to worry Evan Anderson might show up at the door of Engaging Events.

Not that he had come to the office since he kissed her. Since she kissed him back. The only door he'd shown up to was Yaya's two weeks ago with Zeke. In reality, they hadn't even gotten out of the car. He had texted that he wouldn't force himself on her, that if she was willing to listen to his apology, she should come outside. If she wanted him to go away and never come back, she should stay inside.

She'd chosen to stay inside. It had been the hardest thing she'd ever done. That kiss… That kiss had rocked her world. It had been everything she'd ever wanted in a kiss from the one person who shouldn't have been giving it. She'd been so blissed out in that moment it was criminal. Every kiss would be compared with that one for the rest of her life.

Watching Evan get married tomorrow would be worse than the stomach flu. If she could change places with Fallon right now, she would. She didn't have the luxury of choice in this matter, though. She had to suck it up and do her job.

"I've got this," she promised Fallon. "You rest and stay hydrated. This was my baby to see through to the end anyway."

Sophia would have to push her feelings aside and focus on helping to host the greatest wedding event of the year. She hung up with Fallon and went back into her office to sign Miss Pretty-in-Pink and her fiancé to a full-service wedding package. Her father wanted his little girl to have everything she wanted, so he would pay any price. Sophia was out the door and in her car before the ink was dry.

She had another bride who wanted the best

of the best on her wedding day and wasn't prepared for the woman who almost wrecked it to show up.

Once she was in her car, she dialed Jamie. It was surprising when she answered right away. "Hi, Miss Wharton, it's Sophia."

The silence on the other end of the call said it all.

"I'm calling because we have a slight problem," Sophia tried to explain.

"We don't have time for problems, Miss Reed. I am getting married tomorrow. Could you please not do anything to ruin that?"

Sophia winced. It shouldn't have been a surprise that she assumed Sophia might try to break things up. She had kissed the woman's fiancé, after all.

"No, I am not trying to ruin anything. I'm calling because my partner is sick and I'm going to be managing things in her place. I just didn't want you to be confused about why I was there."

"There's no one else who can manage things? You have to be there?"

"Fallon and I are the only ones who can run point. I want to assure you that making sure this wedding goes off without a hitch is my number one priority."

Another pregnant pause. "Then I guess I'll see you tonight."

Jamie ended the call without a goodbye. The last thing Sophia wanted was to cause a bride any unhappiness on her big day. Jamie deserved a drama-free wedding. Sophia's presence would make that more difficult to achieve. Staying as far away from Evan was the only way to avoid trouble.

"YOUR RESPONSIBILITY IS the groom and his brother," Sophia explained to Olive, her second in command. "You can have Ian help you out if you need backup, but I think you'll manage fine on your own."

"Did Fallon tell you she threw up all over some prizewinning roses? I heard the gardener was crying."

Sophia made a mental note to send an apology to the gardener. "What time are the guys with the Ferris wheel supposed to be here?" She couldn't find it on the list.

"I think Fallon was expecting them around four."

There was so much to do in such a short

time. It was already three. The rehearsal was in two hours and the massive lawn was still a blank canvas. Her job was to make certain it came to life with classy carnival booths and an actual Ferris wheel. It had been the most exciting find during the planning. Sophia knew Zeke was going to love it.

"Sophia, where is the videographer going to be set up?" Ian asked. "We have chairs for guests in the area where Fallon said it was going to be."

She followed Ian to the garden to help map out the seating plan. Fallon had not been in her right mind when she gave out orders earlier. But with Sophia's help, everything was soon exactly where it belonged for the ceremony. Tomorrow morning, they'd add bunches of pale pink roses and white dahlias as well as ivy vines to the trellis. Evan and Jamie would be married surrounded by the beauty of nature.

Seeing all of her ideas come to life was Sophia's favorite part of event planning, and she tried to convince herself to stay positive about it this time, too. If she couldn't marry the man of her dreams, she could at least give him the wedding of his.

"Miss Reed, I wasn't expecting you to be here. Jamie said your partner had taken over."

"Mr. Wharton. Good to see you again. Unfortunately, my partner fell ill, but I guarantee you that the show will go on. This wedding will be the talk of the town for years to come."

"I would hope so. My niece deserves the best." He surveilled the progress and moved one of the chairs an inch to the left. "Don't disappoint, Miss Reed."

"Yes, sir." The old man made her feel like a little kid. He also seemed very easy to disappoint. The pressure weighed her down as she finished setting up.

At four thirty, Jamie arrived. She was on her phone and followed by her bridesmaid. Jamie's bridesmaid, Arianna, was a friend from London. Sophia had made all of her travel arrangements last month.

Sophia swallowed down her nerves and ran a hand over her hair to smooth down any flyaways. She had to push her feelings away and focus on her reason for being there. Sophia had to convince Jamie that she was up for this, that she wanted nothing but the best for the two of them. She grabbed Heidi, one of the newer people they had hired for event days, and headed over.

"No, I'll be free to take a call tonight. I have a thing and then I'll be available to talk," Jamie said, which stopped Sophia in her tracks.

She had *a thing*? Sophia closed her eyes and took a deep breath. She was not here to judge whether Jamie and Evan should get married. She was here to make it happen.

Jamie ended her call and her icy-blue eyes glared at Sophia. "Is everything ready to go?"

"For tonight, yes. We'll be back first thing in the morning to put the final touches on everything else."

Jamie avoided eye contact. "Evan and Zeke will be here soon. I assume you have assigned someone else to get them where they need to be."

"Olive will run Mr. Anderson and his brother through everything. My other assistant, Heidi, is here to be at your beck and call. Anything you need, you just let her know."

Glowering suspiciously at Sophia, Jamie asked, "Then why do you need to be here again?"

Sophia pushed her chest out and stood tall.

She didn't blink or break eye contact. "This is my show to run. My job is to oversee all the moving parts and make sure they flow together as one, because I want tomorrow to be the best day of your lives."

The suspicion seemed to shift to respect. "Good."

Jamie led her friend into the pool house to get ready. Sophia sent Heidi with them and went to check in on the kitchen staff and how dinner prep was coming along.

The menu for the rehearsal dinner was almost as impressive as the reception buffet they had planned for tomorrow. Evan had chosen a pig roast with an abundance of decadent sides, including garlic mashed potatoes, honey-glazed carrots with caramelized onions and pesto pasta salad. The smell of freshly baked corn bread wafted through the kitchen.

"Will they have peanut butter and jelly?" Zeke's voice carried down the hall and into the kitchen.

Sophia thought about running, but greeting them here in front of all these people was probably the safest plan. She steeled herself for the emotions that were sure to come when she set eyes on him.

"We're having barbecue, remember? We can have peanut butter and jelly tomorrow before the wedding, okay?"

Evan, Zeke and a woman entered the kitchen. Evan stopped moving the moment he laid his eyes on Sophia. He was every bit as handsome as he was the last time they had been in the same room. He was dressed in all black like he was coming to a funeral instead of a wedding rehearsal.

"Sophia!" Zeke came at her with his arms wide open. "You're here. Evan said you were, but I said he was pulling my leg."

"I'm here." Sophia let herself enjoy the embrace. "Are you excited for the big party tomorrow?"

Zeke pulled back. "Jamie and Evan are having a wedding."

Sophia glanced at Evan, who had his hands in his pockets and his eyes cast downward. "Yes, they are," she said.

"I'm glad we're friends again. I miss Yaya and her stories."

Clearing her throat, Sophia tried not to show how her heart was breaking. She placed a hand on Zeke's cheek. "You are so sweet."

"Okay, buddy. Let's keep moving." Evan

stepped closer, and every hair on Sophia's body stood at attention. "It's good to see you, Sophia."

"You, too, Mr. Anderson," she said, knowing that not using his first name would make it clear that there was no chance for a real reconciliation.

He grimaced ever so slightly at her formality. "This is my mom, Valerie. Mom, this is Sophia, the wedding planner. She's the one who thought of everything. She's the best."

Valerie Anderson held out her hand. "It's so nice to meet you. The boys were talking about you in the car. I can't wait to see what you've come up with. It all sounds very magical."

Evan's mom was a beautiful woman. Her skin was Florida sun-kissed, and even though she'd been a widow for years, she still had on her wedding ring. The navy floral wrap dress she wore was simple but flattering. Evan had mentioned that Jamie's family's wealth intimidated her, but she had nothing to worry about. They might all be dressed in designer clothes, but Mrs. Anderson had a smile like her son's—warm and welcoming. That was what people would notice.

"It's lovely to meet you, Mrs. Anderson. I

hope you have a wonderful time tonight and even more fun tomorrow."

"It's all a bit overwhelming, but exciting."

"We should probably get outside," Evan said, placing a hand on his mother's lower back. "Sophia has work to do and we need to figure out what Jamie wants us to do."

Sophia leaned against the counter to hold herself up. The first couple of hurdles had been jumped. She saw him, spoke to him, managed not to kiss him or make a fool of herself. Now she just had to watch him practice getting married to Jamie before he actually married her tomorrow.

Yeah, it was only going to get worse.

"LET'S RUN THROUGH it one more time before we move them to the tent for dinner," Sophia said so everyone on her team with an earpiece could hear her.

Olive and Heidi approached the happy couple and let them know they were going to do it one more time. As soon as they were back in their starting places, Sophia spoke with the minister.

"One more time to make sure everyone feels good about the flow. You're doing a great job, but make sure we can hear you in the back," she said with a wink.

Sophia always started the rehearsal in the middle of the ceremony, with everyone standing in their place and getting a feel for the order of events. Once that was established, they practiced the recessional. The last run-through put all of it together in order, starting with the processional and handoff of the bride to the groom.

"Okay, let's start from the beginning and go until the end. Cue the music… Groom and best man…"

Gordon and Jamie stood at the end of the aisle behind Arianna. Olive nudged Evan and Zeke to make their way to their spots. Heidi nodded to Arianna to let her know she should start down the aisle.

Sophia moved to the back so she could see everything and everyone. She smiled at Jamie. "Go ahead."

Gordon and Jamie started down the aisle. It looked like Evan and Zeke were both finding it difficult to stand still. Zeke bounced on the balls of his feet. Evan scratched the nape of his neck and rocked back and forth on his heels.

When Gordon and Jamie got to Evan, the two men shook hands like Sophia had instructed them to in the first go-around. Gordon kissed Jamie on the cheek and left her in front of the soon-to-be-flowered trellis with Evan.

The minister listed the order of things. The bride and groom didn't want any extras—no lighting candles or filling a jar with sands to show they are bringing two families together as a new one. They were content with simple vows, an exchange of rings and a pronouncement that they were husband and wife.

"And then I would tell you that it's time to kiss the bride," the minister said, his comb-over blowing up in the breeze.

Typically, the groom would take full advantage of the permission to kiss the bride during rehearsal—it was usually the part he'd been waiting for all night. Not Evan.

He looked at Olive. "And then we walk out?"

"Yes," Sophia answered. "This is where you turn and make your way back up the aisle. Zeke and Arianna will follow."

Ian was waiting and directed them when to stop. That was it. They would be married and ready to celebrate. Tomorrow, the final nail would be hammered down and Sophia would have to move on.

"Let's eat!" Jamie shouted to her and Evan's family and friends.

Sophia had to stop everyone and ask them to exit a row at a time so there wasn't mass chaos. They all made their way across the lawn to the tent for dinner. Part two of the night was about to begin.

The rehearsal dinner was set up quite differently from how things would look tomorrow when they had a couple hundred people here. Tonight, there was one long table for everyone to gather around.

Once everyone was seated, Jamie stood and clinked her spoon against her champagne glass to get their attention.

"I just want to take a minute before we eat to thank you all for coming tonight. Evan and I really appreciate that you're here." She put a hand on Evan's shoulder. "Marriage is a big commitment and one we are ready to take on. With the love and support of our family and friends, I know that this is the beginning of a happy life together."

Evan smiled up at her and put his hand over

hers. Jamie raised her glass and everyone followed suit. It was very sweet, but something felt off. Sophia watched. There was no kiss again. She didn't bend down and kiss him. He didn't stand up, take her in his arms and make a show of their love.

She thought about how even Zeke said he had never seen them kiss. Not that she wanted to see it. Sophia should have felt relieved that they didn't kiss in front of her. Still, something about their lack of affection made her pause.

The man could kiss. Sophia touched her lips as the memory of the one they shared caused a faint tingle. How could someone who kissed him even once not want to kiss him every chance she got?

"Sophia, the kitchen wants to know when you want them to start bringing out desserts for the dessert table," Ian said in her earpiece.

This was as good a reason as any to go inside and put some space between her and the currently kissless couple. It was only a matter of time, though. They would kiss. They'd be kissing each other the rest of their lives.

Once they were halfway through dinner, Sophia helped the staff carry out desserts.

Everything needed to be better than good. It needed to be perfect. She had to prove to Jamie that her head was in the game and that their wedding was her only priority.

"Wow, everything looks delicious." Evan's voice startled her as she set the platter of mini cheesecakes on the table.

"Only the best for the bride and groom," she said, hoping he'd be on his way back to his bride before she turned around. Unfortunately, he was still there...and dangerously close. The memory of him holding her, of him kissing her, made her knees go weak.

"Are you all right?" he asked, concern emanating from his eyes. He reached for her arm to steady her.

"Don't," she snapped. She didn't mean for it to sound so harsh, but he recoiled immediately.

He appeared repentant. "Sorry."

She straightened and tucked some hair behind her ear. "Go back to your guests. Dessert will be ready in a minute."

He nodded and backed away. Once he was back by his seat, Sophia could breathe. One more day. She had to see him only one more day and then he would be nothing but a memory.

"Sophia!" Olive was in her ear. "There is a giant black dog on the lawn and coming this way."

Not the dog. Sophia scanned the table for Patrick, but he was nowhere to be found. Figured. Given what happened a month ago at brunch and the great lake debacle the first time she had visited here, Sophia was not going to let that animal get anywhere near this rehearsal dinner. Hopefully Buster would let her bring him home before he ate her for dinner.

She found Olive by one of the concession stands they had set up for tomorrow's reception. "There he is." She pointed.

Sophia didn't have any experience with dogs other than the poodle Yaya had years ago. Of course, Gigi weighed about eight pounds and rolled on her back anytime anyone came near.

"Give me your belt," Sophia whispered. She held out her hand and waited.

"What are you going to do with my belt?"

"I'll use it as a leash. What else can we do?"

"How are you going to get it on him?"

"I don't know—just give it to me."

Olive obliged and pulled her belt through the loops of her black pants. "Good luck."

Sophia hadn't come empty-handed. She had a mini cheesecake with her that this big guy might eat along with her hand if given a chance. It was a risk she had to take.

"Here, big boy. Come here, boy. You want a treat?" The word *treat* must have been a magic word, because he came running at her. Her heart raced as the adrenaline kicked in. Fight or flight was a real thing and, right now, she wanted to run. She stood her ground, though. "Whoa. Sit. Sit. Sit!" she commanded.

She closed her eyes and braced herself for the attack, but it didn't come. She opened one eye and then the other. There was the dog, tongue hanging out of his mouth, sitting in front of her.

"Good boy," she said, astonished. "Here you go." She held out the cheesecake and with the other hand pushed the belt under his collar. He didn't bite off her hand but finished the treat in one gulp. She held on tight to the belt. "Let's go home, big boy. Come on."

A gentle tug was all it took to get the dog to follow her all the way to the guesthouse.

No one answered when she knocked on the front door. She walked around back to see if Patrick was there.

"I hear what you're saying," she heard Patrick say. "You know I've got you. We're on the same team here."

"We better be," another voice said.

"You have to get out of here, though. Stick to the plan and everything will work out exactly like we want it to."

"Until we meet again, Patty boy," the voice said.

Sophia dropped the belt and froze. Fear like she'd never felt before paralyzed her. She couldn't breathe. She couldn't scream even though that was what she wanted to do. She knew that voice. She had nightmares about that voice.

Her nightmare had come true.

CHAPTER SIXTEEN

"Are you nervous about tomorrow?" Evan's aunt Sheryl asked.

"Not really. I'm actually looking forward to it." *Being over*, he wanted to add.

"Are you two going on your honeymoon right away?" she asked. "And where are you going? Your mom said something about Jamie's uncle wanting to give you a honeymoon as a gift."

"Jamie can't take off work right now, so we're going to try to plan something later. Her uncle did offer to send us to his villa in Italy. I don't know if that will still be an option when we finally decide to go, though."

"Italy! Oh, I would die to go to Italy. The food, the history. Honey, did you hear this?" She tugged on Uncle Lonnie's arm. "Evan and Jamie might go to Italy for their honeymoon."

People were always impressed with the

wrong things. Evan checked his watch. All he wanted to do was go home. Tomorrow was going to take every ounce of energy he had. Acting like a happily wedded man wasn't going to be easy.

Something caught his eye outside the tent. Sophia was running for the pool house. He had already been given the cold shoulder twice tonight. He wasn't in the mood to take a third hit, but she looked distressed. Extremely distressed.

"Excuse me a second," he said to his family. He had to make sure she was okay, even if that meant she told him to get lost one more time today.

He strode toward the poolhouse with purpose. The hairs on his neck were standing on end. He knew something was wrong. He yanked on the door and Sophia nearly jumped out of her skin. Her face was streaked with tears. The sun was setting and there wasn't much light coming through the windows. He went to turn on the light, but she stopped him.

"Don't! He could see me. Please don't!"

Evan's heart began to race. All he wanted to do was hold her and keep her safe. "Who will see you? What in the world happened?"

She was shaking like a leaf. She collapsed on the couch and cried into her hands.

Panicked, he sat next to her and put a hand on her back. "What's wrong? Did someone hurt you?"

Sophia sat up and fell into his arms. She clung to him like she was scared for her life. He kissed her head and hugged her tight. He wouldn't let anyone hurt her. If someone hurt her, he would hunt them down and show them exactly how that made him feel.

"He-he-he-he's here," she stuttered.

"Who?"

"The man in the mon-mon-monkey mask."

A chill ran down his spine. How was that possible? He held her tighter. She had to be mistaken. "I don't understand. There's no one here but our family and friends."

"At Patrick's. He was talking to Patrick."

He had never felt anyone tremble the way this had her shaking. "Patrick was talking to the man in the monkey mask? You saw him?"

She shook her head. "I *heard* him."

He held her face in his hands. "Are you sure?"

The complete terror in her eyes answered

his question. Of course she was sure. That man's voice was stuck in her head.

Evan let her go and got to his feet. He had told her so many times there was nothing to worry about and now the guy was here at his rehearsal dinner.

"What are you doing?" Sophia jumped up and pull on his arm.

"I'm going to get this guy. I'm gonna…" He actually had no idea what he was doing. He just needed to do something. "Where were they?"

"Behind the guesthouse. Please don't go. Please. Let's call the police. Don't leave me here by myself."

How could he resist a plea like that? Evan held her again. "I'm right here. He's not going to get anywhere near you. I promise."

"What do we do? Call the police?"

"I guess," he said.

The door opened and Evan was quick to shield her body with his as he turned to see who was there. Jamie stared at them wide-eyed.

"Are you kidding me right now?"

"It's not what you think," Evan tried to explain.

"It's not? You didn't sneak away from our rehearsal dinner to come make out with the wedding planner? Because that's what it looks like, Evan!"

"One of the bank robbers is here. He's up by the guesthouse talking to Patrick."

It was as if he had thrown a bucket of ice water on her. Jamie's anger completely fizzled out. "Talking to Patrick?"

"Sophia heard them talking."

"What did they say?" Jamie moved to turn on the lights.

"Please don't!" Sophia shouted.

"Don't turn on the lights. We don't want to call any attention this way. He knows what Sophia and I look like. If he sees us, who knows what he'll do."

Jamie held her hands up. "I won't turn on the lights. Is she okay?" The look she gave Evan was full of worry.

He shook his head. He guided Sophia back to the couch and had her sit with him. "Can you tell us what he was saying to Patrick?"

"They were arguing," Sophia explained. "Patrick was trying to convince him to be patient. That he needed to follow the plan and they would get what they want. Then he said…he said, 'Until we meet again.'" She whispered the last part. That was what had triggered the panic attack.

Evan held her hands. "I'm so sorry. That had to be terrifying for you."

"That son of a—" Jamie paced in front of them. "This was his doing. He did this. He's behind it all."

"We need to call the police," Evan said. "We should call the detective in charge of the case."

"No, wait," Jamie said. "What would we even say? Sophia *heard* the guy? Is he even here still? Maybe I should go up there and pretend I'm looking for Patrick. Maybe I can trick him into telling me who the guy is."

"It sounds like he was leaving. We should call Detective Thatcher and tell him what we know. The man was here and was talking to Patrick. Let the detectives do their job."

"Fine," Jamie relented. "You call the cops, and I'll go find Patrick. I didn't even realize he left the dinner. I could pretend I did."

"His dog was loose. I was returning his dog. Olive's belt is still hooked onto his collar."

"Perfect," Jamie said as she headed for the door.

"Please be careful," Evan begged Jamie. "This is wilder than we ever imagined."

"I'm not afraid of Patrick, but he should be afraid of me." Jamie stormed out of the pool house and up the hill to the guesthouse.

Evan stayed focused on Sophia. "Let's call the detective, okay? It's going to be all right."

"He was here. Do you think he knew we were here? Do you think he knows who we are?" She was still shaking.

"I don't know," he answered honestly. If Patrick was behind this, anything was possible. "Let's call Detective Thatcher."

While they were on the phone with the detective, Jamie came back, holding a belt and looking quite triumphant. "I took a picture of the call history on his phone. Can you believe he left his phone on the counter for me to see? One of these numbers has to belong to the man Sophia heard tonight."

Jamie offered to meet the detective at Wharton Bank's offices and gave permission for them to search anything they'd like, including Patrick's office.

Evan ended the call with Detective Thatcher. "Okay, we need to get back out there and end this party so Jamie can get to the city to meet them."

"I have a call planned for later tonight. I can use that as an excuse why I have to bail. Things were already winding down when I came to find you. Can you handle wrapping things up here?" Jamie asked Evan.

"I'll do whatever I have to. Are you okay?" he asked Sophia, who had finally stopped trembling. Her breathing was almost back to normal.

"Whoever Patrick was talking to is gone," Jamie reassured her. "He was alone when I went up there."

"I'm okay," Sophia said, standing up. "I can finish what needs to be done here."

Jamie surprised her by giving her a hug. Sophia's arms were pinned to her sides. "I'm sorry for everything that has happened to you. And I'm sorry for being such a jerk to you. You didn't deserve it."

"Thank you," Sophia replied. Still trapped in Jamie's hug, she side-eyed Evan for help.

He tried to suppress a laugh and patted Jamie on the back. "All right. Let's get moving."

Jamie left and Sophia went to the bathroom

to freshen up. Evan tried to work up what he would say to her when she came back out. His need to protect her, to comfort her, overrode every other instinct at this point. He still had to get married tomorrow, but if it was true that Patrick knew anything about the bank robberies, perhaps this charade could be over sooner than expected.

Sophia returned, sweeping her hair over one shoulder. The urge to press his lips to that exposed curve between her neck and shoulder was overwhelming.

"I'm ready," she stated with conviction.

He needed to hold her one more time, perhaps to comfort himself more than her. He reached for her and she didn't recoil or reject him. Sophia pressed her cheek against his chest and wrapped her arms around his waist.

"I cannot wait until this is all over. I can't wait to tell you everything."

"Everything like what?" she asked, remaining in his arms.

"The Wharton family is complicated. It definitely isn't always what it seems."

She tilted her head up. "Why are you marrying into this family, then?"

"That's the part I can't explain yet, but I

will." He cupped her cheek. "Just know that I am here for you whenever you need me. I won't let any of this ugliness touch you again. I won't."

"I don't understand."

"I know. I'm sorry," he said, touching his forehead to hers. All he wanted to do was kiss her. Reassure her that she wasn't losing her mind. What they had was more real than anything that had happened here tonight or any vows he would make tomorrow.

Both of them were breathing hard. His heart beat so hard against his chest, it was like it wanted to bust out so it could attach itself to her. It was hers now anyway.

She closed her eyes and finally pulled away. "We need to get back out there."

No one seemed to notice Evan had been missing. Patrick had already returned to the party and had Gordon's ear. Jamie had left. Evan's family was sitting around the outdoor fireplace on the patio. Sophia gathered her team to start cleaning up for the evening.

"Maybe we should head out. You ready to go, Mom?" he asked.

"Whatever you want, sweetheart." She

stood up and held her son's hand. "I can't believe Jamie still has to work. Shouldn't she be thinking about you tonight?"

Lying to his mother was almost as bad as lying to Sophia. "Trust me, she's thinking about all of us."

His mom shook her head. "If you say so. I just want you to be happy, and you haven't looked happy all night."

"Weddings are stressful. It will all be better soon. I promise." He watched as Sophia grabbed one of the centerpieces off the table. "I'm going to check in with the wedding planner and make sure we're all set for tomorrow, and then we can go."

"Whatever you want, honey. You're the groom. This is your big weekend."

He stopped to say good-night to Jamie's mom and Gordon, choosing not to acknowledge Patrick at all. He couldn't risk speaking to him directly. He wasn't a good enough actor to not let his true emotions show. Sophia was giving directions to her team when he found her under the tent. No one would suspect she'd been an anxious mess a few minutes ago. There was no way she was going to sleep tonight. Neither was he.

"I'm going to take my mom and brother home. What's your plan after this?"

"I don't know." The sun has dropped behind the house. Night was upon them. Her stoic facade fell for a second. "I'm still freaking out."

"I could come over. Sit with you until we hear back from Jamie."

"You don't have to do that," she said.

"I know. I want to."

"You're getting married tomorrow," she reminded him like he could forget.

"It doesn't matter."

Her brows pushed together. "How can it not matter, Evan? I'm too exhausted to make sense of everything that's happened tonight."

"It means who knows what's going to happen tonight or tomorrow. The only thing that matters to me is that the people I care about are okay."

"And I'm one of those people?"

"Absolutely."

She worried her bottom lip with her teeth. "Fine. I'll text you the address."

That was all he needed to hear. He took his family home and waited for Sophia's text. It was as simple as making up an excuse about wanting to see Jamie before the big day to avoid any questions from his mom when he took off.

Sophia answered the door in an oversize T-shirt and black leggings. It was the first time he'd ever seen her dressed casually. It didn't make her any less attractive.

"I messaged Jamie to meet us here when she's done with the police. Is that okay?"

"Yeah, it's fine," she said, opening the door wider so he could come in.

Sophia's home was so…her. It was extremely neat and orderly. Nothing was out of place, there was no clutter. The wall color was neutral, and the gorgeous trim work added a touch of class and character. Her accent colors were warm and inviting. The furniture, pillows, blankets and rug provided the space with a softness he could not only see but also feel. It was sophisticated comfort. This was a place that made him want to be there. Made him want to stay.

"Have you gotten any updates from Jamie?" Sophia asked, motioning for him to take a seat. "I mean, what are the chances they're going to solve this thing in the middle of the night? Don't they have to get search warrants and stuff like that?"

She remained standing, keeping as far from him as she could get. The proximity that she allowed him when she was in the throes of her panic attack was no longer acceptable. Her walls were back up.

Evan shrugged. He had no idea what was going to happen. They would have to wait for Jamie to get here.

"We can hope they find what they need. The sooner those criminals are off the street, the better."

"Why would Jamie's cousin be working with bank robbers? That doesn't make any sense."

Evan struggled with what he could say and what he shouldn't say. "It's complicated... And I can't truthfully say I know for sure. What I can tell you is that Jamie and her cousin are both vying for the same position in the company, and it's making them both a bit desperate to get their uncle's attention. It's possible that Patrick did something to make Jamie look bad and cast himself as the hero."

Sophia nodded and pulled her legs up,

wrapping her arms around her knees. "Can I ask you something else?"

He turned his whole body in her direction. "Sure."

"Is the wedding Jamie's way of getting Gordon's attention?"

"I can't really explain it to you the way you need me to."

"Are you in love with Jamie?" she blurted out. "Wait. Don't answer that. I don't have any right to ask you that."

He knew why she'd asked. Clearly, he had feelings for Sophia. They were impossible to hide. He knew better than to answer that question with a lie.

They sat in silence for a minute or two.

Sophia growled and threw her arms up. "See, right there, that's what confuses me. I know I told you not to answer, but the fact that you didn't answer anyway is so frustrating. If you were madly in love with her, you would shout it to the rooftops regardless of what I said. Am I wrong?"

This was a test he would never pass. He didn't know how he was supposed to respond, because he didn't feel that way about Jamie.

"I love her," he tried. "She's been my best friend for years."

Sophia shook her head. "What are you doing? Why are you getting married tomorrow?"

"Why do you care?" he threw back at her. "Do you have a reason I shouldn't get married tomorrow?"

Sophia jumped up and started to walk away. "Forget it. Forget I said anything."

"Too late. You said it, so you must have a reason why you don't think I should get married tomorrow."

"I'm going to get a glass of water. Do you want anything?" she asked, ignoring his words completely.

Evan wanted to kick himself. He was rude. He'd put her on the spot when he knew darn well why she said what she said. He had kissed her. He had done that because he wasn't in love with the woman he was supposed to marry tomorrow. Anyone really paying attention could see that.

Jamie needed to arrive soon or he was going to spill the beans and tell Sophia the whole story. Right on cue, his phone chimed with a text from Jamie saying she was outside.

"Jamie's here!" he called to Sophia. He got up and opened the door.

"Well, that was interesting," she said as she walked in.

"Did they find anything?" he asked.

Sophia reappeared with a glass of water in her hand. "What happened?"

"I don't know what they found. They took stuff out of his office that they said was potential evidence. They're going to work on those phone numbers I gave them and figure out who he's been talking to recently."

"Are they going to bring Patrick in for questioning?" Evan asked.

"Not yet," Jamie said. "They want to gather some more evidence against him before they bring him in. He wasn't even on their radar, so they have work to do."

"But what about the man? The man who was at the estate today? The robber?" Sophia asked, her volume rising with each question.

"We don't have a lot to go on. Like I said, they are going to look at those numbers I gave them."

Sophia was agitated. "Why don't we just tell your uncle? The guy who robbed his bank was at his house tonight. Don't you think he should know?"

Jamie's eyes went wide. "Whoa, whoa. *We* aren't going to tell my uncle anything until we know how deep Patrick is in this."

"Who cares how deep Patrick is in this? The actual bank robber was at his house. The bank robber is deep in it." Sophia began to shake again.

Evan was compelled to go to her. "Hey, we're going to get that guy. The cops are looking for him, and they'll find him."

"What about security cameras? Her uncle has security cameras. We could give the police the footage and maybe they can identify him."

"That's a good idea," Evan said, looking back at Jamie.

"After the wedding, I can ask him."

"Why would we wait until after the wedding? Let's call him tonight," Sophia said frantically. She pleaded with those eyes of hers.

"I gave them the phone numbers. Isn't that enough? The police will find the guy."

"They'll find him a lot faster if they have

your uncle's security tapes tonight rather than a week from now."

"We're not going to wait a week," Evan assured her.

"I'm not ruining my wedding day by accusing my cousin of knowing a bank robber. Something like that could cause us to postpone. We can't postpone."

Sophia put a hand on her forehead. "You have to be kidding me."

Evan reached for her other hand. "Hey, I get it. Let me talk to her," he whispered.

Sophia didn't bother to lower her voice. "She doesn't care about the bank robber who almost killed us. Who put a gun in our faces." She had tears in her eyes.

"I don't understand what you're so worked up about. The bank robber isn't going to show up at your house. I'm positive he's been retired by my cousin."

Evan turned his glare on Jamie. "Can you stop? You don't get it. You weren't there."

"Why are you yelling at me?"

He hadn't even raised his voice, but Jamie didn't like being challenged. Right now, though, Evan didn't care what she liked or didn't like.

This was about treating Sophia's feelings like they mattered.

"I'm not yelling. I'm asking you to have a little bit of compassion. I know you have a lot on the line, but she lived through a traumatic experience. *I* lived through a traumatic experience. One that we can't just forget about and get over, but one that keeps us up at night."

"I'm sorry for what happened to you, *both* of you."

"*Sorry* doesn't help, Jamie. Getting that video helps. It would give us peace of mind."

Jamie had both hands on her hips and looked like she could spit nails. "We have to get married tomorrow, Evan. There are no guarantees that Patrick did anything or that they'll catch him if he did. You promised to do this with me."

"I know I did. Can't we get the tape from Nelson or someone else who works there? We don't even have to ask your uncle. No one needs to make Patrick suspicious."

"I'll try," Jamie conceded.

"Okay. See? She'll try," he said to Sophia. "We'll try. I'll do what I can, too. Nelson likes me. Maybe I can get the footage."

"We should go," Jamie said. "We have a big day tomorrow and we need to be well rested."

Evan felt trapped in the middle. Part of him wanted to stay with Sophia and the other part knew he had to be loyal to Jamie and go.

"It's going to be okay," he said to Sophia, who had calmed down. "No one is going to let this guy get away. The police are on it and we're going to get the security footage."

"We'll see you tomorrow, Sophia," Jamie said, holding her hand out for Evan.

He didn't take her hand, but he walked to the door. Sophia was mute. She closed the door behind them as soon as they stepped out on the porch, leaving Evan feeling rotten.

"You're really in love with her, aren't you?" Jamie asked.

Evan headed toward his car. "Don't start."

"Don't start? You couldn't be more obvious. If you look at her like that tomorrow, everyone will know."

"Then I won't look at her. I'll close my eyes. I'll look away. I'll do whatever you want as long as you give the police the security footage, okay?"

"Fine."

"Great."

"Look at us. Compromising like we're already married."

It was as if all the joy had been sucked out of his life. He felt numb. "Don't worry, Jamie. I'll marry you tomorrow, and I hope you get to be the big winner. That's all you really care about, isn't it?"

He didn't wait for her to answer. He got in his car and went home.

CHAPTER SEVENTEEN

FLOWERS WERE A huge part of any wedding and this one was no exception. The trellis was the focal point and there were hundreds of flowers to attach to it before the ceremony.

Olive helped Sophia arrange them. The roses were fragrant and perfect shades of pink and white. They were absolutely gorgeous, and Sophia hated them.

Sophia hated everything about this wedding, but she couldn't show it. From the cloudless blue sky to the adorable carnival booths—everything was flawless. Jamie would get her dream wedding and Sophia would despise every minute of it.

Lack of sleep probably had something to do with it. As did Jamie's insistence that this wedding was more important than finding the men who'd robbed the bank. In Sophia's opinion, nothing was more important than finding the robbers. They had terrorized people. They needed to be in jail.

"Wow. This is the most beautiful thing we've ever done," Olive said, taking a moment to appreciate their hard work.

"Yeah. It's nice."

"Oh, come on, Sophia. You outdid yourself with this one. It looks magnificent."

"Fine, it's *very* nice. Now, can I count on you to check with Ian and make sure the drive is properly decorated?"

"On it," she said with a salute.

Checking the carnival booths was next on Sophia's list. There were three concession stands that would each offer a different elevated carnival snack after dinner. Evan had chosen corn dogs, funnel cakes and snow cones. The funnel cakes could be ordered sweet or savory, and the snow cones came in flavors like watermelon-basil and blackberry-lavender. There would also be servers walking around with popcorn, cotton candy and french fries in pink-and-white-striped paper cones.

Sophia inspected the game booths, as well, stopping in front of the balloon darts. This would be Evan's favorite. As thoughts of him danced through her head, she noticed him walking with Zeke toward the pool house. That was their home base to get ready for the ceremony, while Jamie was in the main house.

Sophia had seen to it that the bride and her bridesmaid had breakfast brought up to the room. The hair and makeup people were here. The photographer had been here for an hour already. Zeke and Evan would have lunch in the pool house before they got ready and had to take some pre-ceremony pictures. With the timeline for everything memorized, Sophia knew where Evan would be at all times.

That was a blessing and a curse. She could avoid him pretty easily, but it also allowed for the chance that she'd give in to the urge to talk to him. Right now seemed like a good time to find out if they were able to get the security footage.

Zeke was practicing his dance moves when she stepped into the pool house. He had a peanut butter and jelly sandwich in each hand and a smile on his face. She had planned for them to enjoy his favorite lunch.

The music was so loud, Sophia put her hands over her ears. She spotted Evan in the corner by the sound system. He was pressing buttons and turning knobs, clearly trying to find the one that would turn the volume down to a reasonable level.

"That's better." He turned and noticed Sophia was there. He rubbed his hands on his pants like he was nervous. "Hey."

"Sophia! We got peanut butter and jelly for lunch," Zeke exclaimed.

"I know." She smiled at him. "I told them it was your favorite."

"What do you say to Sophia for making sure you got peanut butter and jelly?" Evan asked.

Zeke opened his arms. "Thank you, thank you!"

She happily accepted his hug. She was dressed to set up in an Engaging Events T-shirt and running shorts, so her clothes could handle peanut butter fingers.

"You're very welcome, buddy. I just wanted to make sure everything was set up for you."

Evan plucked a bottle of his favorite beer out of the ice bucket. "It's great. You've thought of everything."

"You get what you pay for."

He nodded and his gaze fell to the ground. "Right."

Why was he getting married to someone he didn't love? What was he getting out of it? Money? He just didn't seem like the type who cared about that kind of stuff. Last night, she'd gotten the distinct impression that Jamie needed this to happen more than he did.

"Any word on the security footage from last night?"

"I asked Nelson about it when I got here. He said they have cameras everywhere. I told him I heard Patrick's dog was loose last night and that we suspected it got into some trouble. Asked to see the cameras around the guesthouse to get a timeline for when he was out. Since he's not a big fan of Patrick's pup, he said he would send it to my email when he had a chance."

Relief flooded her body and Sophia finally felt some of the tension in her neck and shoulders ease. "That's great news. Any word from the detectives?"

Evan shook his head. "Nothing."

"You don't think that anyone involved in the you-know-what might be invited today, do you?" This was something that had kept her up all night. What if Evan knew the bank robbers without knowing he knew them?

"I don't think so. Even if Patrick is involved, he wouldn't have gotten support from people who know Jamie. At least, I hope not."

Sophia felt the pinprick tingle of anxiety at the thought of overhearing that voice again. "I'm going to be on high alert all day."

Evan had drifted closer. She wondered if he felt the same pull that she did. Her whole body reacted to him with a need to be as close as possible.

"I'm sorry for that," he said. "I hate stressing you out."

"Well, it's a good thing I have plenty to keep me busy today. Don't worry about me. You shouldn't be spending a second thinking about anything but your happy day."

"Right," he said, rubbing the nape of his neck.

"This is what you want, right?" She moved in his direction.

"Right. There aren't any other reasons not to want it."

"I can think of a few," she admitted.

He tilted his head and closed the space between them. "A few? Like what?"

Sophia swallowed hard and tried to look away, but she couldn't. She imagined herself taking his face in her hands and kissing him the way he had kissed her. She imagined giving him the biggest reason she had for him not to marry Jamie.

Her.

Sophia's pulse beat in her ears. She had never wanted someone so much. He was a cool breeze on a hot day. The full moon in a dark sky. It wasn't right for her to make this about her, though. This decision needed to be his.

"If you need me to tell you what they are, then maybe they're just my reasons and not yours."

Evan leaned in ever so slowly. Sophia struggled to keep her breathing even. His hand touched her elbow and gently glided up her arm.

"Sophia?" Olive said into the earpiece. "Where are you? We need you in the garden for a minute."

The interruption broke the spell he had her under, and she stepped back. She pressed the button so her employees could hear her. "I was checking on the groom and groomsman in the pool house. Coming to the garden now."

"Duty calls," Evan said, shoving his hands into his pockets.

She nodded. "I'll send Olive to check on you from here on out. She'll make sure you get where you need to be the rest of the day."

"Where I need to be…" he repeated with a bit of melancholy in his tone.

She backed away. "Bye, Zeke. I'll see you at the wedding, okay?"

"Do you want a peanut butter and jelly before you go?" he asked.

"I'm good, buddy," she replied. She ran all the way to the garden, fighting the tears that wanted to fall.

MR. WHARTON HAD provided the staff with a room to change and freshen up before the ceremony. Sophia had retreated there once she was confident everything was ready to go. She changed out of her dirty T-shirt and used a washcloth to wipe the dirt and sweat off her arms and legs.

She always tried to coordinate her outfit with the wedding so she would blend in seamlessly. Today, she slipped into her blush-colored halter-neck jumpsuit and nude heels. She pulled her hair back into a low ponytail, letting a few wisps of hair frame her face.

Checking her makeup in the mirror, she fought the memory of almost kissing Evan in the pool house. If Olive hadn't interrupted, she would have let him kiss her again. She would have kissed him back even though Zeke had been in the room with them. That made her a terrible person, didn't it?

She put on her earrings and placed her ear-piece back in her ear. "How's it going out there?" she asked her team. "Heidi?"

"Bride finished pictures by the lake and is headed to the house to touch up hair and makeup."

"Ian?"

"Guests are arriving. We're checking them in as I speak."

"Olive?" She'd saved her for last for a reason.

"Groom and his brother are back in the pool house, waiting for the ceremony to start."

Sophia resisted the urge to ask if he looked happy or not. She couldn't bear it if he wasn't. But she couldn't bear it if he was happy, either.

"I'm on my way out. I'll check in with the

kitchen and then head to the garden to help with seating the guests. Let's make this a wedding to remember, everybody."

Patrick was standing outside her room when she entered the hall. He seemed surprised to find her there. "Wedding planner, right?"

Fear slithered up her spine. "Right. Can I help you, Mr. Wharton?"

"Where is my cousin? I have a little something for her. I thought Nelson said she was in this wing."

"She's on her way back from getting some pre-ceremony pictures taken. I can escort you to the room where she'll be getting ready, if you like."

Patrick gestured for her to lead the way. The bridal suite was empty when they arrived.

"They should be up here in a minute."

"That's fine." He grabbed a bottle of water from the table of refreshments. "This is quite a production. A Ferris wheel? Whose idea was that?"

Sophia forced herself not to tremble under his glare. "It was mine, sir. It went with the theme."

"Do you know that those two never even dated before getting engaged? At least no one I know ever suspected they were anything more than friends. Weird, huh?"

"Love surprises us sometimes."

"Yeah, sure. But sometimes it's just a means to an end. My cousin is one smart cookie, let me tell you."

Sophia kept close to the door for an easy escape. She could hear Jamie and her entourage coming down the hall.

"Can someone make sure that Evan's mom is allowed in the pool house to be with the boys before the ceremony starts?" Jamie asked.

"No problem, Miss Wharton," Heidi said.

Jamie's concern for Mrs. Anderson only added to the complexity of her character. Sometimes she was completely apathetic, but other times she demanded complete control. She obviously cared about Evan but could turn around in an instant and dismiss his thoughts and feelings. Last night, she'd shown such compassion in the pool house but had cared only about herself when she came by Sophia's.

Jamie and Arianna entered the room each holding a glass of champagne.

"What are you doing here?" she asked as soon as she noticed Patrick was there.

"Can't a guy wish his cousin good luck on her wedding day?" he asked glibly.

"I need to get ready. You might want to make sure you get a good seat. I wouldn't want you to miss me committing to my new husband."

"Ah, commitment. Yes. I just thought you should know that I've been talking with Uncle Gordon quite a bit and I have a good feeling he and I have come to an understanding about what's next for me at Wharton Bank and Trust. He didn't want to say anything to you, with the wedding and all, but I felt it was better to give you a heads-up in case there's a chance this wedding is part of some plan to convince our dear uncle you should be his successor. I would hate for you to enter into a loveless marriage for naught."

Jamie's face turned bright red. "You think you're so smart, don't you? I can't believe you forget who you're up against. I'm getting married today to Evan, the man I am madly in love with, the man who is madly in love with me. As for Uncle Gordon's retirement plans, we'll see how he feels in a few days. Something tells me there's a storm coming, but it's not going to rain on me because my hands are clean. Can you say the same?"

Patrick leaned closer. His jaw ticked. "You never could admit defeat, could you?"

"I haven't lost yet."

"Yet," Patrick said, bumping her shoulder as he pushed past her. Sophia jumped out of the way as he barreled past her and out the door.

"I am so sorry I let him come in here." Sophia apologized even though she knew he probably would have found Jamie without her help.

Jamie took a deep breath and straightened her shoulders. "Make sure nothing else goes wrong today, Sophia."

Sophia nodded and took off for the garden, her head spinning with what was said in that confrontation. It reaffirmed her fears that Evan was not getting married because it was what he wanted or because Jamie was whom he wanted to spend the rest of his life with. Sophia thought about how Evan had said something about the Wharton family not being what they seemed. They were much more dangerous than she had ever imagined. How could she let Evan get trapped in their claws?

Instead of going toward the garden, she hurried to the pool house. Olive, Zeke, Evan and Mrs. Anderson were in the middle of a heated billiards game.

"Nice shot, Z-Man!" Evan gave him a high five.

"I'm starting to feel a little hurt that you didn't choose me as your partner, Ezekiel," his mother said.

"Girls against boys, Mom. Sorry."

Evan noticed Sophia first. "Are we okay? Is it time to go?"

Sophia shook her head. "I need to talk to you for a minute. Can we go outside?"

"Yeah," he said, hanging up his pool cue. He was so handsome in his tux. He made her heart beat double time. The suit looked better than she had imagined in her head when she picked it out for him.

He held the door open for her. This had been so impulsive, she wasn't sure what she was going to say. All she knew was that he couldn't get married. Not to Jamie. Not into the Wharton family.

"What's the matter?" he asked as soon as they were alone.

"I want you to think about what you're doing. I need you to think about what's best for you before you go down to that garden."

His hands were on her again. He was always touching her. And it centered her, helped her feel safe and focused. He never touched Jamie.

"What happened?" he asked.

"Patrick came to see Jamie. He said he was there to wish her well, but it was clear that he wanted to intimidate her. To make her think he had some kind of upper hand, that their uncle was going to choose him for something. I don't know. He accused her of getting married as a ploy. He said she shouldn't be in a loveless marriage. Are you guys getting into a loveless marriage? I don't want you to be in a loveless marriage, Evan."

"Hold on, Patrick told her that he had the upper hand? What did he say exactly?"

He seemed to be missing the point. "I don't know what he said exactly. All I know is that this is not one big, happy family."

"I know they aren't happy, but I really need to know what he said. Did he imply he knew something about me and Jamie?"

"He said that if she thought getting married was going to make her the 'successor,' she should forget it. He implied that he was and that this wedding was a waste of time."

"Shoot." He scrubbed his face with both hands.

"Please, Evan. I don't feel good about this. Think about what you're doing."

He shook his head. "I've thought a lot about what I'm doing. I'll admit, I have questioned myself more than once, but I have to marry Jamie today. Patrick's desperate. He wants to see if she's bluffing."

"What are you talking about?" This was the strangest wedding she had ever helped plan. "You're making your wedding sound like it's part of some high-stakes card game, like it's a chess move in the most messed-up chess match. That is not exactly the best foundation for a marriage."

Evan rubbed his temples with the heels of his hands. "I appreciate your concern, Sophia. I want to get married today. Jamie is my best friend."

"You obviously don't want to tell me the truth. That's fine. Misleading me is something you've been good at since we first met." Maybe it was a low blow, but she was tired of getting the runaround every time she asked him to be honest with her. Another part of her selfishly hoped that calling him out would push him to tell her what was really happening.

"I'm sorry," he said, opening the door to go back inside. "Please let me know when it's time for us to come down to the garden. We'll be ready."

Disappointment consumed her. There was something wrong, but Evan didn't want to let her in. There was nothing she could do about it.

"Sophia, can we get some help in the garden?" Ian asked in her earpiece.

She pinched the bridge of her nose and gathered her wits about her, then pressed the button to respond. "I'm on my way."

Once the guests were all seated, Sophia checked her watch. It was go time. "Places, everyone," she said. "Olive, let's have Zeke and Evan escort their mom to her seat and then take their place in front of the trellis."

Sophia let herself feel the ache as she watched Evan walk down the aisle. This wasn't the way she wanted to end things with him. She watched as he kissed his mom's cheek and went to stand in the spot where he would marry his best friend.

She signaled the string quartet to play the wedding processional song. "Heidi, cue Arianna."

The sole bridesmaid glided down the aisle like a fashion runway model. Once she got to her spot, it was time for Jamie to make her grand entrance. "Heidi, cue Miss Wharton and her uncle."

The guests rose from their seats, and Jamie and Mr. Wharton entered the garden. She was a sight to behold. No one there would question why Evan would choose her to join him in a life together.

Gordon Wharton gave his niece a kiss on the cheek and shook Evan's hand before leaving the couple to greet one another.

"You look amazing," Evan said—it was too soft for Sophia to hear, but clear enough for her to read his lips.

The song came to an end and the minister welcomed everyone to the ceremony. Two months of Sophia's life had been spent working toward this moment, but she wasn't sure she could bear to watch.

Was he making the worst mistake of his life? Was she just projecting her feelings onto him? She would never know. Jamie and Evan would go on with their life and Sophia would move on and plan someone else's wedding.

"Excuse me," someone said behind her.

Sophia turned to find Detective Gibson and Detective Thatcher standing there with three uniformed officers.

"Sorry for the interruption, but we're going to need Patrick Wharton to come with us."

CHAPTER EIGHTEEN

"PATRICK WHARTON?" THE detective called out.

Evan's eyes darted right to the man of the hour. Patrick looked panic-stricken. He also looked like he was considering making a run for it. That was not happening.

"He's right here," Evan called, blocking his way out.

The two detectives came down the aisle. "Patrick Wharton?" Detective Thatcher asked.

"What in the name of all that's good in the world do you think you're doing?" Gordon asked, stepping in between Patrick and the police. "Do you see that we are in the middle of a wedding ceremony?"

"We apologize for the timing, sir. Patrick Wharton, you are under arrest. We need you to come with us."

"Under arrest?" Gordon's face flushed. "I want your names and your badge numbers.

You two will never work another day for this city if I have anything to say about it."

Patrick let his uncle fight his fight as Eliza sunk into her chair. Evan wasn't surprised he was such a coward, unwilling to accept the consequences of his own actions.

"Mr. Wharton, I think you should move out of the way and let the police do their job," Evan said.

"Let them do their job? Exactly what has my nephew done that requires them coming here and ruining your wedding?"

"Mr. Wharton is under arrest for conspiracy to commit a bank robbery and for being an accessory after the fact."

"What?" Gordon almost fell over. He gripped the back of the chair that Jamie's mom was sitting in for support.

"We're going to need you to step aside, Mr. Wharton."

"This is a big mistake," Patrick assured his uncle. "I have no idea what they're talking about. I've obviously been set up. Probably by her!" He pointed at Jamie. "Did you do this? Are you really that desperate?"

Jamie held her hands up. "I'm just up here trying to get married. The only one I know who's been desperate is you, Patrick. What did you do?"

"Whatever she told you, she's lying. I have nothing to do with the robberies. Eliza, tell them I had nothing to do with this."

Detective Gibson turned his attention on Eliza. "Mrs. Eliza Wharton?"

Eliza's face paled. "Yes?"

"Ma'am, you're going to have to come with us, too. You are also under arrest for being an accessory after the fact."

Evan glanced over his shoulder at Jamie, whose expression told him she was just as shocked as he was.

"You have the right to remain silent. Anything you say can and will be used against you. If you cannot afford an attorney, one will be provided to you. Do you understand these rights as they have been explained to you?"

Eliza looked like she might throw up. She nodded as they handcuffed her in front of everyone.

Detective Thatcher read Patrick his rights and tried to get the handcuffs on him, but good ole Patrick wasn't going down without a fight.

"I don't know what they're talking about,

Uncle Gordon. I didn't do anything. You know how hard I've been working to stop these crimes against our banks. You know this company means everything to me."

Detective Thatcher gave him a warning to cooperate. Patrick had no intention of going peacefully, however. He continued to fight until the detective knocked him to the ground and cuffed him while his face was in the grass.

Evan wished he could feel bad, but he did not. He was overjoyed at the sight of Patrick finally getting what was coming to him.

The officers in uniform escorted Patrick and Eliza out of the garden. Patrick's parents followed them out, his father swearing to Gordon that he would get to the bottom of this.

Detective Thatcher pulled Jamie and Evan aside. "Thanks to you we were able to ID the guy that Miss Reed recognized as one of the men from the robbery. We found a ton of stuff on Patrick's work computer. Went to his house up in Davidson and, lo and behold, there were four guys living there, including our friend who sounded very much like the man in the monkey mask. Not only did we find the suspects, but all of the stolen cash was there, as well. We believe they've been hiding out there this whole time."

"No wonder your cousin's remodeling job was taking longer than expected," Evan said to Jamie, who was grinning from ear to ear.

"So you got them all?" she asked.

"We believe so. We still have work to do, but we'll keep you updated. Again, we couldn't have done it without both of you and Sophia. Thank you, and sorry about crashing your wedding."

"Yeah, don't worry about that," Evan said, feeling giddy. "This is the best thing that could have happened."

Jamie covered her mouth. "I can't believe this," she said.

"It's over." Evan hugged her and lifted her off the ground. "You've got nothing to worry about anymore."

"I seriously can't believe it."

"Honey, what is going on?" Jamie's mom sounded completely dismayed. She obviously couldn't understand why the two of them were celebrating. Jamie grabbed her mom's hand and motioned for her uncle to come talk to her.

Sophia stood at the end of the aisle wide-eyed and confused. He strode as quickly as he could to her.

"They caught them. All of them. They were hiding at Patrick and Eliza's house. That's why he's been staying here. It's over. They're all going to jail."

Her face lifted and those green eyes looked up at him bewildered. "They caught them?"

"All of them." He couldn't stop smiling.

A laugh mixed with a cry bubbled out of her. He opened his arms and she jumped in. He picked her up and could have spun in circles, he was so happy. He felt such relief, he could have cried.

"It's over. You never have to be afraid of them again," he promised her.

"Evan," his mother said behind him. "What is going on?"

He set Sophia down and tried to reassure his poor mother that everything was fine. Better than fine.

"Is the ceremony going to be postponed? I've never been to a wedding with this much drama. The worst thing that's ever happened was the time your uncle had too many drinks at your cousin's wedding. This is a whole different level of drama, son."

The wedding. Evan glanced up front where Jamie was explaining everything she knew to her family. He looked back at Sophia. His heart still had strong feelings about whom it belonged to.

"I don't know, Mom. Let me talk to Jamie." He stole one more glance in Sophia's direction before jogging up the aisle.

"That's all I know. I'm sorry I didn't come to you, but truthfully, I was afraid you wouldn't believe me. He's had your ear for so long, I feared you'd give him a chance to manipulate the facts, cover his tracks. I couldn't risk it," Jamie said to her uncle.

"This is unbelievable." Her mom shook her head with her hand on her cheek. *Stunned* was an understatement.

"Maybe we should make an announcement to the guests. Start sending people home," Evan suggested.

"Why would we send everyone home?" Gordon asked. "As disappointed as I am, if what you say is true, I will not let that weasel ruin your wedding day. This is your day. You deserve it."

Evan looked to Jamie to say something. Did they need to get married now that giving control to Patrick was no longer an option?

"Can I have a minute to speak with Evan in private, please?" Jamie asked and her family complied.

What was there to talk about? Why would they have a wedding when they didn't have to?

"I know what you're going to say," she said when they were alone.

"What? That we should send all these people home and get on with our lives?"

Jamie grimaced. "I get it. We could bail, but Gordon still wants the same things out of me that he's always wanted from me. He needs me to exhibit those qualities more than ever given the fact that he's been betrayed by Patrick."

"You still want to go through with this?" Shocked, Evan raked a hand through his hair. "Are you kidding?"

"How do you think it'll go over if I tell him we aren't really in love? That I was planning to marry you to trick him?"

Evan didn't know what to do. There wasn't anything he could say that would change her mind. He had made her a promise and she was holding him to it.

"We got this. Come on. Stick it out with me," she begged. Jamie waved Olive over. "Can you tell Sophia to come up here?"

"What are you doing?"

"We need her opinion on how to proceed. Do we start over or just continue on from where we were? I don't know what to do when a wedding gets interrupted by a police raid."

"How can I help?" Sophia asked. "We can start having guests exit the garden."

"No one is exiting. We want to carry on," Jamie said.

Sophia flinched. She stared at Evan. "You're still getting married?"

"Should we start over or just continue from where we left off?" Jamie asked. "I'm leaning toward just starting from where we were. The minister had barely said hello. What's your experience with an interruption?"

"I've never had an interruption like this." Sophia seemed to be searching for her bearings. "I guess whatever you want is what we'll do." Her gaze was fixed on Evan. When he said nothing in reply, she suggested they take a five-minute break and then start from where they left off.

"Okay, good." Jamie grabbed Evan's hand. "We're good, right?"

He nodded, unable to say anything because the lump in his throat felt like it was the size of a golf ball.

Sophia pressed the button to talk to her team. "Wedding is still on. Five-minute break to regroup. Everyone back to their places."

"What are we doing?" Zeke asked Evan. "Did you know the police were going to show up? I thought we were in a movie."

"Me, too, buddy. That was pretty cool, huh?"

Zeke pointed to the Ferris wheel. "Can we go to the carnival now?"

"I still have to get married. The ceremony isn't over yet."

"Oh. This is the boring part."

"I know. Sometimes we have to do things that we don't want to do so we can do the things that we want." Like get married to someone he wasn't in love with so he could take care of his brother.

"Fine," Zeke said with a sad sigh.

"Okay, I need you guys back in your spots," Olive said, guiding them toward the trellis.

Sophia was fixing Jamie's veil. She said something, and Evan watched as Jamie's face fell. Sophia walked away and Heidi led Arianna and Jamie back.

"What did Sophia say to you?" he asked.

Jamie stared down at the flowers in her hands. "That I'm the luckiest woman in the world and I should remember not to treat this wedding like a business deal that needs to get done before the end of the day."

Even snorted a laugh. "She just put you in your place."

Jamie's gaze lifted and she scowled at him. "Shush."

"Hey, truth hurts."

"She loves you," Jamie said with full sincerity. "She's in love with you."

Evan looked down the aisle. Sophia stood with her finger pressed against her earpiece. She nodded at the minister, who picked things up right where he'd left them.

She was in love with him? He had lied to her about how he felt about Jamie. He had kissed her when she was innocently trying to teach him to dance. He had pursued her that afternoon after the bank robbery and failed to mention that he was engaged. He'd behaved badly and needed to make it up to her because, in all honesty, he'd fallen in love with her on that very first day.

He wasn't listening to a word the minister said. He couldn't even look Jamie in the eye. If he did, she would see it. She would feel it and it would make this farce that much harder to play out.

Jamie's mom read a passage from the Bible about love and patience. Would love really be patient? It certainly wasn't kind. Was there any chance that Sophia would wait for this nightmare to be over? Love rejoiced in truth. How could Sophia ever trust him when she learned the truth? Could their love persevere? Would it?

He gave Mrs. Wharton a smile in thanks for her participation as she went back to her seat. It was time for him to play his part.

"Now for the good stuff," the minister said.

Jamie handed her flowers to Arianna and held Evan's hands. He did his best to maintain eye contact.

"Do you, Jamie, take Evan to be your lawful wedded husband?" the minister asked.

"Do you promise to love and cherish him, in sickness and in health, for richer for poorer, for better for worse, and forsaking all others, keep yourself only unto him, for so long as you both shall live?"

Evan waited for her to say *I do*, but she bit her lip. He gave her hands a squeeze. Maybe she wasn't paying attention and didn't realize this was her part.

"I'm sorry," she said. "I love you. I love you for standing up here with me, but I do not promise to be your wedded wife."

Evan could feel his eyes nearly bulge out of his head as the whole crowd gasped for the second time today.

"What are you doing?" he asked, letting go of her hands.

"What I should have done in the very beginning." She turned to face the guests. "Evan is my best friend in the whole world. He's literally the greatest guy I have ever met. He's honest and hardworking, and when he cares about you, he'll go to the ends of the earth for you if you ask him to.

"I have wanted to run Wharton Bank and Trust since I was in high school. I studied harder than every one of my friends because

I knew I needed to be the best if I was going to be trusted to do that someday. I have risen to every challenge that's been given to me. I have proven my loyalty to the company even when others came courting me with promises of bigger and better things.

"But there was one thing I didn't have. I didn't have a husband. I was told I needed a husband to prove that I understood what commitment meant. I was supposed to be balanced. I needed to show everyone I could do it all, so I asked my best friend to do me a favor. I asked him to marry me so I could meet that criteria—even though we learned a long time ago that we make much better friends than lovers.

"Evan is standing up here today because I asked him to, not because he's in love with me or because I'm in love with him. I realized while my mom was up here that my best friend shouldn't have to pretend and make a pledge in front of God and his family and friends just because I'm too scared to admit that I don't want to be married. I want to do my job because I am really good at it. I am committed to Wharton Bank and Trust, and if that's not enough to prove I deserve to be in charge someday, then so be it. I will have to live with that."

Evan had never been so proud of her. She was incredibly brave. He took her by the hand and stood beside her, because she deserved his support.

Everyone sitting in front of them was slack-jawed. Her uncle stared at her in disbelief.

Jamie said the only thing she could. "I'm sorry I lied."

Gordon stood up and rubbed his beard as he contemplated how to respond. He spoke first to the guests. "Please excuse all the disruptions. I ask for your patience. Apparently, there is more to talk about."

He motioned for Jamie and Evan to follow him. They went to another part of the garden, away from prying eyes and ears.

As Gordon paced in front of them, his silence was more intimidating than if he had started yelling. Evan tightened his grip on Jamie's hand. He would stand here and take the heat with her. It wasn't like she was the only one who had lied. He had played along this whole time.

Evan couldn't stay quiet any longer. "You know there's no one like her. You will never find anyone as impressive as her. If you pass her up because she's single, she should leave and go somewhere she's appreciated. The only loser would be Wharton Bank and Trust."

Gordon folded his hands together. "You think so, huh?"

Evan nodded. "I know so. You know so, too."

"First, I'd like you two to know that I'm a little sick and tired of these very private matters being put on public display. The police come charging in and I have to explain to members of the board why my nephew is being dragged out of here in cuffs? Then you two stand up there and declare this whole thing is nothing more than a joke?"

"It wasn't a joke. We were seriously going to do this. We care about each other. We could have been married and not been completely miserable," Jamie said, speaking for herself.

"Don't try to sell me that. You tried to deceive me and your mother. We're invested in your happiness, Jamie. I have felt like your father was looking down on you all day, beaming with pride. Now I wonder if he wasn't trying to warn me something wasn't right."

Evan felt that. They both were guilty of not making their fathers very proud today. Both of their dads would have been against this plan from the start.

"I don't get it, Mr. Anderson. You tell me that Jamie is the most impressive woman alive, but you don't want to marry her? How is that possible?" Gordon challenged.

"He's in love with someone else…someone who's just as impressive," Jamie answered. "That's why."

Evan's defenses were up. He didn't want her to say anything else. He didn't want any of this to reflect badly on Sophia. She should not have to pay for his mistakes.

"Someone else as impressive as you?"

"You've met the wedding planner," Jamie said much to Evan's dismay.

Evan's frustration had to have shown on his face. "Let's leave her out of this."

"The wedding planner?" Gordon's gray brows furrowed. "You're in love with the wedding planner. *Your* wedding planner?"

"They met and fell in love before she was the wedding planner, Uncle Gordon. They were both at the bank during the second robbery. That's where they met, and I think that's where they both fell for each other."

"Please don't ruin her career. She's an amazing event planner. The best, in my opinion. Please don't hold her accountable for my mistakes. All of this is mine and Jamie's mistake. Sophia had no idea we weren't getting married for the right reasons."

Gordon crossed his arms over his chest. "Now, why would I ruin that poor girl's career? Have you seen how hard she's worked to make this fake wedding a masterpiece? This would have been the best wedding of the year, of the decade, if you two hadn't screwed it up!"

Evan had to laugh, because he was right about that. This wedding would have been featured in magazines. Maybe it still would be. "Couldn't the greatest wedding that didn't happen get a little bit of press?"

"Oh, we're going to get press, all right. I'm not sure you're going to want the press, but you're going to get it. In fact, I don't know why you'd want to take over for me now that your cousin has sullied our reputation," he said to Jamie. "Our bank could be the last place you'll want to work."

"You know how I love a challenge," Jamie said with a smirk.

"I think you and I better sit down and figure out how we're going to handle this PR nightmare. And you," Gordon said to Evan. "You need to go find that wedding planner and let her know that we're going to have the reception as planned so we can celebrate the fact that you two numbskulls didn't make the biggest mistake of your lives today. Maybe she'll take pity on you and give you a second chance."

"A second chance? I'll be happy if she doesn't hate me."

Jamie gave him a jab with her elbow. "She does not hate you, Ev. Go talk to her."

CHAPTER NINETEEN

"WHAT ARE WE DOING?" Olive asked.

"This is seriously the biggest disaster of all time," Ian said.

"Do you think they're going to come back?" Heidi asked.

"What if they come back and say, 'Just kidding, we do want to get married'?" Olive asked.

"I'm pretty sure she made it clear that they are not getting married," Heidi said. "She basically said he'd been friend-zoned from the beginning."

"Her loss, man. He is so nice. I don't think I have ever worked with a groom this nice before," Olive said.

"Sophia? Are you there?" Ian asked. "Did we lose Sophia?"

"I'm here," she replied. She was recovering from a heart attack, but she was there.

"What's the plan? Do we just provide

crowd control until they come back? Do we let people leave if they want? What do I say about dinner?" Olive had a million questions. Sort of like how Sophia had about a million questions for Evan if he ever came back.

"We're going to give them a couple more minutes, and then we're going to ask the mother of the bride and the mother of the groom how they would like us to proceed."

"Can I get everyone's attention?" Evan reappeared in front of the flowery trellis. "I want to apologize for everything that's happened today. Jamie and I want you all to stay and enjoy the food and fun we have planned for the rest of the evening. We promise no more police and no more surprise announcements."

Everyone had something to say inside Sophia's ear. Ian and Olive were talking over each other, and Heidi kept repeating that this was unbelievable.

"You're welcome to head on over to the tent for some food and drink. I'm pretty sure we all could use a drink right about now. And if someone knows where my wedding planner is, can you tell her I'm looking for her? I would really like to talk to her."

Sophia directed her crew to jump in and get everyone to the tent in an orderly fashion. As the garden began to clear out, Evan could see her standing in the back. He didn't wait for her to come to him, he went to her.

"Sorry, did I do that wrong?" he asked with his crooked grin.

"It would have been nice if everybody didn't trample one another on the way to the reception."

"I'm new to the whole 'got my wedding stopped by police and then was left at the altar by my best friend who confessed the whole engagement was a sham but let's still party' thing." Leave it to Evan to find the humor in all of this.

"Let's hope this is a one-and-only kind of experience."

"Oh, I sure hope so."

He was painfully handsome. Sophia had to stare at his shoes to think straight.

"You would have gone through with it, though. If Jamie hadn't stopped it, you would have married her." That was the part of this whole thing that ripped Sophia's heart out. He'd chosen Jamie. Even though he wasn't in love with her, he would have chosen her.

"I don't know if I would have. The whole time the minister was talking and Mrs. Wharton was reading about love, I kept thinking about you."

She looked up. "About me?"

"The last two months, all I've thought about is you. I had convinced myself that even though I was falling head over heels for you, the only way I could protect you and take care of Zeke was to marry Jamie."

"Protect me? How did marrying Jamie protect me?"

"If I had backed out of the engagement because I wanted to be with you, that would have been a huge scandal. I didn't want to ruin your career. I also had Zeke to think about. If I lost my job, I wouldn't be able to support Zeke the way he needs me to."

Sophia wrung her hands. She took a step back to fight the urge to fall into his arms. This whole night was a lot for Sophia to process. "I don't know what to say."

"I don't want you to say anything, because I am scared to death that you want to run away from me as fast you can, and I don't blame you for feeling like that." He slowly moved closer and placed a hand on her arm.

His touch was electric. "But I really want you to think about giving me a chance to be in your life."

Always touching, always wanting to be close. It was completely the opposite of how he was with Jamie. He had always shown her more affection than he did Jamie.

She turned her body to release his hold. She couldn't make this decision while she was still managing his weddingless reception. "I need to focus on this job right now. I need to finish this before I decide what I want. Or *don't* want."

It was as if she had slapped him. He winced with pain. "I won't get in your way."

For someone who had been so persistent in the beginning, he sure was willing to step aside these days. Sophia couldn't take the heartache of getting involved with someone who had no idea what he was doing.

"Sophia, the kitchen wants to know if they should start passing out hors d'oeuvres or not," Heidi said in her earpiece.

"I'm coming now," she replied, backing away from Evan. He didn't stop her.

The reception went on as planned. There was plenty of whispering among the guests, but everyone seemed to be enjoying themselves. Dinner was as spectacular as they'd planned. Jamie was absolutely glowing, smiling like Sophia had never seen in the two months she knew her.

The only one who seemed glum was Evan. He had joined his mom's table with Zeke and the rest of his family. Mrs. Hamilton kept trying to cheer him up from what Sophia could see.

After the cake was cut and served, it was time for the first dance. Sophia wasn't sure if they were still going to do that or not. She waited for a chance to talk to Jamie when she was alone at the bar.

"Are we doing the first dance or just starting the music so everyone can dance?"

"Did Evan talk to you?" she asked instead of answering.

"We spoke for a minute before the reception started."

"And…"

"And?"

"I'm sorry I made him lie to you. I'm also sorry I didn't let him back out of this when he wanted to—and he did want to."

Sophia tried to stop her from apologizing.

It made Sophia uncomfortable. "You don't need to explain anything to me."

"Please. I need you to know the truth. Evan came to me the day after he met you and tried to convince me to come up with another plan. At the time, I didn't understand why he was getting cold feet, but I know now that it was because of you."

"Me?"

Jamie smiled and touched Sophia's shoulder. "You. I have never seen Evan fall for anyone the way he fell for you."

Sophia had to let that sink in. Why didn't he tell her that he had gone to Jamie and tried to end all this right after they met? Because he couldn't. He had chosen Jamie.

"You should know that I smacked a guilt trip on him that made it impossible for him to say no to me. I made him think he wouldn't be able to do right by Zeke if he didn't go through with this idiotic plan." Jamie glanced around the room, her shame clear in her expression. "It was not my proudest moment. But I would *never* let anything bad happen to Zeke or Evan, and it was wrong of me to hold that over Evan's head. I was desperate, but it was wrong."

Sophia felt the weight of her misplaced disappointment lift. Her heart swelled in her chest. She had thought he had chosen Jamie over her, but that wasn't the truth. Evan had chosen Zeke over everyone, because that was the kind of man he was. His brother was his first priority, as he should be. There was little reason to doubt he was being honest about how he felt for her.

"Let's do the first dance," Jamie said, switching gears. "Can you have them announce it?"

Her complete one-eighty made Sophia's head spin. "Sure."

Jamie grabbed her drink and gave Sophia a wink before heading back to her table. Sophia went over to the band and asked them to announce it was time for the first dance.

The guests clapped for the happy noncouple as they made their way to the dance floor. Evan looked like he'd rather be anywhere else.

"We're going to do things a little differently," Jamie announced. "Surprise, surprise, huh?" She got some laughs. "Zeke, will you come dance with me?"

Zeke jumped up and looked the complete

opposite of his brother. He was thrilled to be singled out.

"Looks like I've been replaced," Evan said, ready to bow out.

"Not so fast," Jamie said, grabbing him by the arm. "Sophia?"

Sophia cautiously made her way over. She had a sinking feeling that she wasn't being called over because she was the wedding planner.

"You guys, this is Sophia, the wedding planner. I think we should all give her a round of applause because this is probably the most unmanageable wedding she has ever had to manage. Am I right?"

Everyone clapped for her. Evan mouthed he was sorry. He could clearly tell she didn't like to be the center of attention.

"Sophia and Evan worked tirelessly to plan this evening, and it's pretty spectacular. Just wait until you see the fireworks display later tonight. I really wasn't much help, as work always comes first for me, but these two created an amazing party for all of us, so I think it's fitting that they share this dance with me and Zeke."

Sophia was going to throw up. Fallon's

stomach flu would be nothing compared with Sophia losing her lunch in the middle of the dance floor in front of more than a hundred people.

"Jamie," Evan said, reading Sophia's expression.

Jamie tugged them both together. "Just dance, you two." She motioned for the band to play.

The music started, and Evan was quick to give her an out. "You don't have to do this if you don't want. She's bossy, but she's not the boss."

"She kind of is my boss right now."

"I don't want you to feel uncomfortable."

He was always sweet and considerate. He had done what he thought was right for his brother, for his family, and that was the kind of family she wanted to be part of. Sophia put one hand on his shoulder and held the other one out. "Dance with me?"

His Adam's apple moved up and down his throat. "Are you sure?"

"I'm sure."

He put a hand on her waist and the other in her open hand. He pulled her close until their bodies were flush together. For a moment she feared she might explode into flames, but then that familiar sense of safety settled deep in her bones. Being in his arms was like being home.

"Do you remember the steps?" she asked him.

"I think so. Left, touch, right, touch, left, touch, spin." He led them in a circle. "Is this right?"

"It's perfect." He was perfect. He was everything she wanted. He was her person. The reason her heart raced. Her butterscotch candy. Her favorite song. The one. Just like Papou was Yaya's great love.

"I had a good teacher."

She smiled up at him. "I don't want to be finished with you. I want to see if this can be our start."

Evan stopped moving. His eyes kept dancing, though. "For real?"

"You're not the only one falling. I fell a long time ago."

As if they were the only two people in the room, Evan cupped her cheek and lowered his mouth to hers. "I love you, Sophia," he whispered before his lips pressed against hers.

The fireworks they had planned for later had

nothing on the way Evan Anderson kissed. She felt like she was the center of his universe and that everything would be right with the world as long as they stayed right here—together.

"STEP RIGHT UP! Step right up! Come throw a couple darts. Pop a balloon, win a prize."

"This is my booth, Z-Man. This is where I am going to win big." Evan rubbed his hands together. "I'll take some of those darts, sir."

Zeke held out his hand, too. "Me, too."

"What about the lovely lady?" the man running the booth asked. "Are you playing, too?"

Sophia stepped back. "I'm just watching."

"Are you sure?" Evan asked. "You can play the games, too."

Officially, she was still very much in charge of making sure this event ran smoothly. Just because the former groom was her new boyfriend, she wasn't off the hook for doing her job.

"I'm sure. You two play."

"You first, little brother," Evan said.

Zeke licked his lips and was laser focused on the balloons in front of him. He threw his first dart and it landed in between two balloons.

"Oh, man, nice try," Evan said to rally his spirits. "That was a good one. I thought you had it."

"Your turn," Zeke said.

Evan inspected the tip of his first dart. He glanced over his shoulder at Sophia. "These actually look pretty sharp."

"I promised you nothing less."

"You always deliver, Miss Reed," he said with a sly smile.

Evan threw his first dart and it missed, as well.

Zeke patted him on the back. "Nice try, bud. I thought you were going to pop one."

Sophia couldn't love these two more. They went back and forth, taking turns throwing their darts. Finally, on his last throw, Zeke popped one of the balloons.

Evan and Sophia cheered and high-fived him. The pride on his face was priceless. The man running the booth let him choose his prize, and Zeke went right for the giant lollipop.

"Surprise, surprise. Of course you picked candy, Mr. Candy Man," Evan teased.

"Don't be jealous," Zeke said. "You still have one more dart. You can win one, too."

"I think I need a kiss for good luck," Evan said, looking back at Sophia.

She didn't mind obliging. Wrapping her arms around her neck, she kissed his lips. Being able to do that brought a joy she had never experienced before.

"I didn't know I could ask for one of those!" Zeke complained.

Sophia laughed and let Evan go. "How about a kiss on the cheek for popping the balloon?"

Zeke turned his head and pointed to his right cheek. "I'll take it."

Sophia planted a chaste kiss on his cheek.

"Jeez. Guy wins a lollipop and he thinks he can try to steal my girl? You better watch it, mister. She's mine," Evan said.

Zeke tugged on the lapels of his tux jacket. "I can't help it that the ladies love me. Especially when I look this good."

Evan and Sophia looked at each other and busted out laughing. "Do you see what I'm dealing with?" Evan asked. "This guy. Forget Mr. Candy Man. I'm going to call you Mr. Ladies' Man."

"Throw your dart so we can get a funnel cake," Zeke said.

Evan shook his head. Sophia realized she'd been wrong a minute ago—she was going to love them both a little more every day. It was inevitable.

"All right, here I go." Evan threw his last dart and popped the pink balloon in the center. He threw his arms up triumphantly.

"Another winner!" the man running the booth shouted.

Sophia gave him another kiss. "You didn't even have to spend all your allowance."

"You must be my new good-luck charm." He kissed her one more time. That was never getting old.

"Pick your prize," the booth man said.

Evan chose the teddy bear and immediately gifted it to Sophia.

"For me?"

"I always wanted to win a stuffed animal for the pretty girl I had a crush on. It took twenty years or so, but it was worth it. There's never been a prettier girl or a bigger crush."

"Funnel cakes?" Zeke asked.

"Go ahead," Evan said. "Meet us over by the Ferris wheel when you're done."

Sophia checked her watch. It was almost showtime. She pressed the button to talk to her team. "Fireworks in ten minutes. Ian, are you still with the crew?"

"We're good to go. They have it all set up. Just waiting for the okay to start."

"Heidi, make sure that everyone in the tent knows the fireworks will be going off soon— we want to give them a chance to come out on the lawn for a better view."

"Got it."

"I'll be offline during the fireworks. If you need me, I'll be on the Ferris wheel."

"You go, girl," Olive said before Sophia popped the earpiece out and slipped it in her pocket.

"Going off duty for me?"

"I have a surprise for you," she said, pulling him toward the Ferris wheel.

They waited for Zeke, then put him on the ride with his mom. Evan and Sophia got into the next seat. They went all the way around once, and the second time, the wheel stopped when they got to the top.

"Uh-oh. Do you think it's broken?" Evan asked, craning his neck to see what was going on down below.

Sophia shook her head. "Look," she said, pointing out over the water.

The first firework exploded in the sky, reflecting off the lake down below. Up here, they had the best view of the show.

"You planned this?"

"It pays to be friends with the wedding planner."

Evan's smile was lit up by the next explosion in the sky. "It sure does."

He threw his arm around her shoulder, and she snuggled up against him while they watched the fireworks. He kissed the top of her head.

"Just to be clear, I do not want to be just friends," he said.

She kissed him under his jaw. "Good, because neither do I."

CHAPTER TWENTY

Six months later

"I WANT TO thank everyone for being here today. I know I'm an old man, but I always thought I would die before I retired. My late wife used to accuse me of not wanting to retire because I thought no one could do something as well as I could. I mean, it's true, but I digress." The crowd laughed at Gordon's attempt at humor. "Thankfully, I have complete faith that I am leaving the family business in good hands. My niece, Jamie, is probably the only person in the world who can do things better than I can."

Sophia noticed someone from the kitchen staff putting the wrong-sized plates by the salad station. She headed that way but was quickly intercepted by Fallon.

"You are a guest at this retirement party, not an event manager. Trust me. I got it. You can relax."

Sophia held her palms up. "I knew you had it. I was just stretching my legs."

Fallon shook her head but smiled. "Right, sure you were."

"Everything is amazing, by the way. You did great."

"Thank you. Now, go back and stand next to your gorgeous boyfriend and enjoy the party." Fallon gave her a push in the direction of Evan. He *was* gorgeous.

Jamie addressed the guests. "I know I have big shoes to fill, but I promise I will do my best to run this company in a way that will make you proud."

Gordon wrapped her in a warm embrace. It was official. Jamie was now the CEO of Wharton Bank and Trust. She was the first woman under the age of forty to be named CEO of a major bank in all of history. Sophia and Evan were both so happy for her.

She had hired Engaging Events to host Gordon's retirement party at the Wharton estate. It was one of many events they had been hired to do lately, even after being attached to the wedding fiasco of the year.

The luncheon today was much less chaotic than the last time they were here. It was also a beautiful tribute to the years of hard work Gordon had put into his business.

"What time is it?" Evan whispered in her ear after they had lunch and shared a piece of cake.

It was after two. "Almost time to go."

"Let's start making the rounds to say our goodbyes."

Evan took her by the hand and led her over to Jamie.

"Evan and Sophia! Thank you so much for coming." Jamie hugged Sophia.

"Sorry we can't stay longer. We have to pick up Zeke from work at three."

"And it's Sunday," Jamie said. "Yaya will be expecting you."

"Family dinner night," Sophia confirmed. "I'm not sure who is more excited every week, Yaya or Evan."

Jamie patted Evan's stomach. "By the look of it, I'm going to guess Evan."

"Hey, if Yaya wants to cook for me, who am I to tell her no?"

"I'm happy for you two. Really happy." Jamie gave Evan a hug and whispered something in his ear.

He playfully pushed her away. "Shush." He laughed and shook his head.

"Thanks again for coming, you guys. Call me later."

"I'm not calling you," Evan said as they started to walk away.

"Yes, you will! I'll be waiting."

"What was that about?" Sophia asked.

"Nothing. Jamie just being Jamie."

They picked up Zeke from work and took him home so he could get ready for dinner at Yaya's. If there was anyone who loved Sunday dinner as much as Evan, it was Zeke.

"Can you carry this for me?" Evan asked, handing Sophia a bottle of wine.

"You know you don't have to bring anything."

"Your aunt Calista said this was her favorite last week, so I picked up a bottle when I was at the store the other day."

"That was so thoughtful of you."

He kissed her on the nose. "I'm a thoughtful guy."

He was. He always did little things for people just because. It was one of the many things that Sophia loved about him.

They drove to Yaya's and had to park on

the street since the driveway was packed as usual. The little kids were outside, playing Wiffle ball in the front yard.

Evan couldn't resist joining in for a couple of plays. He was such a kid at heart. Another thing that made him so lovable.

Sophia opened the front door and was immediately pounced on by her aunts. Cheeks were kissed, compliments were accepted. She gave Aunt Calista the bottle of wine from Evan.

"Oh, you picked a good one, Sophia. He's a keeper."

She couldn't argue with that. Yaya asked her to taste what she was cooking before giving her a kiss hello.

A horn honked outside. Loud and obnoxious like it was trying to get the whole neighborhood's attention. Everyone ran to the front door to see what was going on. Someone was parking a huge RV in front of Yaya's house.

Sophia's eyes widened, and she pushed past her cousins to get outside. The door to the RV opened and out jumped a woman and man Sophia hadn't seen in much longer than she would have liked.

"Mom? Dad?"

SOPHIA RAN TO her parents and greeted them both with hugs and kisses. It warmed Evan's heart to see the reunion. Everything was coming together just as he had hoped.

He made his way over to them, rubbing his hands on his jeans to make sure they weren't sweaty. He didn't want to make a bad first impression when he shook hands with Sophia's father.

"I can't believe you're here. Why didn't you tell me you were coming home?"

"It wouldn't be much of a surprise if we told you we were coming, now, would it?" her mother asked. She looked so much like Sophia it was scary. No one would doubt they were related.

"This must be Evan," her dad said.

"Mr. Reed, Mrs. Reed, it's so nice to finally meet you." He stuck out his hand. Mr. Reed shook it firmly.

Mrs. Reed was a hugger like the rest of her family. She kissed both of his cheeks and then held his face in her hands. "Oh, Sophia. He's darling. Look at those brown eyes. I can see why you are so smitten."

"Okay." Sophia tugged her mom away. "Let's not manhandle my man."

The rest of the family didn't wait for them to come inside the house. Everyone came out for the big reunion. Even Yaya.

Tears were in the old woman's eyes before she even got her arms around her daughter. Evan found himself getting a bit choked up. He knew how much it meant to Sophia's grandmother to have her whole family there.

Evan introduced the Reeds to Zeke. They were as friendly as their daughter. It was no surprise given how incredible Sophia was. Evan knew he had nothing to worry about.

Everyone piled back inside. Dinner was an even bigger production than usual. Everyone was here tonight. All the aunts and uncles. All of Sophia's cousins. All the kids, big and small. Uncle Gus even brought his new puppy.

They were their loud, exuberant selves. The only thing he noticed was that no one dropped their usual hints about the fact that Sophia and Evan were the perfect couple and should be married immediately.

They all knew better than to mention it today.

As dinner came to an end, Evan felt the nerves kick in. He had gotten Yaya's blessing over two weeks ago. She had helped him get in contact with Sophia's parents, who agreed to come home for this week's Sunday dinner, so they would be here for the big moment.

Her dad had been wary about giving his permission without meeting Evan first, but Yaya vouched for him and the last blessings were given.

Now all he had to do was ask. He didn't have any doubts she would say yes, but he was still anxious. Sophia was the best thing to ever happen to him, and he'd almost blown it. He didn't want to ever be without her by his side again. That gave him the courage to do what he planned to do.

Sophia sat on the couch next to her mother. They were deep in conversation. Her mom showed her some pictures of their latest adventure on her phone.

Evan made eye contact with Yaya so she knew it was time. "Sophia," Yaya said, interrupting. "You know that scarf you borrowed a couple weeks ago? I can't find it anywhere. I thought you brought it back last week."

"I put it in your closet. I hung it with the other scarves."

"Are you sure? I couldn't find it."

Sophia got up. "Let me look. I swear I put it in there, Yaya."

As soon as she went into the bedroom, the whole family kicked into action. The five-dozen roses that Evan had dropped off early this morning that were hiding in the garage were brought out. The champagne bottles were ready to be uncorked. The ring box came out of his pocket.

Zeke put a reassuring hand on his brother's back. "Evan and Sophia are getting married," he said. This wasn't like being engaged to Jamie. Even Zeke could tell the difference.

"Man, I sure hope so. She's got to say yes first."

"She'll say yes. She kisses you. *A lot.*"

Evan's cheeks hurt from smiling so hard. She did kiss him a lot. He wasn't ever going to complain about that.

"I found it. It was hidden way in the back. I don't remember putting it—" Sophia came to a dead stop when she saw what was going on.

Evan went to her and took her by the hand. He guided her a little farther into the room. The tears were already welling in her eyes. She covered her mouth with her hand.

"Sorry," he said. "I think I put it back there."

She laughed and wiped the tears as they fell. Evan cued Zeke to come stand beside him.

"So, Zeke and I have been talking, and we've decided that you are the most important person in our lives and there's no way that we could imagine not having you in them. If you ever left, we would hate that more than Zeke hates cucumbers."

The whole Markopoulos/Reed family chuckled. Zeke really hated cucumbers. Sophia laughed through her tears.

"We know that you have this big family who loves you fiercely and unconditionally. They all think you're pretty special, but we were kind of hoping you would consider joining our family—we're a little smaller, a little quieter, but we also think you're pretty darn special."

Evan got down on one knee. "Sophia Reed, you have shown me what it means to love with my whole heart. You have taught me what grace is—you have shown me more than I probably deserve. I am madly, deeply in love with you." He held out the ring box and opened it up. "Will you marry me?"

She wiped her tears while nodding. "Yes,

yes, I'll marry you. I don't ever want to leave you, yes."

Evan popped up so fast she was in his arms before the whole family began to clap and cheer. There wasn't a dry eye in the house.

"I love you so much," he said as he pressed his forehead to hers. The sound of champagne bottles popping came from the kitchen.

She held his face in her hands. "I can't believe you did this here with everyone I love. No one gets me the way you do."

He kissed her there in Yaya's living room with the whole family watching. When he let her go, she turned to her family.

"Who's ready to help me plan a wedding?"

And the crowd went wild.

* * * * *

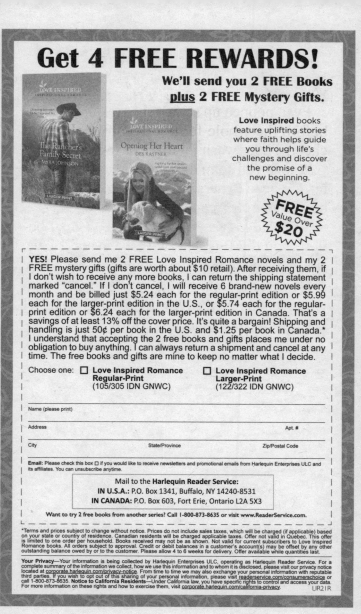

Get 4 FREE REWARDS!

We'll send you 2 FREE Books plus 2 FREE Mystery Gifts.

Love Inspired Suspense books showcase how courage and optimism unite in stories of faith and love in the face of danger.

FREE Value Over **$20**

HARLEQUIN SELECTS COLLECTION

19 FREE BOOKS IN ALL!

From Robyn Carr to RaeAnne Thayne to Linda Lael Miller and Sherryl Woods we promise (actually, GUARANTEE!) each author in the Harlequin Selects collection has seen their name on the *New York Times* or *USA TODAY* bestseller lists!

YES! Please send me the **Harlequin Selects Collection**. This collection begins with 3 FREE books and 2 FREE gifts in the first shipment. Along with my 3 free books, I'll also get 4 more books from the Harlequin Selects Collection, which I may either return and owe nothing or keep for the low price of $24.14 U.S./$28.82 CAN. each plus $2.99 U.S./$7.49 CAN. for shipping and handling per shipment*.If I decide to continue, I will get 6 or 7 more books (about once a month for 7 months) but will only need to pay for 4. That means 2 or 3 books in every shipment will be FREE! If I decide to keep the entire collection, I'll have paid for only 32 books because 19 were FREE! I understand that accepting the 3 free books and gifts places me under no obligation to buy anything. I can always return a shipment and cancel at any time. My free books and gifts are mine to keep no matter what I decide.

☐ 262 HCN 5576   ☐ 462 HCN 5576

Name (please print)

Address   Apt. #

City   State/Province   Zip/Postal Code

Mail to the **Harlequin Reader Service:**
IN U.S.A.: P.O. Box 1341, Buffalo, NY 14240-8531
IN CANADA: P.O. Box 603, Fort Erie, Ontario L2A 5X3

*Terms and prices subject to change without notice. Prices do not include sales taxes, which will be charged (if applicable) based on your state or country of residence. Canadian residents will be charged applicable taxes. Offer not valid in Quebec. All orders subject to approval. Credit or debit balances in a customer's account(s) may be offset by any other outstanding balance owed by or to the customer. Please allow 3 to 4 weeks for delivery. Offer available while quantities last. © 2020 Harlequin Enterprises ULC. ® and ™ are trademarks owned by Harlequin Enterprises ULC.

Your Privacy—Your information is being collected by Harlequin Enterprises ULC, operating as Harlequin Reader Service. To see how we collect and use this information visit https://corporate.harlequin.com/privacy-notice. From time to time we may also exchange your personal information with reputable third parties. If you wish to opt out of this sharing of your personal information, please visit www.readerservice.com/consumerschoice or call 1-800-873-8635. Notice to California Residents—Under California law, you have specific rights to control and access your data. For more information visit https://corporate.harlequin.com/california-privacy.

50BOOKHS22R

#375 ROCKY MOUNTAIN BABY

The Second Chance Club • by Patricia Johns

Taryn Cook is pregnant with her own miracle baby...but she hadn't anticipated that the father, Noah Brooks, would want to be part of her baby's life. Can a man who never planned on being a dad truly be the father this baby needs?

#376 AN ALASKAN HOMECOMING

A Northern Lights Novel • by Beth Carpenter

To fix a family matter, Zack Vogel wishes he were married. His old friend Rowan O'Shea is happy to help him out...and the closer they get, the harder it is to imagine a future without one another.

#377 A FAMILY FOR THE FIREFIGHTER

Polk Island • by Jacquelin Thomas

After rescuing a toddler, firefighter Leon Rothchild faces the flames of his past. Finding himself drawn to the child's mother, Misty Brightwater, he has to decide if his attraction is worth tearing down walls he's spent years building.

#378 HER RODEO RANCHER

The Montgomerys of Spirit Lake

by M. K. Stelmack

When rodeo celebrity Will Claverley persuades city girl Krista Montgomery to become his fake girlfriend for a few days, old emotions flare up. Is there any way these two opposites could attract...and develop lasting love?

Visit ReaderService.com Today!

As a valued member of the Harlequin Reader Service, you'll find these benefits and more at ReaderService.com:

- Try 2 free books from any series
- Access risk-free special offers
- View your account history & manage payments
- Browse the latest Bonus Bucks catalog

Don't miss out!

If you want to stay up-to-date on the latest at the Harlequin Reader Service and enjoy more content, make sure you've signed up for our monthly News & Notes email newsletter. Sign up online at ReaderService.com or by calling Customer Service at 1-800-873-8635.

RS20